Nice 2 Meet U, Marcos

A Novel

Sharon Smith

by @sharimc

ISBN: 13: 978-1503331136
ISBN-10: 150333113X
Library of Congress Control Number: 2014921081
BISAC: Fiction / Literary

DEDICATION

To the youth of Skyline Church's Living Proof (1992-1995) who
are now all grown up, but their stories have inspired
me through the years.

DISCLAIMER

All characters appearing in this work are fictitious. Any resemblance to real persons, living or dead, is purely coincidental.

FOREWARD

By Christopher Yanov,
Founder and President of Reality Changers

The world in which we live often provides no easy answers. Everyday situations can turn on a dime and become entanglements that we could have never imagined possible. What does one do when something happens during a routine stop at a supermarket and abruptly changes that person's life trajectory forever? Life can seem all mapped out until suddenly… it's not.

So what transpires when two such worlds collide? Sharon Smith's Nice 2 Meet U, Marcos ups the ante by weaving a narrative across two families trying to do right by the young boy at the center of the story, Marcos. As each family struggles to do what is best, their options get more and more complicated, as if trying to undo a stubborn knot only to see that knot get tighter and tighter.

San Diego, California, is the perfect setting for this story to take place. Being a border town that has long sought to cement its own identity while sitting in the shadow of a certain giant metropolis to the north, an overwhelming number of San Diegans do their very best to also ignore the world's busiest border crossing on the city's doorstep to the city's south. In fact, less than 10% of San Diego residents have ever even crossed by land into Mexico, even though the sprawling city of Tijuana – with over 1,000,000 residents itself – is less than a 15-minute drive from San Diego's downtown neighborhoods. And despite about a third of the region's population being of Latino origin and seemingly every road and landmark having a name with Spanish roots, a white, middle-class family in San Diego could easily go about its daily business without being impacted by the culture that existed in this region long before California ever became part of the United States of America.

That family could continue with its monolithic cultural lifestyle until, of course, an unexpected event occurs and members of both cultures must interact. Such instances beg many questions: Why is it so difficult for members of different cultures to interact with each other sometimes? Why hasn't there been more interaction before? What keeps cultures apart when they practically live side by side? What can bring them together? Why should they even interact at all?

Smith hopes that young Marcos can provide the reader with some of the answers to these questions, even though he doesn't even quite yet know how to navigate this world (or either culture) himself. Furthermore, Smith surrounds Marcos with characters that have few, if any, easy decisions. Every right choice may not be good; every good choice may not be right.

While Marcos finds himself in the middle of a unique situation, as the founder and president of Reality Changers, I witness young people in San Diego facing cultural challenges every day of their lives. The program aims to build first generation college students and works with youth whose low-income families have come from every corner of the globe. Sometimes the students feel that they will never be accepted as true Americans, and yet their parents' customs feel as distant as the countries from which they came. That leaves such students stuck somewhere in the middle – of both cultures, yet of neither culture. While Reality Changers' mission is to secure scholarships for these students and prepare them to be the first in their families to attend a four-year university, perhaps what goes unsaid is that Reality Changers must help these students carve out a space in this world that each student can truly call his or her own.

Marcos, I hope, would fit right in….

Contents

Life As We Know It

The Meeting
(Evelyn)

The baby-blue Suburban sputtered and lurched up the hill just outside of downtown. It crossed through the valley and merged into the marine haze of the morning. It felt unusual to Evelyn to sit so high above the road, above the road rails, the bushes, and all the little cars that paid her no mind as she pushed the accelerator farther down—not that it made much of a difference going uphill in that car. She looked over San Diego's skyline with its downtown hugging the bay; the heart of the town was known as "Tool Town," due to a skyline that vaguely resembled screwdrivers, socket wrenches, and, some say, electric shavers.

To drown out the whirring of the engine and the clank of the big, ancient car's changing gears, she switched on the radio and turned the knob, but since it was such an old radio, its antenna bouncing on the hood, it could only get a faint signal.

Garbled Spanish music or a crooning country singer was all that would come weakly through the speakers. Dejectedly, she switched it off and listened to the engine moan in fourth gear.

Finally, the car rumbled through the parking lot and coughed when she turned it off. Evelyn had arrived at her destination, her home away from home, a place where she spent more hours than her own house, where she started and ended most of her days. Today, however, she wasn't going to be at her desk to watch the sun go down because she had other plans.

She swung her legs out of the car and slid to the ground. Evelyn walked quickly to the back door of her company's building with intensity. Rather than take the elevator, she climbed the four flights of stairs in an effort to get in as much exercise as she could, taking two steps up at a time and timing herself, trying to beat her time from the day before. Today, she smelled McDreamy Cologne lingering in the stairwell, and as she hit the third floor, the cologne was faint, and she identified the new aroma as hazelnut coffee. Once she got to her floor, she checked her watch: fifteen seconds, two seconds faster than her time the yesterday. She smiled as she opened the door to the hallway, proud of beating yesterday's time and identifying the hazelnut.

Once she got to her desk, she typed in her password, and soon, the screens on all three of her monitors lit up. She opened TweetDeck, which displayed her company's Twitter account, the company's Facebook page, her work-focused Facebook account, columns for the five words she followed and commented on, and a column on trending hashtags. On the monitor to her left on Twitter, she kept up on five blogs, read three different newspapers, and updated posts on the company's blog. On the monitor to her right—which she had put in a special request for—she kept her email up and responded quickly to inquiries. She also had NPR streaming as she kept up-to-date on the news in countries she tweeted about.

Her friend list and Twitter followers were increasing at a rapid rate, faster than her peers'. She was proud of the fact that she had been voted one of the "Top 100 Women Who Rock Social Media" by *Online Marketing* last year. She was trying to make the top-twenty-five list this year.

Evelyn noticed Irene sitting at her desk, peering through her office window to see who had arrived at work on time. Her boss was usually the first one in the office, and like a vulture, she watched as her staff got their morning cups of coffee and settle in at their desks. Irene always had a watchful eye on the staff, especially where Evelyn was concerned. Evelyn could feel Irene's piercing eyes on her. She bit her lip as she read her email.

Irene had been with this global company, Medicomm, for fifteen years, the last ten as head of communications. Upper management and the board of directors respected Irene, and she was in good standing with them; they listened and responded to her ideas. Irene was the catalyst for the department's success, and she had the vision and implemented the strategic plan for a global reach. She knew she was the driving force when it came to the department's growth. The business had a global presence, but the corporation wanted to pursue aggressive international expansion. At Medicomm, it was their job to educate medical facilities around the world on wireless health the globe over. They connected with doctors and technicians through cloud technology and could remotely diagnose and help others in isolated areas speaking in a universal language in radio frequency. Their team did their best to keep abreast of world politics and watched streaming weather and international news all day on the flat screens in the lobby and the break room. They spoke to Doctors Without Borders on a regular basis via Skype, and the entire staff lived on adrenaline.

Irene had hired Evelyn as the senior manager of public relations and corporate communications to expand their global social media presence. She had been searching for a savvy, high-energy candidate who had a strong sense of urgency and the ability to turn on a dime, who could balance a polished presentation for upper management and the media, yet possessed the edginess to communicate with younger generations. The right candidate would need to utilize all the social media tools and to be available to travel globally at any time. She would act as a responsive, informative public persona to high-profile local, national, and international news media and be able to handle interviews with magazines such as *Forbes*, *Money*, and *The Economist*. She would be the company's face for the northern hemisphere. Irene had hired Evelyn three years ago, and ever since, there had been tension between the two of them. Evelyn was exactly who Irene was looking for, yet she was everything Irene was not, which ideally would have been a good hire, as their strengths and weaknesses could complement each other, but their ideas and directions often clashed; Irene knew Evelyn would run the office differently if she had the chance, and Evelyn didn't respect Irene's decisions. Irene did try to make Evelyn's work environment a bit more challenging, albeit subconsciously. In turn, Evelyn did her best to outshine her boss at all times.

When it was almost noon, Evelyn started to log out of her blogs and social platforms. She glanced quickly at her shirt to check that her top button was still intact and that she wasn't showing any cleavage. She routinely dressed modestly but always added some sort of flair to her outfit—an unusual color, detailed stitching, a bright belt or shoes, or a very loud pattern—and she always wore the highest-heeled Mary Janes she could find. Evelyn was determined to stand out from the crowd.

Everyone knew Evelyn wanted her boss's job. The staff watched her from afar and was entertained by her colorful clothes and brilliant performances. Everything she did was done with great gusto, and she was secretly referred to among the staff as "the Shark." Evelyn didn't seem to care what the women's opinions were of her, but it was obvious that she did care what the men thought of her, as she made every effort to make sure she was accepted and included among them. She did what she could to keep up athletically with the men. She ran as hard as they did, leg lifted as much weight, and ate the same portions as them. She also wore high heels to make sure she was as tall as most of the men at the company. Evelyn made a concentrated effort to be equal on every level with the men. Finally, the car rumbled through the parking lot and coughed when she turned it off. Evelyn had arrived at her destination, her home away from home, a place where she spent more hours than her own house, where she started and ended most of her days. Today, however, she wasn't going to be at her desk to watch the sun go down because she had other plans.

She swung her legs out of the car and slid to the ground. Evelyn walked quickly to the back door of her company's building with intensity. Rather than take the elevator, she climbed the four flights of stairs in an effort to get in as much exercise as she could, taking two steps up at a time and timing herself, trying to beat her time from the day before. Today, she smelled McDreamy Cologne lingering in the stairwell, and as she hit the third floor, the cologne was faint, and she identified the new aroma as hazelnut coffee. Once she got to her floor, she checked her watch: fifteen seconds, two seconds faster than her time the yesterday. She smiled as she opened the door to the hallway, proud of beating yesterday's time and identifying the hazelnut.

Men were easier to make friends with, and they were not as complicated as women. Evelyn learned early on in life that she felt more comfortable around the other gender. She moved around a lot as a kid, since her dad was in the military. Their family had moved six times while she was growing up and had spent two years overseas in Japan. Since she wanted to make friends quickly after each new move, she'd noticed that it was the boys who easily took to accepting a newcomer—that is, if she could talk the talk and play sports, understand and laugh at their jokes, and keep up with them. She went mountain biking, skateboarding, and became an excellent swimmer and runner. She learned the boys' jargon and kept up on the football, basketball, and soccer games. She didn't even bother trying to hang with the girls from about third grade on, and so when she was hired on at Medicomm, she knew she had to keep up with the male employees. She ran at lunchtime with the boys, she had drinks after work with the boys, she communicated via Lync with the boys, and she rarely associated with any women. Even the men were reluctant to ask the other women to join them after work—they liked their guy time. She would hear the women grumble, as she and the guys walked by for lunch, "There goes the 'Men's Club' and the Shark."

It was a year after she was hired when she noticed a gal there who seemed to be interesting, tough and girlie at the same time, and she didn't take guff from anyone; she just didn't have time for it. Although they had different roles, they were in the same department. Evelyn appreciated Monica and thought that maybe she would make a good friend. One day, Evelyn just walked over to her at her desk and asked if she wanted to go get lunch. Monica looked shocked.

"What? Leo, Johnny, and Brad are all busy?" Monica said sarcastically and didn't give Evelyn time to respond. "Well, Miss Isabella over there just asked me to McDonald's. So it's between you and Mickey D's." Monica paused as she looked down at her desk and fiddled with a pen, acting as if she really had to think about it. "Why the heck not?" Monica shrugged her shoulders and stood up, and off they went to lunch. It turned out that Monica was easy to talk to, and thus began their friendship. After moving from city to city, school to school, and then being the newbie at work, Evelyn had learned how to scope out people quickly and usually decided immediately who would be her friends. Monica was her first female coworker friend.

Finally, the car rumbled through the parking lot and coughed when she turned it off. Evelyn had arrived at her destination, her home away from home, a place where she spent more hours than her own house, where she started and ended most of her days. Today, however, she wasn't going to be at her desk to watch the sun go down because she had other plans.

She swung her legs out of the car and slid to the ground. Evelyn walked quickly to the back door of her company's building with intensity. Rather than take the elevator, she climbed the four flights of stairs in an effort to get in as much exercise as she could, taking two steps up at a time and timing herself, trying to beat her time from the day before. Today, she smelled McDreamy Cologne lingering in the stairwell, and as she hit the third floor, the cologne was faint, and she identified the new aroma as hazelnut coffee. Once she got to her floor, she checked her watch: fifteen seconds, two seconds faster than her time the yesterday. She smiled as she opened the door to the hallway, proud of beating yesterday's time and identifying the hazelnut.

That afternoon there was another department meeting, and Evelyn gathered her pen, notebook, smartphone, and lunch, and then walked with an attitude down the hall to the small conference room. Irene had sprung a noon meeting on them, on a Friday afternoon no less, knowing full well that Evelyn planned to leave early. Evelyn's intentions were to run a few errands for party supplies for Chad's birthday extravaganza. Her plan was to zip over to Costco and buy party supplies for Chad's birthday party, which was scheduled for the next day. After four years of marriage, she still loved to surprise him.

She entered the conference room and tried to refrain from rolling her eyes. It was important she kept her composure in front of her peers, but Monica, who walked into the conference room after her, must have noticed. The entire international Internet marketing team, all six of them, sat and looked at each other and quietly grumbled as they waited for their boss to arrive; they pecked at their devices, catching up on emails and news. Their reach was global, and no matter where their target market—be it India, China, Russia, Brazil, or Australia—they always stayed culturally appropriate and on message. However, when it came to the boardroom and the absence of their boss, their guards were down and their words flowed with little filter. Evelyn impatiently jiggled her foot on her chair and clicked her pen.

"What's up with you? A bit of attitude? So unlike you," Monica said sarcastically with a wink and then slipped into the chair next to her.

"I told Irene earlier in the week I was going to leave at noon today," Evelyn said, gritting her teeth. She glanced over at Monica. "I need to get ready for Chad's birthday party tomorrow, but I didn't tell her that." She put her hand down and spoke in her normal, raspy voice. "And lo and behold, here we are for a meeting at noon with no Irene. I'm sure she's on her way. When do I ever leave work early? Even on Fridays, I stay late. And the one day I do, we have an 'emergency' noon meeting? What a coincidence."

"Some kind of timing, eh? Maybe she knows what you are up to and figured out she wasn't invited to your husband's birthday party, hmmm? Well, you're rarely in the office, usually off traveling somewhere like Timbuktu, so maybe Irene wanted to take this opportunity when we're all here," Monica said, raising her eyebrows and tilting her head.

"Yes, that's true. I'm occasionally in a place I don't have cell phone reception and can't call in for a conference call, such as when I was in the small village outside of Nairobi, I swear I couldn't call in," Evelyn said.

"So, hey," Monica said, scooting closer to Evelyn's chair and lowering her voice, "what's the plan for your party prep today?"

"Well," Evelyn said, drawing out the word, "I am picking up appetizers from this place downtown, then the gluten-free cupcakes in Hillcrest, and onto Costco off the 15 to pick up all the party drinks and supplies. I borrowed my brother-in-law's ancient Suburban so I can haul all the party stuff home, because my Mini Cooper is not big enough to fit all that party paraphernalia. Oh, man, I drove that Suburban to work today, and its top speed is fifty-five miles per hour, and even that was a struggle for it."

As Monica chuckled, Irene finally waltzed in, without apology for her tardiness, and proceeded to talk about next week's assignments. Everyone was attentive, though they all shared glances of frustration over the pointless meeting that had started late and was likely going to last too long.

Irene talked about their global campaigns and their need to keep consistent with company branding and international initiatives in all their communications. She spoke of their efforts and outreach, and needing to be on the same page. They were bracing themselves for weekend assignments when she asked what everyone was doing, specifically, on Saturday. A trace of fear crossed their faces, and they all claimed they weren't doing much, nothing really. Irene was somber and, looking a little disappointed, walked toward the door, flicked her hand in the air, and said, "Well, back to work then."

They all looked at each other, sighed in relief, and went back to their offices.

Not wasting any time, Evelyn headed back to her desk, grabbed her purse, and raced out the office door, down the four flights of stairs, hopped up into the Suburban, and pulled out of the parking lot and onto the freeway.

The 1972 Suburban belonged to her brother-in-law, Brian, who had nursed that poor, neglected vehicle back from near death and an almost-fatal trip to the junkyard. This Suburban was the first car Brian remembered his family owning. He could think back to when he was just five years old, when his father had first ordered the car from the dealership. According to Brian's father, it was the biggest vehicle a family of seven could find. After ten years of being parked on the side of the garden shed, Brian fixed it and resurrected it from the graveyard. He cleaned all the moss away, rebuilt the engine, and had the Suburban painted its original color. Brian loved this car, and Evelyn knew it. The Suburban had three big bench seats with a light-blue-and-white herringbone pattern covered in plastic. The stick shift was on the steering column, right next to the steering wheel. The outside door handles were metal with a button on the end, which you pushed in with your thumb in order to open the door. Every door had an armrest with a metal ashtray in it. The Suburban could fit nine to eleven people, and Brian, who was raised in a large family, had harbored hopes that he and Evelyn's sister, Emily, would fill the car with their own kids, but Evelyn was pretty sure her sister, after only two kids, had no plans for more children. They kept a booster seat in the vehicle, as there was plenty of room for all to sit and still always be prepared for a little one to join them on their outings. It was an old one they thought they would just store in the Suburban.

Evelyn drove to Hillcrest to pick up the cupcakes and a heck of a time parallel parking the beast of a car on the narrow street. From there, she dropped by Rafael's Party Rentals to pick up the rented chairs and folding tables, and veered onto Highway 15 south, on her way to a place she hadn't been before: Costco, a large warehouse that sold in bulk. She didn't have a membership, but borrowed her sister's "Executive Member," black card so that she would be allowed in and buy merchandise.

She checked the GPS on her phone to make sure she'd gotten off at the correct exit. As she approached her destination, she noticed that a cemetery was across the street from the warehouse. It wasn't like any cemetery she had seen before, with its twirling pinwheels and bouquets of balloons blowing in the stale breeze—not just at one plot, but at most of the sites. The cemetery hugged the street and Evelyn slowed to observe. It struck her as odd; she'd never noticed celebratory items so prevalent in a cemetery before, and she tucked the thought in her mind as she turned away from it, toward the massive warehouse and sprawling parking lot across the street.

With her list in hand, she trotted off to the large, metal warehouse doors. It wasn't her usual means of grocery shopping, going to such huge facilities, as she made every effort to shop at local farmer's markets and stayed away from mass-produced items. But she had heard from others that this was a good place to purchase all the goods for the party in one stop, and soon, she was overwhelmed and lost among the tall aisles and boxes.

After collecting the wine, beer, mixed drinks, meat, cheeses, bread, plates, and cups and paying, she was finally ready to head home. She wheeled the cart along and tried to slow down as the lady checked her receipt at the door. Then, she smacked into the sidewall on her way out, challenged by the cart's lack of maneuverability—much like the Suburban's. She picked up some speed in the parking lot and stepped up on the cart to ride between cars, and she careened right into Brian's precious vehicle. She shook her head, thinking about Brian's reaction to the new dent, hoping he wouldn't even notice it. Unlike her little two-door Mini Cooper, there was plenty of room for all the party goods in Brian's vehicle, and she stood there appreciating how everything fit with extra space. She was reaching up to close the Suburban's back door when a little boy came up beside her and said, "*Hola, Mamá.*"

Caught by surprise, she tried to reach into her brain to find the limited Spanish she had learned in high school. "*Hola, niño, ¿Como estás?*"

"*Bien.*" He smiled. Right away, she noticed his red, curly hair, freckles that peppered his nose, and the cutest, chubbiest cheeks she'd ever seen—and that she just wanted to pinch.

She kneeled down to get a better look at him. He had probably become separated from his parents in this huge facility; it seemed easy to get lost in this big warehouse parking lot too. But he didn't look scared. "Aren't you the cutest thing ever? But don't tell my niece and nephew that; they would be super jealous." He stared up at her, not understanding a word she said. He looked well dressed and clean, and he gripped a stuffed animal in his hand. She couldn't guess the boy's age, maybe three or four. "Are you looking for your parents, your mama and papa?" she asked slowly, wishing she had paid more attention in her Spanish classes.

He looked up at her blankly with a faint smile.

"Who do you have there?" she said, pointing to his tattered stuffed animal.

Noticing she was pointing to his bear, he exclaimed, "Pooky!" as he held the bear out to show him off.

"Aaahh, Pooky," she said excitedly, trying to match his enthusiasm. "Okay, sweet little boy, do you want to find your mama and papa?"

He looked up at her with no new response; he still wore a smile and looked enthusiastic about his bear.

Wracking her brain to retrieve her limited Spanish, she asked, "*Como sé llama?*"

"*Me llamo Marcos.*"

"*Me llama Evelyn.*" Then she stood up and continued, "Okay, Marcos. Let's go find your parents."

She touched his shoulder to move him back a step, so she could close the Suburban door, and reached down to offer him her hand. She was surprised at the touch of his hand as he grabbed hers; it was so soft and warm. They walked around the parking lot as Evelyn looked for a mom or dad who were looking for their lost child. After a prolonged search of the parking lot, she took him into the warehouse to report a missing child. They called on the loud speaker, and the warehouse security looked up each of the rows and made themselves available, but no one came forward, and no one asked about the missing child. While they waited for any response to the announcement, Evelyn bought Marcos a chocolate ice cream cone and a vanilla one for herself. They leaned against the bumper of the Suburban and licked their ice cream while enjoying the sun.

It appeared to Evelyn that Marcos wasn't scared or anxious, but as if he enjoyed her company. And suddenly, she was in no hurry to get back to her party planning.

The Release
(Santiago)

Santiago watched the woman in the parking lot as she pushed the shopping cart, picking up speed with long strides, jumping on its lower bar, and holding tight to the handles. Leaning forward, she let her hands go, spreading her arms wide, shaking her head as if she was enjoying the wind in her hair, and then pounding her fists to her chest like Tarzan. As she caught more speed, her cart went faster down the slope through the parking lot. She put her foot down, skidding it across the asphalt, slowing her motion only to careen into her car, banging the cart into the thick bumper. The groceries spilled over the sides of the cart, but it didn't seem to bother her. She laughed and her wide smile reminded him of happier times and his own Katiana's melodic laugh. He smiled and chuckled to himself at her display of whimsy. It had been a long time since he'd heard himself laugh, much less even felt a smile on his face.

He continued to observe her from the hill alongside the parking lot, above the gigantic warehouse just east of his neighborhood. His foot was jammed up against a tree trunk, bracing him from sliding down the slope, which was covered in small eucalyptus leaves and Manzanita bushes. The trees and bushes shaded him from view. He tugged at his ear, stretching his earlobe unconsciously. He then adjusted his hat and rubbed his forehead, moving his bandana farther back on his head. He wanted to stay calm in front of his son, who was twirling a leaf between his palms, sitting on a nearby rock. He had told Marcos earlier that they were going out to look for his new *mamá*.

Santiago turned his focus back to the lady in the parking lot and took note of her car, a Suburban, big enough to haul a boat trailer. Quite a sizeable car with what looked like a baby seat in the back. She piled plenty of food in the trunk, enough to feed a dozen kids for a month. He wasn't close enough to see what kind of food it was, although he suspected it wasn't all rice and beans, as he typically ate at home.

She wore dark jeans, a frilly lavender shirt, and high heels. It was a Friday, midafternoon, and he assumed she'd stopped by the warehouse to pick up food before heading off to pick up the kids from school. She looked like a fun mom. The kind of mom who would play games, kiss a boo-boo before putting on a Band-Aid, read stories, build forts, sing songs, and offer cookies and milk before bed. Santiago hadn't had any of these things in his own life, and he wanted more for his own son.

He moved his leg; it was shaking from resting all his weight on it. He pulled his khaki pants up by the empty belt loops. He had put his pants under his mattress last night to crease them down the middle—now that his grandmother was no longer ironing clothes, it was the best way he had to press them. He put a finger between his collar and neck, trying to loosen the flannel from his skin. The top button of his shirt was too tight, but he refused to unbutton it.

He had been watching women come and go all afternoon at the warehouse. He thought that this warehouse would be a place that a mom would go in the middle of the afternoon, and it was relatively close to his neighborhood. He didn't go to the megastore himself but had heard it was a good place to buy food in mass quantities.

Most of the women he observed were frumpy and very serious; many were older, some appeared too stern, and others looked overloaded with too many children already. He was initially looking for a Mexican woman, but this *mujer* made him laugh and, judging from the few moments he observed of her, she also seemed to have it together. He felt deep down inside that she would be right for his Marcos. And of course, Santiago thought he was a good judge of character. When he had first met one of his friends, Rubén, his other friends had said that Rubén was a no-good, conniving spaz who could not be trusted. Rubén did have a nervous twitch and talked nonstop, but Santiago befriended him, and it turned out that Rubén was a faithful *compradre*. Santiago believed others weren't as good at judging character as he was.

He pulled out his silver necklace from under his crisp, white undershirt through the tight top button of his flannel shirt, and he held the Virgin of Guadalupe. When he was little, his mother would take him to Mass, and he had always believed in God, even though these days it was hard to believe that Godwas looking out for Santiago and his family. Santiago knew he had done some bad things in his life, and it had been so long since he had been to Mass or even prayed, but today, he hoped that Godwas listening. "*Ayudame Virgencita, Cuidamelo*, please take care of him." He kissed the necklace. "Sweet Mary, mother of Jesus." He tucked the cross back underneath his shirt.

He turned to his son, who was sitting on the stump now, dancing his Pooky Bear on his lap as he hummed "*De Colores.*" Santiago remembered the song from his own childhood. His *abuela* would sing it to him while she tucked him into bed, and Santiago knew she had done the same for Marcos while she was still healthy. He knew no one had tucked Marcos into bed with love and kisses and wishes for sweet dreams for a while now.

"*Mi'jo*, lucky Marcos, listen to me. This is important. I found your new mom. You are going to be well taken care of." He knew his Marcos was ready for someone to take care of him—to sing and laugh, to eat regular meals, and to go out and play on a playground.

"*¿Mami?*" inquired Marcos.

"*Sí, mami.* Listen to me, my lucky Marcos." Santiago sat next to him on the tree stump and put his arm around his son lightly but protectively. He touched his freckled nose with the tip of his finger. "Always remember that I love you. Can you do that for me?" Marcos got up and crawled onto his father's lap, standing on his legs, and gave his dad a bear hug around his head, then snuggled his sweet, soft face into the crook of his dad's neck, where the spider web tattoo left its permanent mark. Marcos grabbed his stuffed bear and let his dad kiss it. Then Santiago reached under his collar once more and pulled out the necklace. He rubbed his fingers on the medallion before he took it off. He held it dangling in front of his son. "*Mi'jo*, I want you to have this. Our sacred virgin will watch over you." Santiago put the chain around his son's neck and then tucked it under his T-shirt.

Santiago pointed down to the woman with the high-heeled shoes and the big car. "There is your new mama." Marcos followed the point of his father's finger with a look of sad loss. "Maybe she will sing to you and give you Maria cookies. She'll take good care of you Marcos, and I will always be here for you."

"You be here?" Marcos asked, pointing to the ground.

"Yes, I will be here for you, always."

"Kiss Pooky one more time." Marcos raised his bear to his dad for a kiss. Once his papa kissed the bear, Marcos gripped its paw tightly, and then slid down the leaves that covered the hill to the parking lot while calling out quietly, "*Adíos, Papá. Asta, Papa*. See you here. *Asta, Papá.*"

"*Adíos*, my sweet Marcos," Santiago whispered to himself as he blew kisses to his son.

He watched as Marcos walked right up to the *señorita* in the parking lot while she loaded her groceries in her trunk. He watched as he greeted her, how she smiled, how they looked around the parking lot for Marcos's parents, and he noticed that his son never pointed to him up on the hill. He watched as they walked inside the warehouse, and he supposed they were looking for someone who would claim Marcos as their own. At first Santiago was pleased that the *mujer* stayed with his son, and he thought everything was going fine and that the lady would know what to do to take care of Marcos. He continued to observe them as they sat on the bumper of her car, the bumper the cart had crashed into, and they both licked their ice cream cones. He saw the police car come and park next to them. He watched the sun get closer to the horizon and how the woman took the booster seat out of her car and put it in the police car. He watched as his son crawled into the cop car and how the *mujer* bent down and buckled him into the seat. He saw the door close behind his son and the police car's red rear lights flashed.

Suddenly the trees were not rustling, the earth stopped rotating, the motors of the cars made no sound, the birds were silent, the world stood still, and his heart stopped beating. Then, his son was gone

The Party

Evelyn clicked the lighter several times as she tilted the votive candle. "No light. Drats," she murmured to herself. She had just used the lighter the other day, and it had worked fine. She ruffled through the junk drawer, which was stacked with small containers in an orderly way, just as Chad liked it. Searching for a match, she didn't have to look long before she picked up a matchbook from Elsie's Wine Bar, where she and Chad had had their first official date. She was so enamored with him that day. They'd talked at the wine bar about the Ensenada bike trip where they had met. She had been so impressed with how he was so strong, smart, and attentive to her. She stared at the matchbook that sported Elsie's big, fancy cursive *E* logo in yellow on a black background. After a few minutes, she realized that time was ticking and her guests would arrive soon. She still had to put together the final touches to the house and food trays.

"Evie, where did you put my brown shirt?" Chad called from the floor above. She hated when he called from room to room, especially from floor to floor. She didn't understand why he couldn't just stop what he was doing, come down the stairs, and enter the room she was in.

"You're wearing brown? Can't you be a little more creative than that?" she hollered back up the stairs, just the very thing she hated him doing.

"Good gawd, Evie," he said as he jumped down the stairs like they weren't even there. "Why does everything have to be different for you? Can't I be plain? Someone has to be plain next to you, so that our guests can admire my extravagant Evie."

She smiled, knowing she would attract attention at the party with her outfit tonight, as she straightened out the spaghetti straps on her bright turquoise dress with the scoop neckline. On the wide waistband, there was an embroidered peacock, Evie's favorite creature and fashion statement, dashing across the dress. Bright little feathers were sewn into the dress to enhance the image. Did she like the peacock for daring to be different, or was it something else? Was it that the brilliant peacocks were known for determination, domination, ornamentation, and pride? Evelyn always wanted to stand out and make a statement, and she was sure that at this party, there would be no duplicates. Evie had seen the dress on a New York fashion runway, and she had hunted down the designer in L.A. She had driven north two hours to the Garment District to buy it for this very occasion. Evelyn had a keen eye for fashion and would go to great lengths to get exactly what she wanted.

"Nice thinking, chap, but it's your big day, so you can play it up, mister. How about the green button down with the dragon on the back that I got for you from San Francisco a couple of months ago?"

Chad had agreed that Evelyn could throw him a party to celebrate his thirty-fifth birthday, but he knew that she would go overboard and invite every Tom, Dick, and Harriet they knew. Although he wasn't as into pomp and circumstance as Evelyn was, he'd accepted the fact that she needed to throw the party of the century, and his birthday was a good excuse to do it.

"Okay, just pick out whatever you want, and I'll wear it for you," he said, putting his hands on her shoulders and bringing her closer to kiss her nose. "Thank you so much for doing all this for me. I could never have made it this far without you." He stared into her eyes with complete sincerity and appreciation.

"Mister, you are worth it. And as much as I love this moment right now, you looking into my eyes so lovingly, we need to get going. I still have to light all the candles and put the flowers on the dessert plates."

"Flowers on the dessert plates? Well, it all looks great, but, Babe, you know I would have been happy with just a small dinner and celebration for two." Chad turned and surveyed his living and dining rooms, stacked with votive candles, bouquets of flowers bursting with color and scent, platters stacked high with foods both savory and sweet, and a full bar that looked like it could keep an entire wedding well stocked until dawn. "Um, how many people are you expecting? There are enough food and drinks to feed a village."

"Well, you are in for a sur-prise, mister." She tilted her head to the side with a smirk, knowing that he would see people he hadn't seen since high school—and some who he hardly even knew at all. She thought people loved getting out and going to parties, and she'd invited every person she could think of to the event.

He wagged his finger at her. "You are so bad," he said, moving to chase her up stairs.

"No, Chad, really I have things to do. Stop," she said as she placed her hand on his chest, locking her elbow to put him at arm's distance, and giving him a determined look.

"Okay, but you're in for it after the party. You just wait." He took a few steps back down the stairs, then turned to look back up at her. "Hey, babe. Did you tell the neighbors we're going to be disturbing their sleep tonight?"

"Yes, not only did I tell them, but I invited them and warned those people across and down the street that there might be some noise." She indicated the apartment complex across the way.

"Oh, gawd," he mumbled, shaking his head as he tried to hide his smile of approval.

Evelyn stood on the landing of the stairs between the first and second floors and looked down onto the living room. When she and Chad were first married, they had lived in an apartment in Hillcrest, near Mercy Hospital, where he'd worked as a resident. They'd lived there for a couple of years, and then they saw an ad for this downtown townhome in the community newspaper. After taking a tour of the facilities and the open townhome, they knew they had to have it. For the last twenty years, the city of San Diego was revitalizing their downtown and doing all they could to become appealing to the young professionals to come and live in the neighborhood. Both Evelyn and Chad loved the downtown scene, with its plethora of restaurants, unique boutiques, and hum of activity. The location was absolutely perfect. They could walk to Petco Park to watch the Padres play, run the boardwalk alongside the cruise ships and sailboats, and spend time with friends who also lived in the area. Their house wasn't near either of their places of work, but they loved the busy downtown lifestyle enough to make the daily commute.

Their three-story townhome had a metal façade, a red front door that opened onto the public sidewalk, and a balcony that looked out onto the sprawling town, and if you stepped up on a chair and looked west, you could also see the cruise ships come into the bay. In the two-car garage, they had the extra space to hang their toys. Bikes were suspended from the ceiling by hooks, their kayaks, oars, surfboards, and paddle boards were all secured along the wall. Backpacks, gym bags, and various running and biking shoes were neatly placed alongside the wall as well as in stacked, white-painted cubbies. Chad and Evelyn hardly had an evening or weekend at home relaxing in the house; they were always active, on the go.

The place had been move-in ready, built five years prior, but Evelyn had decorated it to look as modern as she could, with simple and expensive furniture, cool gray–painted walls, and one huge, oversized canvas with colorful stripes, which took up the entire wall on one side of the room. The citrine silk–upholstered mod couch with oak, curved armrests had a single twenty-inch pillow that rested in the crease of the seat. They had sat it in the middle of the living room, facing the large, flat screen TV hanging over the fireplace. The transparent acrylic coffee table was propped on a New Zealand sheepskin area rug, which rested on the black-and-white, weathered faux wood floors that ran throughout the house. There were many responses when people walked through the door, but there was always some sort of visible surprise, a gasp, eyes opening wider, a hidden smirk, or just raised eyebrows. Some liked it, but some just thought it eccentric and passed it off as Evelyn's personal style. Some commented that the furniture didn't look comfortable, or that it felt more like a design piece and less like a home. Parents, especially those of young children, would comment about how many breakable items were within easy reach of a toddler's hand and how inhospitable it was to children. She knew the criticisms, but she loved the clean lines. And besides, she and Chad didn't plan to have any children, so who cared if it was the sort of home a toddler could tear apart in less than five minutes? And she felt it was comfortable, so she didn't care what others thought of it.

Chad didn't mind what Evelyn did with the place; he just wanted every room and every drawer and every square foot to be neat and tidy. Any kind of disorder made his life impossible.

From the landing, Evelyn looked on her party preparation and was proud to say she was the best hostess around. Streamers dangled from the high ceiling and metallic balloons were tied to every chair and table post. Sushi was displayed on square, white plates, and ingredients for cosmopolitans stood in a row on the console. Fresh Gerber daisies, bought that Saturday morning from the farmer's market on India Street, stood in plain glass vases, and confetti was dispersed on the tables with Happy Birthday punched out on different colored paper. Their favorite indie music reverberated throughout the house thanks to the surround sound system. The song "Hurricane" by MS MR, bellowed through the Bose speaker system, which had been installed on all three floors.

The final touch was a centerpiece of organic cupcakes that were made of vanilla sponge, zesty lemon, and rosewater buttercream, covered in white fondant, finished off with small, white flags with a Caduceus, the symbol of medicine, for embellishment.

The doorbell rang, echoing throughout the house, startling Evelyn back to reality.

She checked her light-pink lipstick in the mirror and tugged on her straight blond hair that fell just beyond her shoulders. She didn't even try to touch up the ends with a curling iron, as she knew they would go limp in less than a half hour. She scrutinized herself in the mirror to make sure she didn't find any flaws in her outfit and overall look. She kept her makeup application to a minimum—a light coat of mascara, a quick rub of blush, and faint lipstick was all she applied. Most days, she wore little makeup, but twice a day she slathered her skin in expensive creams, determined to keep the wrinkles at bay. Her flamboyant style brought attention to what she worked diligently to maintain—her healthy physique. She didn't shy away from biting into a chocolate cupcake with buttercream frosting in public, but stayed away from them in private. She stepped on the scales daily to make sure her one hundred and twenty pounds were maintained. If she gained a pound, she made sure she lost it before the end of the week.

On her way out of the bedroom, she slipped her feet into her bright yellow Mary Janes with four-inch wood heels, which completed her look.

She had started late setting up the house, distracted by the events of the day before. She had been wondering if the little boy, Marcos, had found his parents or if he was still at the center, under the care of Jessica, his social worker. She wasn't quite ready to face the masses and the energy that would fill her house soon. She heard the doorbell ring a few times and Chad opens the door and greet their guest but Evelyn delayed joining the others by busying herself with collecting more candles. She didn't even look toward the door to see who the first guests to arrive were. She had flowers to put in vases and place around the house and ice buckets to fill. While she was focused and running around, Chad announced, "Hey, babe, my mom is here."Soon, more people started migrating into the house, filling it with laughter, chatter, and birthday greetings. The guests included old college and high-school friends, colleagues of both of theirs, current and former bosses, fellow med students, some family, and training partners.

Chad's buddy, Charlie, was one of the early arrivals. Charlie was one of Chad's friends from grade school. They had hung out all through high school and then went separate ways when they went off to college. Charlie had ventured to UCLA to study business, and Chad had gone to UCSB to study biology. When Chad had come down to San Diego to attend med school at UCSD Hospital, they ran into each other at a local triathlon and reconnected.

After graduating from college, Charlie had come up with a concept for a casual shoe, the "Chaz," an almost slipper that could be worn all day. The concept caught on so fast in Southern California, and then eventually started selling in other places in the United States and later internationally, that Charlie set up a *maquiladora* in Tijuana to keep up with the demand. The shoe became profitable for him, and he no longer had to work full-time hours.

Charlie wore fashionable clothing and always donned a hat—a trilby, fedora, or a Panama—on the days he went to Mexico to visit his *maquiladora*. For the party, he wore a beanie and his aviator glasses—even inside—a V-neck T-shirt, and, of course, his Chaz shoes. Charlie was a player; he had a new girlfriend every month. Evelyn wasn't sure how he met so many women, but they were of all types, from lawyers to baristas, from environmentalists to musicians and artists, and even other players like him. For some reason though, Chad had shown up solo to Chad's birthday party, claiming that his date had gotten sick suddenly and was unable to join him.

Spencer, another one of Chad's close friends, was also from Santa Barbara, although he had gone to a private school, and Chad and Spencer were only acquaintances from the surf club. Chad had met up with him again in med school. Spencer wore his hair combed forward like a teenager, which complemented the soul patch on his chin, a distraction from his cleft lip. He was more subdued than the others, somewhat of a quiet type, although when he did say something, it was always worthwhile. He lived at the beach with his wife, Lorena, who was a native of Mexico, had a slight Mexican accent, and wore bright clothes.

These friends worked out, talked about food and health care, were highly competitive, didn't smoke, and usually met up with Chad and Evelyn at the restaurants, wine bars, or for sushi on Saturday nights.

Of course, Evelyn's sport's buddy, Addison, or Addy as she was known, came to the birthday party. Addison and Evelyn had met when they were coupled up in the same boat on the rowing team. Addy had just moved from San Francisco and, without knowing anyone in San Diego, had latched on to the first person she met, Evelyn. They were not particularly the best of pals, but they seemed to be always getting paired together in sports events be it riding or swimming or rowing. They saw quite a bit of each other as they were both committed to rigorous exercise. There was a strong competition between the two of them, but they often found themselves on the same team. They were now in the same triathlon club—the only two girls in the group.

Addy had long, brown wavy hair that she usually didn't comb, which Evelyn noticed she hadn't brushed it out for the party either. She usually had it up in a rubber band and pulled her hair through to create loose hair flying every which way on the back of her head, but today it was down and looked like it was forming dreadlocks. Addy didn't care much about her personal presentation, but she did care that she was healthy; her body could run long distances, resist the common cold, and strong enough to move all the furniture in a house if the circumstance presented itself.

When she arrived at the party, Addy raced over to Evelyn, concerned why Evelyn had missed the group's run yesterday. "Evie, I waited for you about ten minutes and let the group go ahead. What happened to you?"

Although they saw each other frequently, Addy was not the one Evelyn would confide in about her long day with a cute little boy who had lost his parents. She hadn't told anyone about her day with Marcos yet, not even Chad, as she had gotten caught up with the party presentation and figured she would tell him after things settled down. "Oh, yes, well, I got held up going around town, getting all the stuff for the party. Thanks for waiting for me, dear. Sorry you had to run extra hard to catch up."

"No big deal. It actually felt really good to run it out. It calms me down when I sprint once in a while."

"Don't you know it, I feel the same way. Sometimes I just want to run full speed, and I feel so exhilarated that I jump into the Pacific Ocean to celebrate," Evie said with a smile. "There is nothing like it."

Evelyn offered to make her a margarita and showed her where a few friends from the triathlon group were gathered, and there she left her for the night.

Emily, Evelyn's sister, and her husband, Brian, came late. They weren't sure if they would be able to come at all; it was contingent upon them finding a babysitter. Emily looked happy to be out, dressed up, and free from her kids for an evening. She had a drink in her hand and a smile on her face. "Evie! You outdid yourself! What a fabulous party! Can you fit anyone else in here? It is so packed!" Emily was taller than Evelyn, but she always wore flat shoes. Evelyn stood at five foot seven inches with her bare feet, but with her four-inch heels, she stood a couple inches taller than her older sister. Evelyn was a little taken aback with Emily's attire for the party—a glittery top and a pair of dark, fitted jeans—mostly because Evelyn was used to seeing her sister wear casual clothes, anything she could quickly pull on out of bed or grab on the way to a quick shower before her kids woke up. Evelyn forgot that her sister used to join her on her San Francisco boutique shopping sprees and that Emily had been the one who usually found the gems in the back of the shop.

Brian slipped his arm around Emily's waist and reached out his other hand to Evelyn, dropping her Mini Cooper keys into her hand. "How did the Suburban hold out?"

She squinted her eyes trying to appear in some sort of discomfort. "It was a beast, but it served its purpose." Then she put a smile on her face. "Thank you so much for letting me borrow it. I don't think I could have put all this together in one day without it. I have your keys in the kitchen. I'll go get them. Enjoy the party, and I'll be back."

She stole away and wove through the crowd to the kitchen as Maroon 5's acoustic version of "Harder to Breathe" blasted through the speakers.

After growing up in military housing and moving eight times during her growing up years, no one in her family had ever owned a house of their own, never painted the walls or added any permanent structure to the homes, never hung up large shelves—only had removable bookcases. Nothing was permanent; their houses were always ready to be packed up and their stuff organized and set to be moved out at a moment's notice.

Her father was a trainer for the marines. Yes, the one who could be seen yelling into a soldier's face, barking out orders to move faster, carry more weight, climb higher—that guy who no one likes in the boot camp scenes in the movies. That was her dad. He lived a strict, regimented life, not only at work, but at home too. He expected the moon and more from his kids and his wife. His daily routine was always the same: he woke and went to bed at the same time every week day, ate all his meals at the same time, went on a run every morning, and did the same amount of push-ups and sit-ups every day. He expected his family members to follow suit, and therefore, they all lived a disciplined life. His wife, Evelyn's mom, stayed home and made all the meals for the family and had it served and the table set at the same time every day, kept the house cleaned, went shopping on the same day of the week, and followed her husband's orders, no questions asked. Evelyn, her older brother, Ethan, and sister, Emily, sprung out of bed every weekday at the same time and were expected to make their beds as soon as they rolled out of them—the sheets had to be so tight, a penny could bounce off of it. They had to do their chores around the house on Saturday mornings before they even went out to play or turned on the TV or an electronic game. They were enrolled in every sport they could sign up for in the city they happened to be living in.

Everything was timed: their showers, getting from one end of the yard to the other, clearing the dinner table, doing their homework, getting to the end of the street on their bikes, getting through a series of obstacles set up in the backyard, and doing any basic task in the house. At one point, Emily had just stopped caring how long it took to do something and started taking time to draw a picture or bake in the middle in the afternoon when the sun was up and there was a game to play or a bike to ride, she rather take her time and do what she wanted without checking the time. She started hanging out with friends and sitting and talking. With her out of the competition, it was down to just Ethan and Evelyn. At first it was a bit insulting to Ethan that he had to compete with his little sister, but then, when Evelyn was in eighth grade and was on the swim team, she started getting stronger and faster. Ethan would still win in the push-ups and running, but to his dismay, he barely won, and he had to break a sweat. They were both competitive so the race was always on. Who could eat their pancakes faster, who could race up the stairs first, who could take the shortest shower, and who could finish their homework first? There was always a competition going on. When Evelyn hit high school, she started beating him at chess and could jump rope longer than him. There was a day when they stopped competing against each other, and that was the day she swam faster to the other side of Devil's Lake. Her brother looked up from his front crawl stroke and saw that she had gotten to the shore before him. He was shocked and didn't talk to her all day. After that incident, no one raced—not to the end of the street, the other side of the lake, to the end of the hallway. Evelyn felt proud that their races against each other ended with her victory, and she smiled smugly whenever she thought of that day.

Although, the competitions never ended—not even when they became adults. They still waved their grades in front of each other and counted their trophies to see if they had more than the other sibling. Emily had had enough of the competitions, and at one point, she'd just said, "Hey, I dropped out of college first, I got married first, I had a kid first, bought a house first, and settled down first. The race is over. I'm done and out of the family competitions." And she seemed content with her life, but she could still feel a competitive flare even in a friendly volleyball or croquette game in the backyard.

Still vying for first prize, Evelyn knew she won the trophy for best party. There, in their downtown condo, people kept pouring through the door that opened onto the street, and Evelyn began to wonder if some of them were invited by guests because not all of them looked familiar.

The house was filled with energy, yet Evelyn was distracted thinking of her encounter with the little boy named Marcos. Although she was a relatively private person and didn't divulge much, she felt as if she had to tell someone what had happened to her yesterday. She wasn't quite ready to tell Chad; she wanted him to enjoy his party, or so she told herself.

While she mingled among friends, she engaged in mindless small talk. As she passed Monica on the way to the kitchen, she reached out to hold her hand firmly and whispered in her ear, "I need to talk to you about something that happened yesterday. Maybe I can meet you out on the veranda in a bit?"

"What happened yesterday?" Monica yelled above the talking and the music, interested in what could have happened twelve hours since she saw her last.

"That's what I'm going to tell you, silly girl."

"All right, meet you in ten."

Evelyn chatted with a few more people on her way to where Emily and Brian were standing, dropped the Suburban keys off with Brian, and then wove her way to the food table to make sure all the serving bowls were full and that the food and drinks were plentiful. She poured herself another glass of red wine and pushed her way to the veranda. She stood there alone, nervous, and staring out at the downtown lights and the crescent moon while a G-Spliff song played. She was among friends, a crowd of people from her past and present, yet she felt so far away.

The Realization
(Santiago)

As quickly as time had seemed to quit ticking, it seemed to start pulsating double time. Santiago's mind quickened; he was suddenly alert and attentive. He watched his son get into the backseat of a police cruiser, and in a panic, he suddenly realized what he had just done. He ran up the hill to his Impala, peeling out from the curb, and raced to tail the police car that carried his son. Behind the cop car, the woman's Suburban followed every turn and every curve. He breathed deeply and tried to believe that everything was going to be okay.

He followed the caravan to a center for children, a facility far away from his neighborhood. He parked across the street from the building, close enough to view the front door but far enough away so that the cops wouldn't notice him sitting in his car.

There was a warrant out for his arrest, and he wanted to be careful the police didn't eye his car from across the street.

Santiago had been caught in possession of marijuana about four months ago. He had been riding in Rubén's car and Rubén had taken a curve too fast and a policeman had pulled them over. The two policemen had asked if they could search his car, and believing it was completely clean, Rubén had agreed. "Nothing to hide here, sir."

Santiago had shaken his head as he was suddenly suspicious why the cops randomly pulled them over and was trying to give Rubén the message to just say no, but he had let them search all the same, and sure enough, they'd found marijuana under the passenger seat. It had been planted in Rubén's car, Santiago was certain. He wasn't sure by whom, but someone who was trying to frame Rubén. Both Santiago and Rubén were written up and both had already spent time in juvie for theft, and they didn't think the law was in their favor, so they ditched their court date when it came up and now there was a warrant out for their arrests. Santiago wanted to stay low, out of the police's view, not only due to his outstanding warrant, but also because he knew he looked out of place in the white, polished area, and he didn't want to raise any suspicions.

From afar, Santiago observed a heavyset police officer with a brown mustache get out of the driver's seat and open the back door for Santiago's son. Marcos sat there, staring, holding his Pooky Bear close to him. Santiago couldn't see his child's face, but he knew Marcos must be scared. In their neighborhood, a badge and a siren were reasons to run, not trust that they would help.

The officer's partner got out of the driver's seat, unbuckled his son's seat belt, and took him by the hand. Santiago could tell that he spoke gently to his son in Spanish and that he must be someone's father. He led Marcos to the front door of the one-story, tan stucco building. The woman from the warehouse parking lot had parked and ran to catch up to the policemen, completely steady on her high-heeled shoes just like one of Charlie's angels, and she looked like she could run miles. They exchanged a few words, and she went inside with them.

As the sun plunged below the horizon, it left a flash of bright red radiating light throughout the sky. Santiago sat in the car and reached across the passenger seat to roll up the tinted window, so that no one could see in.

His car was old, and he had spent a big portion of his time fixing it up, although he still hadn't put in any power locks or window controls. It was a '64 Chevy Impala with two doors and a hard top. It had 425 horsepower, a 409-cubic-inch engine, and four-speed stick shift with the shifter on the floor. The bucket seats were covered with white vinyl, and there was a center console.

He always liked the '64 Impala, but they were difficult to find. He had been looking for the car for years. Since buying this one, he had made it his own; he painted it a metallic dark green, tinted the windows a dark gray, and installed air-bag suspension, enabling the car to sit lower to the ground and then raise it up to drive. Marcos giggled whenever Santiago raised and lowered the car hydraulically, with the touch of a button. Santiago also put in disc brakes, rack and pinion steering, eighteen-inch wheels, and headers and turbo exhaust system. He had recently installed a sound system with a thousand-watt amp, throbbing beat of which could be felt by any car passing by. He was proud of his car not only because it was a distinguishable sweet ride, but because he had fixed it all by himself.

As Santiago sat in his white bucket seat with the windows rolled up, the car started getting warm. He took his hat and bandana off, and used the bandana to wipe the sweat from his face. He held it up to his eyes, and he felt himself close to losing his fight with tears. He loved his son and wanted the best for him. He really believed it would all work out, but once he realized Marcos might fall into a system and never find a family to take care of him, he regretted what he'd done, leaving his son out in the world, out of his care. He should have known; the world wasn't always good to him, but Marcos was lucky, and Santiago wanted to believe there was still hope for him. Santiago bit his knuckle and tried to pull himself together. He opened his hands, palms down, and looked at the letters M-A-R-C-O-S tattooed between the knuckles of his fingers.

He sat up, alert when he saw the two police officers walk casually back to their car, talking and shaking their heads in what he assumed was disgust.

Not knowing the procedure for the search for the child's parents, Santiago waited until the police drove away, and then he turned the key in the ignition, released the brakes, and lightly touched the accelerator to quietly leave his post on the street. He was not at all familiar with the area. He traveled south to give himself a moment to think. He parked his car in the alleyway of a residential area, killing the lights that pierced the growing darkness. He should have known they would take Marcos to a receiving home of some sort. Here he had tried so hard to keep the social workers and cops and family court judges out of his life, but they always found a way in. He sighed. Maybe he should have brought Marcos there in the beginning, or taken him to the children's hospital, where he had heard of others taking their children for care, but he wasn't going to lose hope in the woman from the parking lot who had made him smile. He wanted to believe she would do anything to make sure Marcos was taken care of and that maybe she would take him into her home.

The sky was now pitch-black, and he still sat, alert, as he watched people come and go from their homes. The houses out here didn't have chipped paint and bars on the window. The yards were all well-tended, and he knew that kids played basketball in the street on the weekends. Santiago imagined that, inside each house, a parent was cooking dinner for their kids. They would all sit down together around the table—dad home from work, the kids tired after a day of school—and eat as a family.

They looked at him, these people, not recognizing his car, knowing he didn't belong in that part of town. He assumed the cops were pacing up and down the streets around the giant warehouse looking for suspects, anyone cruel enough to abandon their son in a parking lot. Santiago didn't want to raise suspicion any more than he already had, so he started the engine of his old but faithful car and headed back to the center for children.

When he arrived back at the Polinsky Center, the big-blue Suburban was still there. Relief washed over him. Maybe the woman from the parking lot was inside signing the adoption papers to take Marcos home right away. He watched the door of the building intently. Finally, after what felt like hours, the *señorita* came out alone. He followed her car out of the neighborhood, across the freeway, through downtown, and down the hill near the bay. Her car disappeared into a parking garage of elegant townhomes fronted directly onto the sidewalks. There were no swing sets, no tricycles, no basketball hoops, and no family life in this area of town.

His stomach turned. He realized he had made a terrible mistake. "*¡Diós mío!* Oh God," he said out loud, to himself. "*¿Qué he hecho?* What have I done?"

The Spider
(Evelyn)

The crisp evening air felt good on Evelyn's skin. She could still hear the beat of the music, the tinkling of glasses, and the excited voices from inside, but outside, she could also hear the wind move through the leaves of the palm trees and the horns from the huge cruise ships blow as they arrive into the bay.

Monica stepped out onto the patio. "Evie, what's wrong? Whatever could have happened since yesterday? Did you have a fight with your mother-in-law or hit someone with that big boat of a car?"

Over time, Evelyn had started appreciating Monica for her blunt and honest-even-if-it-hurts approach, and they both enjoyed sarcastic humor, although it was Monica who was careful not to place judgment and put others down. Evelyn appreciated this, but knew she didn't practice it herself. Monica's laugh was a deep chuckle, which was always a compliment to whomever caused her to laugh. Her cynical, dry comments enlivened most conversations.

Monica had dark, silky hair cut in blunt bangs that hung over her brilliant-blue eyes, and generous lips that stretched across her face to show a warm, toothy smile. Her style was her own, although she always looked as if she'd walked out of the nearest thrift store. Tonight, she was wearing a red dress with white retro boots and exaggerated eye makeup; she looked like she had leaped out of a comic book and she was the hero.

Even with their differences, Evelyn always appreciated Monica's refreshing honesty and never had to guess what she was thinking. Evelyn usually kept her feelings guarded from her circle of friends; she had trust issues, as she had learned to keep her feelings to herself as she traveled from one place to another, moved from one school to another—she just wanted to be liked and didn't want to share her feelings out of fear of rejection. But she felt assured she could confide in Monica because there didn't seem to be the typical gossiping or talking behind others' backs with her. She actually felt safe confiding in her.

On the veranda, in the night air, Evelyn turned to Monica with a sense of urgency. "Monica, you won't ever believe what happened." She took a deep breath and continued, "Yesterday, when I went to pick up party stuff at Costco, a little boy came up to me in the parking lot, lost. We couldn't find his parents anywhere. We walked around, we called on the PA in the warehouse, and then we had to call the police to see if he matched any of the missing person's reports."

"Oh, poor thing! How old was he?"

"I'm not sure, maybe three or four years old. He didn't know a lick of English. And you know my Spanish is terrible! Anyway, I bought him some ice cream while we were waiting for the police, and by the time the police came, there was no way I could just leave him with them."

Monica raised her eyebrows. "Oooh, a little compassion for a child?"

"Why would I not show compassion for a child? I never said I don't like kids."

"Uh, no, honey, I didn't say you didn't like kids either, but you not wanting to give birth to any children gave me the impression you might not want to spend the afternoon taking care of one. And didn't you do some sort of pinkie promise with Chad that you two would never speak of the unspeakable—of having kids? I'm just sayin'…"

"I don't want children because my life is too full already, but that doesn't mean I don't like them. Sure, I feel awkward with kids around, but this kid is different. Plus, Chad and I support a few children through our charity work, one in Africa and one in India…" Her voice was shaky, and she sounded defensive, as if she were being attacked.

"Okay, okay. Carry on with your story," Monica said as she fluttered her hand as to encourage her to continue.

"Well, the police took him to the Polinsky Center, a receiving home where kids go until they're reunited with their parents or placed in foster homes."

"Oh, like a group home? Poor boy."

"Not like a group home, just a place to stay temporarily. Anyway, I followed the cops to the Polinsky Center and went in and sat with the little boy while the police spoke with the workers. I just didn't want this little guy to feel abandoned twice, you know? I felt like I had to protect him." Evelyn thought back to yesterday when she'd sat down on the little blue rug with the hopscotch squares on it. She had found some puppets and tried to keep Marcos entertained, but he didn't understand what she was saying. He laughed, amused, and his eyes sparkled, but then he would go back to looking around at the toys. Thinking he was hungry, even after the ice cream, she dug in her designer purse for food. She wasn't like her sister, who had all kinds of foods in her bottomless bag, but Evelyn had managed to find a cranberry Clif Bar and offered it to him. He took it and then couldn't get the slippery package open, so she bent over to tear the wrapper. Marcos had studied the bar, turning it over, examining it, then had cautiously taken a bite until he eventually ate it all. He might never have had a Clif Bar before, but he'd seemed as though he liked it.

Evelyn had sat there trying to remember songs from her childhood and rhymes she would hear her sister saying to amuse Evelyn's niece and nephew. She had started humming "Mary Had a Little Lamb," then started the story of Goldilocks, but Marcos wasn't following, so she'd put up her fingers and took up the motions and started to sing, "The Itsy Bitsy Spider went up the water spout."

Marcos had stood up and waved his hands and excitedly. "Eety beety! Eety beety!"

Evelyn had looked over at the social worker who was sitting at the table in the center of the small room, watching them out of the corner of her eye. "Excuse me, what is he saying?"

The young lady had smiled. "He knows that song, 'Itsy Bitsy Spider.'"

"Oh," Evelyn laughed. "Of course." She put her hands back up in position and tried again, "The Itsy Bitsy Spider…"

Marcos sang back, "*La Araña Pequeñita.*"

"Went up the water spout."

"*Subió, subió, subió.*" Little brown fingers wiggling in the air. And he'd continued on with the "Itsy Bitsy Spider" motions and words.

"*Cayó la lluvia*"—fingers waving down for rain—"*y se la llevó*"—waved his hands away as the spider was washed by a big wave—"*salió el sol*"—put his arms over his head for a big sun up in the sky—"*y todo lo secó*"—he waved his hands out, as if swatting a fly—"*y la Araña Pequeñita*"—his fingers wiggling together up to the sky—"*subió, subió, subió!*" he exclaimed at the end.

Slowly, Evelyn had become enamored with this little boy's big brown eyes, his chubby cheeks; she noticed his freckles again and how they spread from one cheek and traveled over his nose to the other cheek. He had loopy, big curls of auburn hair. His hands were chubby, with little dents for knuckles. He appeared to be well taken care of, and he seemed calm. He didn't seem to be upset or worried, sitting here singing with a Caucasian woman he had never seen before this afternoon. He had seemed almost happy, and Evelyn had been surprised to realize that she was too.

"I think he likes you," the social worker, Jessica, had observed.

Evelyn had smiled and felt a flush of pride and joy. "Really? You think so?"

Jessica had smiled and nodded her head.

"Well, I think I like him too."

♋

Now, standing on the veranda with Monica, it seemed like that had happened a lifetime ago Evelyn gazed out at the view of the San Diego skyline and the harbor as she tried to summarize her thoughts. "Something happened then, Monica. There was a connection," Evelyn said in a hushed tone.

"Connection?" Monica looked into Evelyn's face, confused. When she thought of Evelyn, she had always thought of her flashy clothes, her endless colors of Mary Jane–high heels, her intense exercise schedule and spontaneous trips overseas with her husband, and her green Mini with a peacock feather painted on the rooftop. She had never known her for having an interest in children. "What are you saying?"

"Oh, I don't know, Monica. You should've seen this little boy. He's just the cutest thing ever. And so gentle and kind. Oh, and he has this enamoring laugh, like a guttural rattle from inside—a most unique laugh." She fidgeted with her wineglass and tilted her head thoughtfully. "Something happened, Monica, and I just can't stop thinking about him."

Life in the US of A

Santiago's mother had had a difficult time adjusting to life in the States—or maybe she had been confused about who she was before she crossed the border, and it wasn't life in a foreign land after all. Nobody was sure; they just knew that Alejandra couldn't quite find her way home, whatever direction home would be.

Santiago's parents met in Tijuana, on his dad's smoke break from assembling sprinkler parts in a maquiladora located in town. His mom had waltzed by, giggling and whispering with her friends. Santiago Senior had seen the young girl parade along the street before, and was surprised when she came over to him. She'd asked if he had another cigarette that he wouldn't mind sharing and that was the beginning of their relationship. He was eighteen and she was sixteen. When she turned eighteen, they were married and crossed the border to what they hoped was a better life, with more work and education opportunities, and then settled into a safe place to raise their children. But for Alejandra, it was the walk across that invisible line that brought confusion and loneliness. She never was able to become fluent in English, and she was separated from her family. Santiago Senior thought that if Alejandra had crossed the border again, back to visit relatives, she might not have been able to cross again.

Santiago Senior thought if they had a baby, it would solve all her problems, and that she would feel a sense of belonging that San Diego would feel like the home she had been searching for. Santiago Junior was born when Alejandra was nineteen years old. She held him and sang to him, but as time passed, she started feeling homesick again, as she didn't have her mother or her aunties there to help her or give advice about raising a baby boy. Santiago Senior's mother would come around once in a while, but she was busy all week cleaning houses, and they only saw her on weekends. As the years rolled on, Alejandra had started drinking and would tell her husband in the evenings to watch the boy because she had errands to run. Several hours later, she would come back with a few groceries. Santiago Senior started getting suspicious when it would take her longer and longer to go to the local market.

A few years later she had become pregnant with a girl, and they'd named her Carmelita. Alejandra had been excited about her baby girl for a while, but then she had lost interest. She felt so isolated in their little house, taking care of two kids, and yet she felt so young herself. She had started hanging out at nightclubs, and when other men gave her attention, she had felt that maybe she still looked good, that maybe she wasn't quite ready to be a *mami* to two kids quite yet. It was then that she began to stay out all night and come back the next day.

As a young boy, Santiago Junior would sometimes see his mother stagger down the street as she came home at odd times of the day, her hair all tousled, as if a she had a bird's nest perched on top. Black would be smeared over her eyes and down her cheeks. Her shirt would be on backward or misbuttoned. Her skirt would be lopsided with the zipper half-down. Sometimes she would come back with only one shoe, limping down the street.

As she came into the house, she would see Santiago Junior and smile and pat him on his head and say, "Well, *hola Santi*, baby boy." And then she would go into her room, close the door, and he would hear her fall onto her bed. About an hour later, he would hear her call out, "*Santi, Santi*, bring me a bucket." And he would fetch the bucket that he kept under the sink for these occasions and take it to her, and she would throw up in it, and he would wet a rag and hand it to her so she could wipe her face. Then she would smile at him from under the vomit in her hair and fall back into her bed without the pillow and no covers and sleep till midday. His dad slept on the couch. The next day, his mom would start the process all over again— she would be out all night and back at a random time during the day.

Santiago Senior had felt as if he'd lost all control or influence over his wife and knew he had to be the one to take care of the kids; he had to be the responsible one. He found Carmelita a day care and took Santiago Junior to school every day. Santiago Senior's mother started coming around to help him with dinner and some of the cleaning. He never raised his voice to his wife, and he never forced her to stay. He knew she felt lost here, and he blamed himself for bringing her over the border and that he was not able to be her everything. He might have gone back over the border with her, but now that they had the children, he wanted them to have a better life, with opportunities here in the United States.

Since Santiago's father he had experience in Mexico assembling sprinklers and had been able to get an assembly-line job soon after he came over to the United States. The company had sponsored him, and he had been able to get his green card to work in the States legally. After working there for several years on the line, Santiago Senior had moved up and was given the job of material inventory specialist, where he had to handle dangerous material. He kept inventory and transported material with his forklift experience, and he oversaw the crane operation. One day, there had been an explosion in the warehouse, and Santiago's father and his assistant in training had caught on fire. Santiago Senior died on the ambulance trip to the hospital, but his assistant lived and suffered severe burns. There were lots of safety protocols on-site, and Santiago's dad had been a stickler for following rules, but he had allowed his assistant to take on much of the responsibility and found there was a mix-up with flammable gas in the warehouse, and somehow it had been ignited. The details were never revealed and a coworker had come over to the Medinas' house to report the devastating news.

It was when Santiago Senior died in the tragic accident that Alejandra decided to cross the border one last time, back to what was familiar to her. She wrote down a contact name and number, gave it to *Abuelita*, and then left. She left without her kids, because she said they were better off here in the States, that there were more opportunities for them here, and that *Abuelita* could take care of them. And then she was gone. Santiago hadn't seen her since that day. He would hear from her occasionally. He was fourteen when she sent him a letter asking for him to send her money. He had to be creative on how to make money, but he would do his best to take care of her the only way he could from the other side of the border, because she was still his mother. He also knew it was what his father would have wanted him to do.

He often thought about how she would titubate down the street toward their house and how he would see people in the other houses peek around their curtains and watch her through their living room windows. He would sometimes recall the smell of her vomit that would penetrate throughout the house. He would also remember looking at his father's face and seeing the shadow of sadness.

He didn't want his child to grow up the way he did. He didn't want him to feel lonely or miss out on his childhood by tending to his parents. He didn't want his child to be without a mother—or a father for that matter. So many of his friends grew up without fathers; the dads would skip town or just leave the house to never come back. These kids should be out playing soccer and hanging out with their friends at that age, not taking care of their parents. They should be laughing and taking trips, not looking for ways to make money to support an entire family. The weight of responsibility shouldn't come so soon. Life was too short to miss out on one's precious few years as a child. Santiago wanted something different for his family.

He was so thankful for his *abuelita*, who saved his life in many ways, but he didn't want his child to grow up without a *mami* and a *papa*. He wanted to break the cycle and see his child become what he dreamed—to be free from the life of the streets and touch life of opportunity. He knew it was out there; it just wasn't in his grasp. But Marcos was young enough to still have a chance. Not only had his *abuelita* save his and Carmalita's life in so many ways, but it was also his friend Rubén who changed the direction of Santiago's life more than he would ever know.

Santiago had met Rubén when they were in third grade. They had played soccer together at recess, but they didn't start hanging out together after school until the end of the school year. They'd both seemed to not have anywhere to go, so they would wander the streets, looking for something to keep them entertained. Rubén had always been fidgeting in his chair, and teachers had kept telling him to pay attention. He had gone to special classes with only a few students, but he hadn't been able to sit still long enough and was just not interested in learning, it seemed. Santiago thought Rubén was smart; he just talked too much and had other things to do than sit and listen to boring teachers.

One day when they were kicking a soccer ball back and forth in an empty lot near Rubén's house, they saw a couple fifth graders walk by. Santiago and Rubén had seen them with a group of boys before, roaming the neighborhood, and Rubén had suggested that day that they ask them if they wanted to play some soccer with them. Together, they had run over and asked if they wanted to play some *fútbol.*

"Join you? You'd have to join our group first, and I don't think you would be able to hang with us," one of the fifth graders had replied. He'd stuck out his chest and looked proud, and to Rubén and Santiago, the two fifth graders had looked so much bigger now that they stood so close.

"Whatcha talking about? We want to hang with you. What do we gotta do to hang?"

The two fifth graders, had looked at each other and scratched their heads, almost shrugging their shoulders.

"Well, you are a bit too young, but if you can show us you can get some stuff for us, maybe we'll consider."

"Sure, whatcha need?" Rubén said, a bit eager to be considered.

"Well, um, I think I'm hungry and need some Skittles and a drink. How about you, *Ese?*" he said to the other fifth grader.

"I want a root beer and maybe an ice cream cone. Yeah, that's it. It's a hot day, and I need some refreshing ice cream. If you get that for us, we'll consider you hanging with us."

Without a discussion, Rubén had gently hit Santiago on the chest and said, "Let's go. But I got to get something from my house." Santiago hadn't said anything the entire time, but he had nothing else to do and he did want to hang with the fifth graders, so he went along with Rubén and decided to join him.

Rubén had run into his house briefly and come out wearing a jacket, which Santiago had thought interesting, since it was summer and warm outside. "I know where to get all that stuff. Follow me," Rubén had said as he picked up the pace to a slow jog and weaved among the streets until he came to a corner 7-Eleven. "We can get it here."

"What do you mean get it here? I can ask *Abuelita* if she has something we can get them if they're hungry."

Rubén had put hands to his face in frustration; his friend just didn't get that they would be inducted into the fifth grade neighborhood gang if they could get the boys their requested items. "No, *estúpido*, just go in the store and get the candy and drink and then come out. I'll take care of the rest and be a distraction."

"What? We can't just go in and take things?" Santiago had said innocently.

"Sure you can. Just go in and get what they want. Don't you want to hang with the fifth graders?"

"Yeah."

"Then go in there, get your stuff, and leave at my cue. Ready?"

"Yeah, okay," Santiago had said hesitantly.

They'd pushed open the glass doors, and a bell had rung at their entrance. Rubén gave Santiago a nod toward the candy and then jetted off in a different direction.

Santiago stood in front of the candy display and stared at the selection. There was candy there that he was unfamiliar with, and he couldn't find the Skittles. He stared at the candy and couldn't escape thinking about what his dad would think about what he was about to do. He knew his father wouldn't have approved. His dad had come over the Mexican border, and every day he was in the States, he had felt thankful to be there. He'd worked hard, paid his taxes, and voted. He had taken his new citizenship seriously, and he always told Santiago to do good work and go to school and be thankful for what the US of A had to offer them. Santiago continued staring at the candy, feeling self-conscious about what he was going to do, when he'd looked up and had seen Rubén flitting around the store. Santiago looked down again, feeling guilty, and still couldn't find Skittles. Then, he saw Rubén at the checkout, paying for some gum, and he heard him say, "Thanks, Mr. White. Enjoy your day." He'd whistled softly, to get Santiago's attention, and nodded toward the door. In a panic, Santiago had grabbed a candy, stuffed it in his back pocket, and caught up with Rubén as he casually walked out the door, whistling a tune while Santiago was wiping the sweat off his brow.

They had sprinted over to where they'd last seen the fifth graders, and Santiago had noticed that Rubén's jacket was bulky but he was juggling whatever it was in there as gracefully as a kangaroo carries her baby in her pouch. They found the fifth graders nearby in the empty lot, kicking Santiago's soccer ball around.

"Well, there are those twerps. You came back, third graders. Did you bring us our snacks, cuz we're hungry?" one of them said, glancing at the other.

"Yeah, we got 'em," Rubén replied.

"Okay, you there," the smaller fifth grader said to Santiago. "What the hell did you get?" He squinted at him.

"I got you some candy." Santiago reached back to his pocket and pulled up out a Snickers bar.

"I asked for Skittles, not a Snickers. And it's smashed. I can't eat a smashed Snickers. And where's my drink?" he said, holding the squished Snickers up in disgust. During his brief panic he'd had in the store, Santiago had completely forgotten about the drink request.

"So, what did you get, little squirt?" the bigger boy said to Rubén.

Rubén had smiled from ear to ear. "Well," he said slowly to build the suspension, "I present you with root beer!" Rubén pulled out a liter of A&W root beer, not just a can of it.

"Good work little, one, but what about my ice cream? It's a hot day, ya know."

Rubén held up his hand to ask for some patience. "Oh, now for the creamy vanilla ice cream," he said as he reached into his jacket again and pulled out a full gallon of Dreyer's vanilla ice cream.

The two fifth graders looked at each other, their eyes wide and their mouth gaping in surprise.

"But, wait. I've got more," Rubén said putting his hand up again and his head down as to present his next item as he stuck his hand in his jacket again and pulled out four red cups and his last item were a package of straws.

"Shit." The fifth graders had exchanged glances and laughed in disbelief of their new found thief. "You're in, little dudes. Good work." They'd slapped them on their backs and given them hearty congratulations. On that day, the three other boys had discovered that not only was this not the first time Rubén had stolen, but that he was an expert bandit.

Rubén had raced back to his house to get a big serving spoon to scoop out the ice cream, and together, the four boys had sat on the edge of the sidewalk and had root beer floats.

The second week of seventh grade, Rubén had enough of school and figured he knew how to read and write and had basic math skills, which, he decided, was enough information to survive in the world. He also needed to make money, and school was getting in the way. Dropping out of school was not an option for Santiago, as his *Abuela* who said she would stop feeding him her carne asada and kick him out on the streets if he dropped out of school—she wouldn't allow it. She was a firm believer in school being a benefit of life in America, and she said that is why she and Santiago's grandfather and then Santiago's father had risked their lives to cross the border: so Santiago could have a good education. When she said it like that, Santiago knew staying in school and graduating was what he had to do. But he also knew he had to make extra money for his family and send money to his mother—his grandmother had no idea that Santiago was sending money to his mother. So Santiago would go to school, cart "packages," freshly delivered marijuana, from the drop house to the client, all in the few hours he had after class. And then after all that running around, he would get home late and sit down to do his homework. He worked extra hard on the weekends. The life of kicking-the-can around or even playing a game of soccer was gone.

Although Rubén and Santiago had been friends for a long time, sometimes Rubén annoyed him, with his constant chatter and his need for approval, but sometimes it didn't matter because Santiago knew Rubén was the most loyal person he ever knew.

Rubén had a difficult upbringing, although he also never complained about being cheated out of a childhood. Santiago and Rubén had one thing in common and that was their mothers had left them at an early age. Rubén's mother had left his family when he was eight years old, and he said he remembered that day, when his mom told him she was going out to get some milk, but then he saw her gently open the tailgate of their family truck and quietly, not asking for any help, started placing bags of stuff in the truck. She went back and forth, from house to truck, always looking around to see if anyone had noticed her. When she was finally finished trekking back and forth, she came over to Rubén, stuffed some bills in his back pocket, and whispered in his ear, "In case you run out of milk again. You be a good boy." He'd watched her from the front porch as she drove away; she never looked back to wave or even to take a final look. Rubén claimed that at that moment in time, he knew he would never see her again, he knew that she was leaving them forever, and yet he didn't run after her or cry later, when he was sitting in his bed. She had left her three boys to fend for themselves. Maybe she thought they were stronger than she was, and she just couldn't face their father another day. Rubén reckoned she was just tired of the abuse. It just wasn't worth it to her anymore.

Rubén was the middle of two brothers. The oldest was ten at the time and had already started smoking and staying out for long periods of time. Their younger brother was five and still sucked his thumb and carried a blanket around. Their dad was a third-generation Mexican American citizen who was proudly honorably discharged from the military. He was discharged due to medical reasons, and every third day of the month, he stood in line at the bank to cash in his check. On the fourth of the month, the boys quietly sat in their room, trying not to bring any attention to themselves. After their dad cashed his monthly check, he bought all the groceries and beer for what was supposed to last for the entire month—lots of beer. And he would drink and drink, until the beer was all gone, which usually lasted for ten days. The refrigerator and cupboards would be empty, and the beer was gone by the fourteenth.

To make ends meet for the last two weeks of the month, they had to be creative. His dad had arranged with a friend to take some paying customers from Mexico over the border. He had a closed-in bench built inside the van, and he would have the people who'd paid curl up inside the oversized bench; he could safely get three average-sized people into the enclosure, four if they curled up very tight. When they arrived at the border, he would have his three boys sit on the bench and have them playing their Gameboys or just arguing to make it look like normal life. They would cross the border and drop their clients off at the mall in Chula Vista. Then, he would drive straight to the nearest grocery store and buy beer, Pepsi, milk, bread, and eggs in that order.

Milk, Pepsi, and bread were not enough to fill the stomachs of three growing boys, so Rubén and his older brother started stealing food. They would go to the 7-Eleven wearing jackets they'd cut slits in the lining of, so they could slip in food quickly without anyone noticing, a bag inside their coats so no one would notice the food. His brother would buy some gum or Hostess donuts with change they would find on the street or in their dad's pockets, and they would walk out without a single sidewise glance or causing any suspicion. They would rotate their visits among three 7-Elevens, a Vons grocery store, and a gas station convenience store. Their younger brother never came with them, and they never asked him to. They also never took food from the local Mexican stores or food trucks.

When his older brother was picked up by the cops for drug possession and his younger brother left to stay with an aunt in North County who was still in contact with their mother, it was only Rubén and his father still in the house. Rubén wasn't about to join his younger brother; he felt his mother was a deserter, and he didn't want anything to do with her or her side of the family. It was then that running drugs for the lieutenants started to appeal to him and that is when he quit attending school and started running packages for the officers. He was able to pay the rent and utility bills and started cooking healthier meals. He also gave money to his dad, who, in turn, would, not surprisingly, spend it on more beer. They no longer brought Mexicans over the border or stole food from 7-Eleven.

After all those years—of his father's neglect, his mother's abandonment, and his brother's extended stay in prison for stabbing someone while in the pokey—Rubén never spoke ill of his father, continued to visit his brother regularly, and never mentioned a word about his mother. He never held anything against his younger brother, who had run to their mother's side and was never to be seen again.

Rubén had already been running drugs when he convinced Santiago that it was good money and that Santiago should join him. They enjoyed hanging out with the guys they worked with and felt like they were part of something bigger than themselves—they felt important. The gang started giving them other projects, just to find out how much they would do for them—they stole food, a computer out the back of a car, a flat screen TV from a store, and they beat a guy up. After their initiation, they could move up in ranks. They joined the gang to have a sense of belonging, to feel protected, and mostly, to make money and support their families. Santiago tried to lay low in the group and focus on his job, but Rubén was eager to move up the chain of command quickly and be accepted by the gang. He kowtowed to whatever the gang members wanted. He frequently said things to other members that would make Santiago cringe. Rubén's attempt to be cool was a bit too eager, and Santiago saw some of other members turn their backs on Rubén and snicker at some of his quirky gestures and offhanded jokes. Rubén was also a sloppy dresser, which didn't give him any more respect, as the gang members prided themselves on their tidy clothes and dressing to represent the group in a respectable manner.

Rubén was a bit scrawny, with a nervous twitch. He was either smoking or thumping his hands and banging his feet. He never stopped moving, and it seemed to Santiago, he never stopped talking either. He wasn't sure who could talk the longest or fastest, Rubén or Santiago's sister, Lita. Rubén wore his hat sideways, in the effort to look cool, of course. He wore a bandana underneath it, one diamond earring, and a black rope necklace with a silver-cross hanging from it.

Although many in the gang didn't give Rubén attention after "work" hours, Rubén worked harder than any of the other soldiers and surprised them all by bringing in a substantial amount of money. He was fiercely loyal and did anything the gang asked him to do without question. For that reason, Rubén was valuable to the group. They may have talked about him behind his back and not included him in some of their insider dealings, but they kept him around and made sure he still felt included enough. Rubén had to grow up very fast when he was out on his own, but despite all his quirks, he was streetwise, sly, faithful, responsible, and a profitable worker. Santiago feared

Rubén wouldn't move up in ranks too fast, but knew the gang would protect him when the time came.

The only time Santiago saw Rubén calm was while he was smoking a cigarette. Rubén didn't do drugs because he didn't like being less in control of his body.

He also knew Rubén was a light sleeper, and it was rare that Santiago ever saw him asleep or even drowsy. He knew Rubén would stay up with him in the wee hours of the morning, waiting for a runner, as Rubén was always alert and noticed any movement in the distance. He was also quick to react. Santiago always felt Rubén had his back and would keep him safe, even if it meant sacrificing himself.

Santiago and Rubén remained close friends, even though it was easy to get caught up in the petty beefs within the gang. Rubén had always been there for Santiago, helping him with his family, keeping an eye out to make sure his sister didn't get in too much trouble, and he took Santiago's grandmamma home several times when she was wandering the streets. Rubén was more than a friend. He was like a brother.

Life
Rearranged

&

The Visit
(Evelyn)

The bed shook as Chad sat up, threw his legs over the side, and put on his Chaz shoes. He rubbed his eyes and unsteadily attempted to stand up. Evelyn rolled over and looked out at the dimly lit sky. She watched as Chad sauntered over to the bathroom, and she glanced over at the alarm clock, not really able to focus on the time.

"Where the hell are you going, mister?"

"Oh, sorry, Evie. I didn't mean to wake you." He turned back around and crawled on all fours across the bed to kiss her on the forehead. "I have to go to work. I have rounds at oh six hundred."

"Didn't you tell them you just had a birthday, and you should have the day off, on a Sunday nonetheless? I didn't know you had to work the day after the party. Are you hung over?"

"No. I only had a couple drinks last night, since I knew I had to work today. I'm covering for someone who covered for me when we went to Colorado on that mountain biking trip. It just ended up being the day after the party. I'm sorry to leave you with the mess. I'll help clean up when I get home."

"Ah, your mom and Monica stayed and helped clean up while you were saying your good-byes. There's not much left to do. Don't you have a twelve-hour shift?"

"Yes, but I'll still help you. Just leave it till I get home." He rolled over her to get up on the other side of the bed and headed toward the bathroom again. Evelyn knew it would bother him all day, knowing that there was anything out of place in their house. He was a clean freak, and every item had a designated spot in their house.

"Do you want to take the leftover cupcakes to work with you?"

"Maybe. Those scoundrels at work eat everything, especially the third shift doctors. They act as if they haven't eaten in days. I think the late hours make them hungrier," he said from the bathroom, leaving the door open as he peed so he could talk at the same time.

"Ha, well, that solves that, but don't worry about the rest of the leftovers. It's not much, and what is left I'll just throw in the trash." Evelyn brushed the hair out of her face and sat up to see if it was cloudy or just still dark outside. "Did you have a great time?" she said a bit more enthusiastically than she intended in the early hours of the morning.

"Oh, Ev, you way outdid yourself. How the hell did you find Stanley Cougar? I don't even remember the last time I saw that guy." He washed his hands diligently, like any good doctor would—even if he was just going to get in the shower.

"Spencer surfs with him, so they've been in contact, Facebook friends or something. You know those surfers all find each other one way or another."

"Yes, yes I know." Chad walked on her side of the bed and smoothed her corn flour-colored hair back. "Hon, you go back to sleep. I had such a great time. Thank you."

She smiled as he looked into her eyes with genuine appreciation. "You're welcome. Now you get out of here before they rethink you joining the fellowship next month," she said jokingly, turning back into her pillow and pulling up the covers. "You've waited so long and worked so hard for this opportunity."

"Exactly. I won't mess that up," Chad replied seriously.

Since Chad had been at the UCSD hospital, he'd developed an interest in robotic urologic microsurgery during his residency, and he'd spent a month undergoing special training. Recently, Chad had been awarded a two-year fellowship in Urology; it sent a wave of exhilaration through him every time he thought about it. It wasn't easy to get such a privileged opportunity as to be included in such a small, select group of surgeons. It was an honor. He hadn't announced it to his friends yet. Evelyn had thought he was going to let people know at the party, but he didn't want any more attention than he'd already had last night. He wouldn't let anything stand in his way of advancing in his career, and he was devoted to his profession and his patients. He had worked too hard to get this advancement, and he was willing to give up his gym time or social time with their friends to make sure he was doing all he could in his job.

Evelyn turned onto her side and stared at the ray of the light coming through the crack of the bathroom door. She thought about how the birthday party had played out. She thought about hers and Chad's friends, their lives together, and their initial meeting six years ago.

Chad and Evelyn had met on a bicycle trip from Rosarito to Ensenada, an organized trip that was an annual tradition for many. Addy had asked Evelyn if she wanted to go with her, and since neither of them had gone on the fifty-mile bicycle trip to Mexico before, they had thought they should go. A "ride along the Pacific Coast and inland through rural countryside from Rosarito Beach to Ensenada," Addy had read from the website promoting the event, "plus a Finish-Line Fiesta on the Ensenada waterfront with food, drinks, and live music until sunset." Of course, Evelyn had been up for the new adventure.

Addy was an intense person and when she spoke, she looked directly into her listener's eyes. If the conversation turned personal or emotional, she would avert her eyes and strike up a different conversation. She read the *Wall Street Journal*, *Science News*, and *Tech World* and she considered herself an expert in politics, she knew all the muscles and parts of the body and their functions, and she was up-to-date on the latest technology trends. It was exhausting for most people to be around Addy for any length of time, but if it involved an adventure, Evelyn wasn't effected by Addy's particularities. Evelyn decided to go.

It was a sunny day in early May. Addy had already had her bike sparkly clean with all the safety gadgets and reflectors on the back, and a little horn she would honk if anyone got in her way. Evelyn had an eighteen-hundred-dollar cross-country bike that she was unwilling to take down to Mexico, so she'd started calling friends the night before, begging to borrow their bike, or in other words, using her "charm," to persuade someone to let her take their bike down to Mexico. A guy named Cooper said she could use his bike for the day. It was old, but "no scratching it, and don't lose it in Mexico," he'd said. "You know how crazy it can get at the party at the end of the race." Evelyn and Addy stood in the parking lot in a line with other bikers as they waited for the bus to arrive that would take them down to Rosarito, Mexico—about a forty-five-minute drive. Evelyn sat on the bike, trying to adjust the seat's height. Cooper was shorter than she'd thought or maybe just had shorter legs than her. She raised the seat and adjusted the gears. "What the hell? This bike hasn't even been used in years and needs a tune-up. What was his problem letting me take it? Was he worried I was going to wreck it because I'm reckless or if I was going to get in a wreck because he hasn't maintained it?" She squinted at the brakes, trying to evaluate if they even worked and if they would stick going down some of the steep hills they'd be riding.

"It was nice of him to get up so early this morning and have it ready for you," Addy said, trying to be the optimist.

"Yeah, yeah. Sure it was. I don't think he's even taken it out of his garage since 1992. He had to get up to clean it, so I wouldn't see the cobwebs weaved among the spokes. Why the hell didn't he come with us anyway? He could have signed up when we asked him in the first place? Although I wouldn't be able to borrow his bike if he came, but all the same, I think he is a wannabe biker and hasn't ridden this bike ever."

"What the hell, Evie? You already have a bike and could have brought that one."

"True, very true, so I'm hoping this one gets me down to the fiest-a," she said exaggerating the *a*.

"I'm rather sure he could beat you in any bike ride. You go to work and sit on your bum, while he goes to work and does yoga. He might even take a spin class every day of the week."

"I could still take him and you know it." Evelyn became somber real quick—she hated being challenged, especially when the person wasn't even there for her to prove she could beat them. She started mumbling to herself about how she was going to show him she could beat him to the finish on the next bike trip.

As they pushed their bikes up on the trailer attached to the back of a truck designated to follow the bus going to Mexico, Evelyn noticed a guy with defined calves placing his bike next to theirs. His tight, black Lycra bike shorts peeked out from underneath blue running shorts with a white Nike swoosh on the bottom left leg. He wore a gray T-shirt that read "Light up the Night," a race she had also run, which led the runners through the streets of San Diego in the slight chill of the October night. Evelyn watched as he and his friend climbed into the bus and sat in the front seat. Evelyn gently tugged on Addy's shirtsleeve and then motioned her to quickly climb into the bus. They nabbed the seat behind the two guys.

"Well, hello, ladies," the friend of the "Light up the Night" said as he turned around in his seat, hand extended. "I'm Charlie."

Evelyn and Addy shook his hand politely.

"Pleased to meet you, and here is my friend Chad," Charlie said as he slapped his friend's arm lightly with the back of his hand. Chad turned around without an extended hand but with a nod and a quick hello. "Yes, Charlie and Chad. We're the C-H friends," Charlie said, "but don't get us confused. Chaddie here might bite or something."

"Screw you," Chad mumbled in jest.

Charlie laughed and then stood up and excused himself as he went to say hi to someone else he'd recognized in the back of the bus. Addy got up to use the little bathroom in the back, claiming it was better to use this tiny bathroom than the germ-infested outhouse in Mexico.

Evelyn and Chad both sat on the right side of their green, padded bus benches, next to the window.

"Have you ever been on this trip before?" Evelyn asked in effort to start a conversation.

"Yeah, a couple of times, although not with Charlie here," he said as he patted the seat where Charlie had been sitting for a brief time. "I think I'll be pulling him up the hill or find him stuck in some Mexican pub along the way."

Evelyn laughed under her breath. "Yes, my friend might be pulling me out of a ditch too. I borrowed a real dumpy bike from a friend."

"I think you'll do okay," Chad said as he turned away. After a moment if hesitation, he said, "So, you don't have a bike?" as if he was surprised she wouldn't have her own bike.

So the conversation began about exercise and their workout schedules. He talked about how difficult it was to exercise now that he was a medical resident, and she laughed about the dinky fitness center at her office.

They stepped off the bus and lifted their bikes off the trailer. Evelyn noticed that Chad led Charlie over to where she and Addy were getting on their bikes, and so together they started cycling on the black asphalt road along the Mexico coast. They weaved among the other bikers and followed the road that sat close to the steep cliffs, which plummeted, with no warning and no road rail or even a rope, down to crashing waves. The ocean escorted them along the old road that weaved next to low-level mountains, dipping them down hills, propelling them up to great heights with magnificent views of the wide, dark-blue waters. As they slowed through villages, Addy and Evelyn watched as Charlie threw out candy to the kids along the roadside and witnessed Chad stopping to help a fallen rider with their scrapes and sprains. Chad had a backpack complete with ointments, ankle wraps, and small and large Band-Aids. Soon, people figured out he was a doctor (he didn't tell them he was only resident at the time), and riders would come up alongside him and start listing off their ailments. Chad would inform them that he was studying to be urologist, and not understanding what a urologist did, they still continued to complain of some sort of discomfort—stomach problems, back pain, joint aches, knee pain, yes, lots of knee pain. An ulcer, arthritis, meniscus? Chad would respond just using common reasons for those pains.

They stopped at a small village, and Charlie entertained the kids with his hand tricks and blew up a few balloons, tying them into Weiner dogs, because that, he confessed, was the only animal he knew how to tie. The kids would holler out to him some other animals, "*más animales*," and Charlie responded in Spanish, "only Weiner dogs," and then that would make the kids laugh and then they would ask again, just to hear him announce again, "*sólo Weiner perros.*"

They stopped at a pub and downed two shots of tequila and then came back out and threw their legs over their bikes, hopped on, and were back on the road again. Evelyn noticed Chad was in excellent shape, and she watched his muscles flex as he peddled up the hill. She herself struggled with her bike, which kept clicking and wouldn't switch into gear. She was completely embarrassed and kept announcing that the only reason she was not in the lead was because of the bike. Cooper had said it was a still a good bike, but she begged to differ. She found that it stopped clicking in third gear, which didn't help her get up the hills.

Chad not only came prepared with simple medical supplies, but he was also weighted down with plenty of water and Powerbars enough to share. He also came with a container of hand wipes, and he kept pulling out those damp toilettes, cleaning his hands vigorously. He came well prepared. Evelyn observed him as he watched his friend, Charlie, entertain the crowds, and stood back and just laughed peacefully, and Evelyn thought he looked so kind and caring. He didn't seem to care that his friend was getting all the attention—it was as if he didn't notice, and she assumed it was because Chad was confident in who he was and didn't need to be in the center of attention. He was not only well prepared, but he was also well educated, seemed kind, and very fit. She was instantly interested in him, and it appeared to be mutual, as he followed her all the way to Ensenada, where the old road ended and the party began.

Together they weaved through the crowds of the fiesta and navigated up and down rows of booths selling handmade ponchos, wallets, and other trinkets, including velvet paintings of Elvis or Jesus, and of course, margaritas and pitchers of beer. They tried on sombreros and tasted the hot sauce. They ate their tacos with carne asada and tried the pozole verde—too hot for their gringo tongues; even though Evelyn pretended it didn't have any effect on her, she knew her eyes were watery and gave her away. She bought a colorful wrap and tied it around her hips, and Chad bought a bandana and tied it around his forehead. Together they bought bracelets and downed more margaritas. Addy didn't seem to mind watching Evelyn and Chad's relationship bloom in front of her, nor did she seem to mind that the budding lovers were not paying any attention to her. Charlie wore a big, colorful sombrero, and he was easy to find among the crowd not only for his hat, but also for his hearty laugh, which could be heard above the cacophony. As he weaved among the crowd, he would find them and hang out awhile, and then he was off carousing and socializing again with his new audience. Charlie was causing either a ruckus or a cheer, as he went through the crowd carrying a margarita with a big umbrella floating in it.

Chad and Evelyn sat next to each other on the bus ride back to San Diego, while Addy fell asleep in the seat behind them and Charlie sat in the back, telling stories to his audience. The two exchanged numbers as they parted, and two days later, Chad invited Evelyn out to Elsie's Wine Bar, and then out again just a few days later. They started running, hiking, and swimming together, and going out on weekends to new, trendy restaurants in town. Soon, they were exclusive, and they started inviting friends along on their outings. They continued to ride bikes together and ran in races raising funds for whatever illness needed more money or awareness. Then they started taking trips together: skiing in Aspen, surfing in Costa Rica, hiking Mount Whitney, and biking cross country. After about a year of traveling and enjoying life together, Chad took her out for dinner and was ready for a serious discussion about their relationship.

"Evelyn, I have enjoyed my year with you, and I think it's been one of, if not the, best year of my life. I just don't want to mess it up. I don't want to ruin what we have…and I just wanted to say…well, I think it would be the appropriate and honest thing in our relationship to tell you now that I want to be exclusive with you, and I…well…don't want to have kids. I mean, I never want to have kids. I'm just not a kid person, and I love the spontaneous lifestyle we have been living, and I think kids would just complicate our lives." He sat there wringing his cloth napkin in his hands, and his eyes darted toward the window and then back at her, and then darted to the corner of the room and then back at her.

"Yes, I know what you mean."

"Really? You do? I've just seen so many people who have been in love and enjoying life together, and as soon as they have a kid, they're trapped. They don't go out, they can't travel, they start arguing about money about responsibilities, and on and on. I just don't want that for us."

Evelyn smiled, looked intently into Chad's eyes, and reached out her hand to touch his. "I feel the same way. I'm not a kid person either, and they sometimes annoy me, actually. They get in my way at the grocery store, and most of them are rude. I would much rather spend my time with you and not complicate life with kid troubles."

"Ahh, I'm so relieved. I wasn't sure how you felt about having kids, but I'm so relieved we feel the same way. I thought this might be the moment that you reconsidered us and our future. I wasn't sure if maybe you had dreamed all your life of being a mom and wouldn't want to have it any other way. It didn't seem as if you were that type, but I wasn't sure, because we've never talked about kids. I'm so thankful we're on the same page."

"Yes, I'm so thankful too. It's me and you, mister." And they sealed their discussion on not having kids with a kiss.

A year later, they moved into together, and year after that, Chad proposed. The year of the party and the year of his fellowship, they'd quietly celebrated their fourth anniversary with a good-morning kiss and a clink of their coffee cups on their way out the door and on to work.

As the warm gray light brightened their bedroom a little the day after Chad's birthday party, Evelyn heard the whir of the blender as Chad concocted some sort of smoothie, maybe something with flaxseed and various greens and beets that they had bought at the farmer's market Saturday morning. She listened to him empty out the dishwasher and could just imagine him taking a clean towel and rubbing the rim of each glass to make sure there were no lip marks on any of them before placing them in the cupboard in a perfect row with the other sterilized glasses.

Evie lay quietly in bed a few more minutes, reliving the details of the party, but every so often, she remembered the large, trusting eyes of a little boy as he had gently held her hand. *Why*, she wondered, *hadn't Marcos seemed more upset about his missing parents?*

When she finally heard the back door shut and the garage door hum close, she jumped out of bed, hurried into the shower, skipped down the stairs, and stopped to evaluate the remnants of the party.

She put her hands on her hips and surveyed the damage, expecting wilted vegetables, glasses tipped over, paper plates with leftover food crusted on them, and an overstuffed trash bin. Instead, the only evidence of a party was streamers and deflating balloons dancing lightly in the almost-still air. She knew that Chad wouldn't be able to leave without everything in the house being in order.

Knowing that it was a free Sunday morning without any commitments, she had originally planned on taking a run in the crisp morning air and then walking down to the farmer's market again—but there was only one thing on her mind, and it wasn't running. She wasn't sure why she kept thinking of Marcos, but she knew she had to go see him and find out if his parents had found their little boy yet. The thought of him being alone in the center chilled her, and she wondered if he felt scared. She walked directly to the door, jumped into her little car, and retraced her path back to the Polinsky Center.

She rummaged through her purse, pulled out her wallet, and stuck her finger underneath the plastic to slide her license out. Marcos's social worker had approved of Evelyn visiting with Marcos while he waited for his parents. Evelyn waited for visiting hours while the police were scouring the community, putting out fliers, and knocking on doors in search of someone who might know a cute, little boy named Marcos.

As she waited, Evelyn looked around the room. It was a wide hallway with blue low-pile carpet, four blue chairs with chrome legs, framed children's artwork hanging on the white walls, a vending machine full of juices and granola bars, and a poster that read, "Fatherhood begins in the womb," with a man with an unshaven face kissing the belly of a very pregnant woman.

Evelyn thought of her own father. She'd learned early on that to get her father's attention, she needed to do just as many push-ups as the men, bring trophies home from her swim meets, or have all A's on her report card, and then her father would chuckle, pat her on the back, report her success to his military drinking buddies, and then, if she did something spectacular, he would announce how proud he was of her. Her life revolved around receiving her dad's approval.

Her mother was all about making her husband proud as well. She got up in the morning and dressed in an outfit as if she were going out every single day and would always do her hair and makeup, even on Saturdays. When Evelyn's dad was sent out early to Okinawa and left the family behind, her mom would actually not curl her hair on some days. Meals started getting pushed back to a later time—first maybe ten minutes, then twenty, and one time, dinner was about an hour and a half late, and Evelyn thought her mother was feeling a bit rebellious. The house wasn't kept up as usual when her dad was away, and her mom actually went out with girlfriends on her own. She also didn't go to all the kid's sporting events and Evelyn's swim meets, like Evelyn's dad would do. Evelyn thought her mom was just tired of being perfect all the time and needed time for herself. When the family arrived in Japan, her dad had been there for a couple months, and Evelyn's mom went back to her old ways; all the meals were on time once again. Evelyn vowed she would never be as passive as her mother, and she set out to prove to men that she was their equal or better.

"Okay, I'll take you back to see him," the Polinsky front desk employee said to Evelyn with a slight smile, and then added, "But I'm making an exception for you, miss, because his social worker said to." She was a heavyset woman with a wide, white, toothy smile. She shuffled over to the side door to let Evelyn through and led her back to the dining area.

She found Marcos eating breakfast. He leapt from his seat and ran over to give her a hug. "*¡Sabía que vendrías por mí!*" He wore a shabby gray shirt with a faded Mickey Mouse on the front and some tattered blue shorts. He had on the same Adidas shoes as before, with socks that had a blue stripe around the ankle. The clothes must have been what the Polinsky Center had on hand.

"May I sit down?" Evelyn asked, as she gestured toward the empty chair next to him.

He smiled at being treated like a grown-up and patted the seat like he'd probably seen one of his parents do for him.

She sat down in the tiny orange chair and leaned over to see what he was eating. "Mmmmm, so what do you think of the oatmeal?" she asked, as she pointed to the soggy mush in a bowl.

He looked up at her and squinted his eyes with a tilt of his head, maybe to say the oatmeal was just okay.

"Is it yummy?" she said, as she rubbed her tummy and smiled. "Or yucky?" She put her finger in her mouth and acted like she was going to puke.

He laughed his cute little laugh and then put his finger in his mouth and coughed. "Yucky," he said, laughing.

His repeating "yucky" surprised her, and she let out a chuckle. Maybe he had already known that word or maybe she had just taught it to him. She looked at him in wonder. Had she really just taught him that? She couldn't remember teaching anyone something—at least not like this—ever before. She laughed delightedly.

Then he put the spoon in the dish and pulled out a big mound of oatmeal, smiling big and letting out a guttural chuckle while he brought the spoon up to her mouth and offered her the bite. In grand, exaggerated motions, she put her hand to her mouth and protested the spoon. Marcos set the spoon back in the bowl, and turning, he propped himself up on his knees in the chair, then bent down to pick up the spoon again while laughing hard in anticipation of what he was planning to do next. She was afraid he would fall down because he was a bit wobbly as he laughed and tried to balance the spoon. She gripped the back of the chair to support him. He offered the spoonful of oatmeal again, but this time he was just a bit more determined to put the spoon in her mouth. Evelyn was so amused by this little boy that she started giggling, and then she couldn't stop giggling, especially when he got some oatmeal on her hand. When she pulled her hand away and exclaimed, "Ew!" he managed to push the spoonful of mush into her mouth.

At first, she was shocked. She looked over at him, as he was watching her with wide eyes, waiting to see how she would react, then with a mouthful of food, she started to giggle. While laughing uncontrollably, she couldn't chew the food and lunged herself back, which tipped the chair backward. Marcos quickly got down from his chair and touched her hand "*¿Estás* okay?"

She nodded her head, and then she rolled off the chair to get up and started to chortle, gasping for air through the soggy oatmeal as she searched for a napkin and could not find one. She grabbed his bowl and spit her mouthful of mush into the blue plastic bowl in desperation.

She looked over at him, and his eyes were even wider than before, as if he couldn't believe she'd spit it out. She had only been in the little dining hall for maybe ten minutes, and this little boy had already made her laugh so hard that she had to gasp for air. One of the workers walked over to them, and Evelyn was sure she was going to ask her to leave, but instead she offered her a rag to clean her face. The worker motioned to everyone with a quick wave of her hand that Evelyn was really okay and please go back to what they were doing. Evelyn started to giggle again, a bit more quietly, thinking about the scene they'd just made in front of all the other kids, and she sat down in where he had been sitting as Marcos climbed into the chair she had been sitting in. He looked up at her with a big smile, as if he was proud of himself.

Evelyn was taken aback by what a sweet and adorable boy he was. She cleaned her face, then wiped his mouth in a silly gesture; she dropped the cloth on the table, and said, "So, how do I look?" gesturing with her hands as if showing off her face and smile. He gave her a thumbs-up. Without even thinking, she reached over and hugged him. He crawled into her lap and let her continue to hug him. She looked up to see if this was approved of here at the center and saw a few young social workers who revealed slight smiles of what seemed like approval. The lady who had brought her the rag looked on and gave a big smile, so Evelyn assumed hugging was approved and continued to hug Marcos, who seemed to melt into her arms. He wasn't laughing anymore.

They spent some time in the little library after breakfast, and she read him *The Cat in the Hat*, *Winnie-the-Pooh*, and *Puss in Boots*, in English, while he played quietly with his Pooky Bear. After a while, Jessica, Marcos's social worker, who had been watching Evelyn and Marcos interact through the window, came in to inform them it was time for Marcos to go to a group activity. Evelyn reached over to hug Marcos and said, "*Adios.*"

"*¿Adónde vas?*" There seemed to be concern in his voice.

"Are you going to be back?" Jessica said, turning to Evelyn with all seriousness.

"Oh yes, if I could, I would like to keep coming back until his parents come to pick him up, if that's okay."

Jessica turned to Marcos and said, "*Ella va a casa pero ella estará de regreso.*" She stood up and faced Evelyn, and said, "I told him you'll be back." She said it firmly, as if saying "since I told him you were coming back, you need to come back."

"Yes. Yes, I'll be back."

Lucky
(Santiago)

Marcos had been born on a Wednesday. Almost seven months before that day, Kat had come to Santiago as the sun appeared to touch the ground, illuminating an orange and yellow haze across the sky, through the clouds. She had been smiling, and her hair had reflected the sun—it looked like it was woven with copper. She'd taken his hands in hers and looked up into his eyes with that constant sly smirk she always had; her teeth seemed to sparkle.

"I have something magical to share with you, *mi amor.* What I'm going to tell you is going to blow your mind." Katiana told him, getting as close to his ear as she could, then stepping back tossing, she tossed her head to the side like she was a little girl again, flirting with the boy next door.

Santiago said nothing. He just continued gazing at her curiously and tipped his eyebrows up, indicating he wanted to hear more. He held her hands tightly in his.

"Santi, I'm telling you, I was taking the pill like you told me, but, my love, it didn't work. This is what I wanted to tell you: I'm pregnant." She gave him a wide smile and tilted her head again.

He continued his stare, but he squinted, examining her expression, checking for sincerity. He dropped her hands, but she quickly picked his back up.

She continued, "I know we never talked about having a baby, and we are young, but, *mi amor*, I think we are the luckiest people ever."

How could he be angry or disappointed? He didn't want to shout or hit anything or run down the street yelling, "This isn't fair!" He just stared at her, not sure how to react. He wasn't sure if he was happy or even if he agreed that they were lucky, but her smile was irresistible, her charm was too alluring, her beauty undeniable, and if she thought they were lucky, by God, they must be.

"Really, Kat. You happy?"

"I know it's going to be tough. I know it's going to be a challenge, but I think this baby is our good luck charm. It will give me purpose in life and bring us closer together. I know you're still building your clientele, but maybe I can leave the grocery store and look for another job to make more money. Your *Abuela* could take care of the baby while I'm at work, since she has wanted to stay home and make tortillas. Anyway, Santi, I think it will work. I think it will be magical."

Katiana and Santiago met at Maria's Grocery Store on the corner of Market and Home. It was Katiana's first job; she was fourteen years old. The minute you walked into the store, you could smell the fresh tangerines and tomatoes, as if the luscious fruit had just been plucked from the tree or vine. Local *mamacitas* sold their homemade tortillas there, laid out on a round table strategically placed between the bell peppers and dried bean containers. There were bins of rice where you could turn a knob on the bottom, and the rice would flow into your plastic bag. The small bakery was a big attraction in the neighborhood, as they sold *budin de pan*, *Tres Leches* cake, authentic Mexican cheesecake, sweet bread, *conchas*, and flan. One of Santiago's favorite when he was a kid was the chocolate cake topped with flan. The local kids raced into the store after school with their coins to buy their spicy and sweet candy that they couldn't find in any gringo store: the *Rolo de Coco*, sugar skulls, *De la Rosa Mazapan*, chili-spiced dehydrated mangos, salted apricots and plums, *Aldama Glorias*, *Coronado chiclosos*, Mexican Liquid candy, or, Marcos's favorite, chili-powdered lollipops.

When Santiago was younger, he would go to the store with his grandma and his sister, and they would buy fresh meat and dried beans, but soon after, he started roaming the streets on his own and coming into the store alone or with some friends from the 'hood. He remembered when Katiana started working at the store. She'd looked so young and shapeless.

Over the next two years, he'd watched her as she interacted with the customers, stacked the plums so they wouldn't fall when stacked high, how she'd kept a Cherry Coke on the shelf under the register and would take a sip between sales, and he also noticed her shape become curvier. He'd watched her hips form, and her shirts get tighter. She'd started wearing mascara and curling her hair. He'd also noticed her wearing a smooth gold bracelet every day that had etching around it—words he couldn't read from a distance. He would come into the store a couple times a week to buy his mandarin

Jarritos and salted plums. Katiana would ring up his items on the little cash register and announce the total price of the items while trying to hold back a smirk. Santiago would give her the money, a five-dollar bill, and he never forget how she would pull out the bills individually from the register and lay each dollar bill down on the counter: "*uno*"—slap down the first dollar bill— "*dos*"—laid down the second one gently—"*tres*"—sealed with a slap, and then she would use English—"fifty-three cents"—and dump the change on the bills. Later she would start adding a Chiclet or a little candy to the change. It would be different flavor each time, and she would never mention that she gave him a candy with the change.

One day, when Santiago had gone in the store with Rubén, his friend kept poking him in the back saying, "Go ask her, man."

"Not yet, man, not yet."

"It's a good time now, homes."

"No, *Ese*, not yet. I'll know when. Not yet, man." Santiago would watch her tidy up the canned goods, stack the tortillas, slap another dollar bill down on the counter for another customer, whisper something to her friend—and all the time, she would keep her eye on him, tucking away a smile.

It was April when he came in for his mandarin drink and forewent his chili lollipop and went for the chips. She was wearing a short, blue jean skirt, a bright pink shirt with a red flowery pattern around the v neck, and big, silver hoop earrings. "*Hola*, Santiago."

It was then that he realized they had never exchanged names. "*Hola*, Katiana. How do you know my name?"

"The same way you know my name." He knew then that it was time, and he asked her out to the taco shop across the street. It would never be the same, after that day in April. That was many years ago.

His grandmother had been excited when they'd told her about the baby. She said she would be delighted to take care of the baby; it would be the best privilege she'd ever had besides raising her own children and her grandchildren, but to take care of her great-grandchild would be a dream come true. She also insisted that Katiana move in with them. "It would make things so much easier, and we can all be in the same house together," she'd pleaded.

The plan was to wait to get married until after the baby, while they saved some money for a wedding.

Santiago's aunt gave them a crib that her granddaughter had slept in. Katiana great-aunt brought over items for the baby from her great-great-grandchild, and they set everything up in the room they shared in the front of the house, facing the road. Katiana was so happy.

It was when he'd felt the baby kick in her womb that Santiago had suddenly realized the baby was real, not just an idea or dream of Kat's—nor was it a burden to be ignored. The baby was real, and Santiago started to care about the life growing inside her. Katiana had taken good care of herself while she was pregnant. She routinely visited the clinic, and they gave her material to read on what she should not do while pregnant. She followed the guidelines completely. His *abuela* made sure Katiana ate properly by adding spinach to pasta and rice. There were no more Cherry Cokes that she liked so much or any other caffeinated drinks. She didn't drink or smoke, and she took all the vitamins they gave her at the clinic. At four months pregnant, she asked Santiago to come with her to the clinic for the sonogram because she was just a little scared. Would he come and "keep her company"?

It was then that they discovered they were having a boy—and when he finally *knew* he was lucky. Santiago was elated and couldn't stop smiling. He couldn't wait to meet his son.

The name "Marcos" was a simple name they had both liked, but the main reason they chose the name was because it was Katiana's grandfather's name. It was her grandfather who had stayed with her grandmother till her death and then continued to take care of Katiana until his own death. Kat had lived with her grandparents, as her parents had never married and her father continued to live a reckless life in Guadalajara. Her mother had been young when she gave birth to Katiana and had moved to Dallas, Texas, to discover herself, always saying she was going to come back and take care of her daughter one day. After her grandfather's death, Katiana lived with her aunt in San Diego, who, although loving, was thrilled when Katiana informed her she was moving in with Santiago. It was her grandfather who had loved Katiana deeply, ignoring Mexican cultural norms and taking up the role of caretaker. She had learned so much from him. Santiago, not having a father figure in his life, willingly accepted his son being named after someone who had been a faithful father, husband, and caretaker until the very end.

Her pregnancy went well. Katiana was seventeen years old and would have just turned eighteen when Marcos was due, at the end of June. Although she was young, Katiana was strong and practiced her breathing techniques she'd learned from the local pregnancy care clinic.

Santiago was there in the delivery room when Marcos was born. His grandmother, his sister, and Katiana's aunt all came and waited anxiously in the lobby, although they kept knocking on the door and sending in notes and snacks to him.

His son was beautiful and looked like his mama. He had round, dark eyes, long lashes, puffy cheeks, and thick, loopy hair. Santiago obediently followed the nurse to the nursery with the baby after the delivery, and he was able to help bathe Marcos and run a comb through his hair. After the nurse placed baby Marcos in Santiago's arms in the nursery, he walked down to the birthing room, opened the double doors, and with significant pride, introduced child to mother. He knew he was smiling big and wide because his cheeks hurt the rest of the day. When she saw the baby, Katiana started to cry. Big tears streamed down her cheeks as she took the baby and hugged him in her arms. They were now a family, united by one kicking, glowing healthy baby.

That night, Marcos slept in a plastic bassinet next to Katiana's hospital bed. Katiana fell asleep, and Santiago slept on a cot that the nurse brought in for him. There were four patient beds in the room, and Katiana's was nearest the door. A parade of fathers, mothers, brothers, sisters, sons, and daughters kept walking past Katiana and Santiago, weaving around the other side of the curtain that separated them. The visitors were loud and excited. They brought flowers, balloons, blankets, and little booties past them, right up to the end of visiting hours.

After a restless night of feeding every two hours and nurses coming in to help Katiana with the nursing, the morning light finally peeked through the curtains, and Marcos started to stir. Katiana responded quickly and picked up the baby.

"Oh god, Santiago. Look at this," he heard Katiana whisper, trying not to wake the sleeping mother and baby on the other side of the curtain.

Concerned, Santiago jumped off his cot and was at their side. "What is it?"

He followed her pointed finger to the top of Marcos's head. "His hair is red! No, no, that can't be," Katiana protested.

Sure enough, Marcos's hair had dried and the sun rays shown through the window from across the room, it revealed a deep red color. They had just assumed his hair was pitch-black, like their own.

"Do you have any Irish blood in your heritage?" Santiago asked Katiana, already surmising her response.

"We are as Mexican as we can get for generations. There is no way this could be. Do you have any Irish blood?" she asked, but she already knew every member in the Medina family had married a Mexican and his heritage was from the Cádiz province in southern Spain. "Oh my god," Katiana repeated. "We have been cursed, Santiago." She put her fingers to her temples, honestly looking concerned and distressed about the red hair.

Santiago turned quickly to her. "What are you talking about?"

"My grandma told me once that those with red hair are cursed," she said, concern on her face.

"Kati, that's crazy talk, superstitious stuff your grandma would say. Have you ever met someone with red hair?"

"No," she said slowly and added, "not from Mexico, just seen photos." Her eyes darted from left to right, never meeting his own. "What could this mean?" Katiana whispered loudly with confusion written across her face. Her grandma had told her all the Mexican myths and legends, and Katiana believed that the badger named the sun, the veiled lady really did bring Pedro down to her grave, that San Pedro helped Jesucristo fight off the devil and tossed him far in the ocean, and if she was around cows, she would never eavesdrop on the cattle at midnight on Christmas Eve. The legends were told as truth to her as a child, and according to Katiana's grandmother, if children were born with red hair, it meant that they were unlucky. Her grandmother had instilled in her granddaughter many superstitions that became undeniable juggernauts in Katiana's life.

And that is how it came to be that Marcos became Santiago's "Lucky Marcos." His hair was the copper color of a lucky penny, but more importantly, he became "Lucky Marcos" because Santiago never wanted Marcos to believe there was any truth to his mother's fear of red hair.

"Kat, it means nothing at all," Santiago said firmly, taking her shoulders and doing his best to assure her. "Now don't you mention it again, you hear? It means nothing at all." He searched her face for a deeper meaning to her fear and noticed a teardrop emerge from the corner of her left eye, which she swiped away before it could fall.

Rubén came to visit on the last day of their stay and brought them tacos. Before he came, Santiago mentioned to Katiana that maybe they should ask Rubén to be Marcos's godfather.

Katiana laughed then looked up into Santiago's face. "Oh, are you serious about that?"

"Yes, why not? Rubén is the most faithful and loyal person I know."

"Yes, maybe, but the other guys you hang with don't respect him, he talks so much, he can't focus, and he just doesn't seem as if he could care for more than he has now. I know he's your friend, and mine too, but he has enough to handle right now with his father and brother and crazy girlfriend. He just isn't a likely choice."

"Okay, I'm willing to consider that, but who do you think it should be? You don't have family, and my kid sister is just too self-centered and not kid friendly. Who then?"

It was then that Santiago and Katiana knew it had to be Rubén. He was a good guy; they knew he would find some way to care for Marcos if anything happened to them, and they knew he would take his responsibility seriously. Rubén was Santiago's oldest and dearest friend, and he knew Rubén was faithful, loyal, and responsible—just what his son needed. He saw how Rubén would take care of his own dad and regularly visit his brother in prison. Santiago felt as if those two people took advantage of Rubén—his family gave nothing to him in return, not even a simple thank you—but Santiago saw Rubén's commitment to the people around him. For those reasons, they both agreed he was the best choice.

When Rubén arrived that night to visit the *bambino*, they asked him to be Marcos's godfather. Rubén was touched and kept wiping his eyes, saying he had dust in them. He sat in the corner chair and put his face in his hands for a few minutes, sitting there quietly. Santiago and Katiana looked at each other, surprised; Rubén was actually sitting without moving and taking the question very seriously. After a few minutes of silence, Rubén lifted his head out of his hands, peered up at them with a big smile and wet, glossy eyes, stood up abruptly, and said, "Yes, it would be my honor." He touched his hand to his heart and fluttered it to indicate his heart was beating and he was touched. He went over to Santiago and kissed him on both cheeks and to Katiana, in bed, and kissed her cheeks, and then to Marcos, lying in his plastic crib, and gave him a single kiss on his right cheek.

After Rubén left at the end of visiting hours and the lights were dimmed, Santiago stared at the ceiling, lying in the last available cot, in disbelief. He was a father at age nineteen, and counting his mother in Mexico, he now had six people under his care. He listened to his son's gentle breathing, listening to the reality of life.

As a family, they went back to the home where Santiago did most of his growing up and his *abuela* made sure that it was kept meticulously clean and smelled of disinfectant. The floors and appliances were shiny, there was a single flower in a vase positioned in the middle of the dining room table, and the knitted afghan was folded neatly in half and hung over the couch. Marcos's crib had a clean fitted sheet on it, and Santiago's grandma had washed all of Marcos's baby clothes by hand.

Katiana did her best to nurse Marcos, but by the third week, she had had enough of it and they went to bottle feeding. Three weeks later, Katiana found a job and started back to work at a new grocery store four blocks away, and it was Santiago's *abuela* who took care of Marcos all day.

Marcos brought much happiness to the house. Santiago's grandmother started whistling and humming again, his sister would carry Marcos around the house and talk to him about who knows what, and Katiana seemed to enjoy her role as a new mama.

He remembered the day he brought home Marcos's first and only stuffed animal. Santiago was sitting at the green table pushed up against the window in his office, waiting for a runner to show up; there was a Garfield cartoon strip taped to the old schoolhouse table. He had liked Garfield in grade school and liked how he would carry his Pooky Bear around with him. The particular cartoon strip taped on the table was of Jon and Garfield in the morning. Garfield, with a smile on his face, lifts his Pooky Bear to Jon's face, indicating to give him a kiss. Jon concedes and says, "Oh, all right. Good morning to you too,

Pooky." *Kiss* Garfield then hugs his bear and says with droopy eyes, "Love me, love my teddy bear." Santiago knew then he had to get Marcos a Pooky bear too. He came home with the loveable bear and gave it to his four-month-old son. Marcos took to the bear immediately, and from then on, that bear was either being slept on, dragged around in the firm grasp of a little hand, or propped up next to him as Marcos ate his lunch. Pooky would be a comfort to Marcos in the days to come, and he never took to any other stuffed animal or blanket.

As Marcos started getting older, his facial features started to form, and his hair became a more pronounced, darker red. People would comment. When they went to the market or to Katiana's auntie's house, someone was sure to say something about how unusual it was for a Mexican boy to have red hair—what did it mean? The more people talked about his red hair, the more Katiana pulled back from Marcos and the more time she spent in their room. She would pull the curtains closed and sit quietly on their bed. Santiago thought she needed time alone or was going through some degree of postpartum depression; he assumed it was best to leave her be, and he or his grandma or sister would take care of Marcos while Katiana withdrew further inside of herself and away from the others.

One Saturday afternoon, Santiago came home from hanging with the boys at the Lemon Grove recreation center and found Katiana and Marcos taking a nap. The curtains were open and the noon sun was radiating through the side windows into the tiny house, giving the feeling that you had been warmed inside by a hot pepper. Katiana had the La-Z-Boy reclined, and she was lying there asleep, with Marcos next to her in the chair. Her arm was around him, and he had his sweet face resting on her chest. Katiana's face was tilted toward him, her nose almost touching his hair. They had been snuggling together when they both fell asleep. Their faces looked so peaceful. Over the years, when the scene came to his mind, Santiago felt the warmth from the sun all over again and the peacefulness on both their faces calmed his heart.

The Hangover
(Evelyn)

Evelyn sat at her desk tweeting, lost in her thoughts. She was supposed to be communicating the strategic business development of wireless health and how the company was diagnosing patients in remote places, such as in the desert lands of Africa and the jungles of South America. She would usually fall into the zone, unaware of what was going on around her, but the events of the past few days were on her mind, and she was distracted. Her cell phone rang, breaking her train of thought as she worked on a paragraph for the company's website, registering a blocked number on her caller ID. She dragged her finger across the bottom of her phone, ready to send it to her voice mail, when she decided to answer instead.

"Hello, this is Evelyn."

"Evelyn, hi. This is Jessica, Marcos's social worker. Do you have a second to talk?"

"Jessica, oh, hi. Actually, can I call you right back?"

"Sure, of course." Jessica gave Evelyn her callback number, and they said their good-byes.

Evelyn turned back to her computer and minimized her TweetDeck, the five blogs she had been reading, and the three different online news sites she followed, grabbed her phone, took the stairs to the ground floor, and went to the employee garden area—the area reserved for smokers, but she knew nobody would be there at that time of day.

"Hello, Jessica? Yes, this is Evelyn. Sorry about that. Everyone can hear everything in my office, so I wanted to get away from all the eavesdroppers."

"Oh yes, I understand. I know offices can be like that. Yes, I just wanted to talk to you about Marcos. I've noticed that you've been visiting him almost every day."

"Yes, I guess I have. I hope that's okay."

"Of course. I'm sure that it's helped him get through this transitional time so much. We've created fliers with his photo and description, and we've posted it in storefronts and out in some neighborhoods. I've put an announcement in the *Union-Tribune*, and the police have made some house visits in the Logan, City, and Sherman Heights areas, but we've not gotten any leads, and nobody seems to recognize or have heard of Marcos."

"That seems so odd. His features are so distinguishable, you would have thought someone must have seen him before, or at least they would recognize him as a kid in the neighborhood."

"Well, that's the thing; they might have, but no one is talking for some reason. It could be that one of the parents has a warrant out for his or her arrest, and they're not coming forward at this time, and the neighborhood could be covering for them. He also might have come over from Mexico and was left stranded. Maybe his parents didn't make it. It could be a number of reasons."

Evelyn suddenly got a deep ache in her belly and felt so sorry for him—Marcos, the cutest, sweetest kid she had ever met. He was gentle and kind, and he had an odd confidence about him. It was what drew her to him the day she'd found him abandoned in that parking lot. He didn't act like an abused or neglected child. He actually looked well taken care of and clean; he had nice clothes on. He smiled easily and was quick to give a hug, unlike a child who might have been in an abusive or negligent family. It felt to Evelyn as if Marcos had known the love of a family and grew up feeling secure and cared for, but then why would a child who was loved be abandoned in a parking lot in the middle of the day? It baffled her.

"Well, we're really doing our due diligence in trying to locate a family member, but I wanted to ask you if you would be interested in filing a 'nonrelated extended family member' status so you could take him home while we continue to look for his family."

"I'm sorry, what is that?" Her mouth suddenly went dry. Her mind was foggy, and she touched a cold hand to her cheek, hoping it would bring her back to reality.

"Since Marcos doesn't have a guardian or caretaker, and you are the closest person to him at this time, you can file for this status. The Polinsky Center is just a transitional place for kids who need to find a new place to live. Kids stay at the center for only two to three weeks while we try to find a place for them to live. Either he goes to live with you, or he goes to a juvenile facility."

Evelyn gasped. She couldn't imagine sweet-natured Marcos in a group home. It was just another word for *orphanage* to her, and she didn't want to think of Marcos as an orphan—not when she was around. She tried to find her words. "Um, well, what is involved in filing this status?"

"Yes, well, we would need to get your fingerprints, do a background check, and come visit your home before we release him to your care while we continue to search for his family members."

"Oh, really? That's all it takes?" Evelyn ran her trembling hand through her smooth, silky hair, trying to comprehend what was going on and how simple it was for the city to release a child into someone else's care. "Okay, well, let me think about it a bit. Can I call you back?"

"Yes, of course. I know that is a lot to take in, but yes, please, think about it."

The next three hours of work were a blur. She wasn't sure if she was making sense on her blog and decided to go for a late-afternoon run. She snuck out of the office about four o'clock, a couple of hours before her usual departure time. Monica might notice she was gone, but she didn't want to talk just yet.

She walked outside, where it was warm but with a feeling of change in the air, as though it were shifting to cool. The leaves rustled in the wind. Autumn was coming.

Chad came home to find Evelyn lying on the yellow sofa, staring up at the gypsum board ceiling. Evelyn had driven up to Torrey Pines after work and decided to hike the trails. When she got home, she'd taken a shower and then felt extremely tired and laid down. She usually felt exhilarated after exercise, not drowsy like today.

"Hey, sweet thing. Are you okay?" Chad set his gym bag down by the door to the garage, concerned about his wife's sloth-like activity when she was usually running up and down the stairs. He sat on the floor next to her, smoothing her already silky hair down the sides of her head.

"Yeah, I'm fine. I felt really tired, and I wasn't making much sense at work, so I thought I would take a hike, but now for some reason I'm just a bit sleepy and the couch looked so inviting," she said with a slight smile as she looked up from the stiff couch pillow. She hesitated to say more. She wondered if she should tell Chad what had recently happened. It had been over two weeks now since she had met Marcos, and she still hadn't told her husband. She kept thinking about telling him, but he was busy with work, and she feared he wouldn't understand why she would spend her time with a little boy she'd met in a parking lot and not training for the next race. The timing never seemed to work out to tell him, and they only saw each other when they were going off to work or when it was late at night and they were tired. Chad had been busy on the weekends, and she had been able to slip away without his notice—or so she thought.

At this moment on the couch, she considered telling him, but her mind was befuddled with the recent request to take Marcos home. She just couldn't imagine how he would respond now. She couldn't process her feelings, her thoughts, or her words. She decided to tell him later.

"What? Your three cups of chai tea didn't do the trick? Maybe you have a fever. Or are you malingering so you don't have to go out with us boys tonight?" he asked as he placed his hand on her forehead, pretending to check for a temperature. "Maybe you have parasite or jungle fever or even the West Nile fever. Maybe I'm the carrier of that germ and brought it home and gave it you?" Chad pretended to look frightened for her.

She hit him gently on the arm. "Stop. I'm fine. I just felt tired. I just took a twenty-minute power nap, so I'm good to go.

Do you mind helping me up?" She stretched her arms up, ready for him to pull her up, off the couch. "Maybe we can stay in tonight? We could play a game or watch a movie, just the two of us?"

He lifted her effortlessly and wrapped his arms around her, nestling his head into her neck, then started nibbling on her. "Maybe you are sick with some sort of neck disease, and you're delusional. It's Friday night. We have to go out and meet Charlie and his new girlfriend."

"Yes, of course. Now let me go, you silly boy. I don't need red marks on my neck. What would the boys say?" she said teasingly.

"Oh, I'm sure they wouldn't even notice."

"Yeah, that would be the first thing they would notice."

Every Friday night, when Chad wasn't working too late, he called his friends Charlie and Spencer, and their significant others, for drinks or dinner, depending on the time they were all available. Besides Elsie's Wine Bar, they'd started hanging out at a relatively new trendy restaurant, Searsucker, on Fifth Street, in the Gaslamp area. They could all make it that night, and Charlie was bringing a new girlfriend.

Two hours later, Chad and Evelyn walked into Searsucker, a chic seven-thousand-square-foot space filled with mismatched, salvaged chairs, ropes hanging from poles, bold wall art, and suspended lighting fixtures. They were thankful the wait wasn't too long and that they were able to snag their favorite spot along the only window. They heard La Roux's song "Bulletproof" blaring through the speakers as they walked to the table.

Chad and Evelyn were the first to arrive. Evelyn had carelessly assembled her outfit for the night; she'd ended up wearing her Dylan George coated skinny jeans in chocolate, a flowing watercolor print sleeveless top of a city street scene she'd picked up in France, and brown crocodile leather four-inch pumps. As they waited for their friends, Evelyn ordered the Peter Rabbit cocktail, complete with a sprig of basil and garnished with a pickled carrot. The drink reminded her of reading that story to Marcos on their second day together. As Evelyn and Chad sat there, she looked down at the cocktail ring with the large apple-green Chrysoprase gem that Chad had given her when they were in Australia. She flipped the sizable stone around her finger, around and around, lost in thought.

"What's up with you?" Chad finally said, after waiting for her to say something.

"Oh, sorry, sweets. I guess I'm a bit more out of it than I thought." She brushed her hand gently along his cheek. She didn't think that this moment in the restaurant would be a good time to tell him about Marcos; their friends were coming soon and their conversation might be cut short, and she wouldn't be able to explain herself completely.

"I hope you aren't burned-out from work. Maybe you can sleep in tomorrow. Maybe you haven't been drinking enough water or you need to take a break from training. Maybe you should take it easy on the drinks? Sometimes you're tired after traveling a lot, but you haven't been sent on any trips lately. Maybe you've been training too hard."

"No, I haven't been that diligent in my training lately."

"What are you talking about? You've been gone every night this week. I thought you were running. Where've you been?"

She realized she'd given a little more away then she'd intended. Her mind raced to cover her tracks. "Oh, you know, I'm still exercising, just not quite at the same pace. Maybe I just need to sleep in tomorrow; that might do the trick."

"Excuse me, ma'am." Chad motioned to a waitress. "Could I get some water? Thank you." Chad was so thoughtful, always trying to take care of her, but sometimes Evelyn felt a little like he was a bit obsessed with her health and pace of exercise.

"Hello, my favorite peeps," Charlie said in a booming, jolly voice as he flicked the back of Chad's ear and then gave him a fist bump. "I want you to meet Veronica. Veronica." He motioned her over, putting his arm around her shoulders and presenting her proudly. Veronica was about five foot three and wore five-inch heels with a tight leather skirt that hit the top of her bare thighs. Her top was low cut and revealed her very robust bosom. She had long, fake nails that were painted dark red; she wore lots of makeup and thick black eyeliner. "Darling, may I present Dr. and Mrs. Hogg?" He presented them with a grand gesture. "Or as I like to call them, Evelyn and Chad."

"Oh my gosh, are you kidding me? Your name is Evelyn Hogg? What the hell? Why didn't you keep your maiden name?" Veronica exclaimed.

Not missing a beat, Chad piped up. "She was happy to drop her maiden name and take on the Hogg name. You know, we have a long heritage of Hoggs as bankers. We're Swiss Italian, from the Alps—"

As if she didn't hear a word Chad was saying, she interrupted, "Have you heard about that girl named Ima Hogg? Oh my gosh"—she turned to Charlie—"can you believe naming your child Ima Hogg? What the hell were they thinking? Parents can be so cruel. And her sister's name was Ura Hogg. Isn't that crazy? What were they thinking?"

Chad and Evelyn stared at her, mostly because they couldn't believe that this was whom Charlie had chosen to bring as his date. He dated many girls, and they had met most of them, and Veronica was not like any of them.

Charlie stood at the bar, looking at the scene with amusement. He grabbed a chair and offered it to Veronica, ordered them a drink, and then sat down.

Evelyn looked at Veronica's long, fake nails and tacky taste in clothes and was annoyed that Charlie brought her to their friend-exclusive dinner. She knew that she shouldn't judge, Ralph taught her that, and there might be some great redeeming value about her and that was why Charlie invited her, but Veronica was certainly not making a very good impression.

Completely unaware of any tension, Veronica asked, "So what was your maiden name that you were so eager to get rid of?"

Evelyn sat staring at her, anger rising in her belly. She twisted her drink and thumbed her ring. "None of your damn business," she muttered.

Chad jerked his head toward her, appalled at her reaction to Charlie's guest.

"I'm sorry? What was it?" Veronica again acted as if she hadn't heard, then turned to Charlie, who was maintaining his cool.

"Knipple." Then he picked up his glass of beer and took a big gulp.

"What the hell? Knipple?" Her loud, braying laugh sounded like a donkey with a slight snort, and it seemed to echo even in the loud room. "Knipple! That must have been torture, especially with a flat chest!"

Evelyn was trying so hard to hold her tongue, but Veronica had crossed the line. Evelyn stood up suddenly, her chair scraping the wood flooring. "Who the hell are you to come in here and insult us?"

Chad touched Evelyn's arm in hopes of calming her down, and Charlie stood up and suggested that he and Veronica go to the bar to get their drinks.

When Charlie and Veronica were out of earshot, Chad turned to Evelyn. "What is wrong with you? You don't even know her."

"I know enough. Chad, she was totally insulting. She doesn't even care about first impressions; she was so brazen and rude. How dare she insult my name and call me flat chested?"

"She didn't call you flat chested. She said it would have been a bummer to have that name and be flat chested."

"That is not what she meant, Chad! And speaking of flat, did you see her butt? Flat as a pancake. She probably hasn't exercised a day in her life. She spends all her time putting on fake nails and makeup—"

"Evelyn, that is Charlie's friend…girlfriend. I know it's not his typical type of girl, and yes, she was rude, but try to be civil. Get a grip. You don't usually talk crap about people anyway."

She fidgeted in her seat and put her hands up to her face. Quietly she said, "I don't know. Her first few words were rude, and I really just wanted to slap her. I'll give her another chance." She ran her hand through her hair. "I think I need another drink."

Charlie and Veronica brought over their drinks and their other friends came with them, Chad's good pal Spencer and his wife, Lorena, who had just arrived.

Evelyn drank a smorgasbord of drinks that night. She sat in the wooden chair, drowning not only in alcohol, but also in confusion. She felt so disconnected from the people around her, her mind returning over and over to a little boy who was sitting alone, waiting for his parents to come pick him up.

The group continued talking. Veronica was laughing, and Spencer tried starting a discussion about some sort of social unrest in Libya or Bahrain. Evelyn, completely knowledgeable about the situation, was feeling her brain lose itself in intoxication, and she watched Spencer talk as she watched his soul patch move in and out from below his bottom lip as he spoke. Evelyn began to laugh too loudly and talk nonsense, and she noticed the others look at her curiously.

"Attention, everyone, I have an announcement," Chad said over the noise of the crowd. Evelyn looked up from her drink and tried to focus on Chad's face, trying to think what he would announce.

"I, Doctor Chad Hogg, have been accepted into the robotics fellowship for Urology."

"Congratulations!" they all responded.

"Well, let's raise our glass for our friend Dr. Chad, saving one penis at a time. Here, here." Charlie held up his glass as the others joined in and raised their glasses, clanking as alcohol splashed over the edges.

Evelyn stood up to reach the center of the table, and as she tried to sit down, her chair wobbled, and she missed her perch. Chad caught her by her arm and kept her from falling into Spencer.

Acting as if nothing had happened, Chad said, "Well, it was a long day, and I have to do some rounds in the morning, so I think we need to go. Thanks for meeting us, thanks for the cheers, and it was nice meeting you, Veronica."

Everyone muttered good-bye and watched, trying not to stare as Chad took Evelyn by the arm and directed her to the door. As they left, Evelyn said, "Yes, nice to meet you Harmonica," and with a smirk, and behind Chad's back, flipped up her middle finger, giggled, and then stumbled out the door as "I Love It" by Icona Pop was blaring from the speakers.

The Medina Family
(Santiago)

Four months before the incident with Marcos in the Costco parking lot, Santiago parked his car alongside the curb in front of his grandmother's house one cool evening, when the sun was low. Her *casa* was a small, drab place, once painted white with a cheerful green trim, but now, after many years of neglect, the paint had no distinguishable color and was chipped and dirty. The lawn was a plot of brown, dead grass, and there were no plants growing in the window boxes. As he walked up toward the house, he saw a pile of cigarette butts in the walkway that Rubén had left last time he was around. His *Abuelita* wouldn't let Rubén smoke inside, so he obediently smoked outside, on his own special wooden chair that he had dragged over from the side yard, blue paint chipped and faded from sitting out in the sun. There was a plastic lawn chair with a broken leg propped among the dead grass. All the windows of the house had iron bars, and the steel front door had double locks. He walked toward the house, up the two steps to the porch, and reached to open the door, only to find it ajar.

The house was about nine hundred square feet, and it was the only home Santiago could remember. After his father died, Santiago and his sister had moved into the little place. Santiago had been ten and Carmelita, six. He had been the man of the house from the first day he'd walked in, even though he didn't do much around the house aside from putting in a new light on the front porch or pulling weeds in the back; it was his *Abuela* who worked tirelessly to make the house welcoming and nice for them. She painted the walls of the kitchen a bright yellow, and she was always sweeping, mopping, dusting, or scrubbing, showing her love through work. He remembered how, when he was a young child, he would come bounding through the front door after school to find a snack of mango with lemon and chili, jicama, and cut cucumber with two *pancrema* cookies and horchata. His grandmother would leave it protected by Saran Wrap on the table, to make sure he had a snack ready. Back then, his *Abuelita* was always thinking of his and Carmelita's needs.

His grandma had always worked hard to support her family. The last ten years, she had been a housemaid at a big, fancy home in La Jolla. She was in charge of the wealthy family's clothes, which meant not just the laundry, but also that their shoes were shined, buttons were sewn on, white linen shirts were pressed, and curtains were ironed and cleaned. Each night, she would come home and set down her purse, which would spill over with a sewing kit, rags, and spray for stains. No matter how tired she may have been after a long day at work, his grandma felt it was her duty to make dinner every night of the week. She didn't take an evening off from making supper, and they never ate out for dinner unless they went over to their auntie's, who made delicious chili rellenos—with spicy roasted and peeled poblano chilies to give just enough kick, filled with lots of stringy Monterrey Jack cheese in light and airy egg batter. They topped it with salsa roja and with a side of arroz y frijoles. Her relleno was always the hit and nobody minded taking a small break from eating grandmama's food.

When his *Abuelita* made dinner for them, she moved around the kitchen in rhythmic motions, like a whirling dervish; his *abuela* slapped the tortillas and plopped them on the flat pan in a systematic way. It was hypnotizing to watch her stream of movements. She made the tacos with care, filling them with freshly made salsa, fried seasoned carne asada, cebolla, cabbage, super-creamy avocado, cilantro, and topped with tangy salsa. In Santiago's opinion, his grandma made the best tacos in Southern California. His *abuela*'s tacos were made with love.

On this late afternoon, as Santiago entered the house, he stepped onto the cracked and faded linoleum floor that was laid throughout the house. The dining area opened onto the kitchen, where the old table that his grandfather had made out of pine wood was standing in the center of the room covered with a flowered tablecloth his grandmother had brought with her from her table in her old house. The vinyl chairs were mismatched, having been found abandoned alongside the road, though a couple of them his *abuela* had bought for a dollar at a yard sale. The kitchen cupboards had been white, but the edges were now worn and brown from hands opening and closing doors without any handles. The faded green refrigerator was set in the corner, and sometimes the freezer door didn't shut and the ice would melt down the door and drip on the linoleum floor, leaving a cold puddle. The sink was white porcelain, with mildew in the corners around the faucet, and the yellow on the walls had faded. In the past, he would have found his grandmother puttering in the kitchen, obsessively cleaning the counters, but it had been a while since he'd smelled the bleach she would use to clean the porcelain.

The family room, off to the right of the dining room/kitchen, had a braided, brown circular rug; he was uncertain the last time it had been shaken out. There was a black, plastic-covered couch, a matching black chair next to it with rips on the side, and a beat-up easy chair. The seating was situated directly in front of the TV for ultimate viewing of warfare on the Xbox. Santiago had spent money on the purchase of a large, flat screen TV, which was mounted on the wall and took up most of the wall space. There were no pictures in the house, except for a framed photo of the Virgin of Guadalupe, next to a crucifix that hung next to the front door.

At first, when Katiana moved into his *Abuelita*'s house, she helped out with the dishes and some of the cooking, but after Marcos was born, she had returned to work at another grocery store. *Abuelita* willingly quit her job to stay home to take care of her great-grandson as her job at the La Jolla residence had started to become too exhausting for her. While Marcos was taking a nap or playing, she would make tortillas and then the two of them would go out, Marcos in his umbrella stroller, and sell tortillas to the local markets for extra money.

Santiago was the breadwinner in the house, paying for the rent, food, and utilities as well the diapers and formula and the extra needs his sister kept having. His grandmother never asked where Santiago made the money, but she knew he was a hard worker and he always figured out how to provide for the family. Santiago was suspicious that she knew how he got the money and that she just didn't ask because she wanted to be kept in the dark about his line of work. She hadn't said a word to him when he and his best friend Rubén had started hanging out with a new group of guys nor had she asked questions when Santiago was able to start paying for the extra things around the house. The less she knew, the better, and Santiago wanted to make sure he kept his business out of the household environment.

Over the last few months, though, something had started happening with his grandmother. Her cooking didn't taste as good; she would forget the salt or the peppers in the salsa. The house wasn't as tidy as it used to be, and his *abuela* looked as if she were lost in her own kitchen. He'd noticed she kept opening cupboards and looking for things, not remembering where she put the tortilla pan or her special knife for chopping garlic and peppers, and she kept asking where the garbage disposal switch was; as many times as she was reminded that the switch was underneath the sink, she would still look around, frustrated, unable to find it. She would touch all along the kitchen's back wall looking for it. She would try switching on and off all the lights in the kitchen and dining room. Santiago had installed the switch to the garbage disposal underneath the sink because it was easier to put it there instead of cutting through the tile on the kitchen wall.

In the past, his son would play on the carpet with his teddy bear, humming, as his grandma sang the old Mexican tunes Santiago remembered her singing when he was a little boy. It made him so happy to know his son was well taken care of, but since his grandmother had started acting differently, more often than not, he had found Marcos up on the counter, opening the cupboard where he thought his grandma kept the Galletas Marias. His *abuela* didn't have a snack waiting for him, as she had for Santiago, when he was a boy; she often forgot to feed Marcos at all. Marcos turned to see his father and said, "*Papá, Marcos no puede encontrar la abuela.*" Santiago was sad to hear that Marcos was looking for his grandma but couldn't find her.

His home had once been filled with happiness, the sounds of a loving and joyful family, and now it was silent as the grave. Santiago sat down on the couch, his head heavy in his hands.

He thought back to the night, just a few months earlier, when he had come home to a hungry, unsupervised son and his girlfriend staring at herself in front of the mirror, scissors in her hand.

Katiana had been laid off from the grocery store two weeks prior. The store had expected more customers at its grand opening, but the store didn't generate the income they had planned on and had to let Katiana go since, she had been the last hire. Ever since then, she'd started hanging around the house again. Santiago would find her in the bathroom most evenings, either contemplating cutting her long black hair or combing it in long strokes, pulling a strand of it, the scissors ready to cut, and suddenly putting the scissors down and deciding today wasn't the day to cut it. Gone was the fun-loving, upbeat girl with the infectious laugh and sunny disposition who had won his heart, and in her place had become a zombie-like being.

On the day that Marcos searched for cookies in the cupboard, Santiago heard Katiana fumbling around in the bathroom. "Katiana, you're home. Were you planning to make dinner for Marcos? He's hungry," Santiago said crossly, hungry himself.

"*Querido*, I know. I told him I was coming," she replied from behind the bathroom door, not defensively but almost carelessly. Santiago opened the door slightly, and Katiana continued to brush her hair in long strokes, looking at herself with empty eyes and not turning to acknowledge him as he stood a couple feet away, staring at her with interest through the crack in the door.

Standing in their short hallway between the bathroom and kitchen, Santiago heard his sister come through the back door. His sister always came into a room quickly, waving her hands in the air in effort to dry the dark raisin polish on her long, fake nails. Her hair smelled of fruit, and her curls bounced as she opened the refrigerator door, grabbing for a Coke and snapping it open while talking about how so-and-so said x and y, and could he believe it?

Carmelita wore thick black eyeliner and big, round silver hoops in her ears that almost touched the tops of her shoulders. Her black hair was meticulously rolled in long curls all the way down her back. It looked as if her hair was unusually longer, but Santiago wasn't sure. Where did she find the money to get all glammed up anyway? It was probably all his hard-earned money that she was using; she never worked, not even helping clean up around the house or making any of the meals. He was suspicious that his grandmother had been secretly giving his sister some of the money she'd earned selling her tortillas at Katiana's old grocery store.

"Carmelita, do you know where *abuelita* is?" Santiago inquired.

"Heck if I know. She goes out; she comes back in. Am I her keeper? I can't keep track of her. She goes to the store and then comes back with nothing. She leaves in the car and doesn't come back until hours later. Here, then gone, here and then gone," Carmelita rambled.

Clearly there was only one person Carmelita thought about and that was herself. She would flutter in then swoop out. Santiago and his grandma had lost track of Carmelita's comings and goings long ago.

"Well, could you make something for dinner? Marcos is hungry."

"What do you think I am? Do I look like his *mamá*?" Throwing makeup and various small items in her purse, which was sitting on the dining room table, she continued, "I don't make the meals around here, Brother. Why don't you make him something? He's your son anyway." Then, in a stage whisper, she said, "If I were you, Brother, I would be home more often. I don't trust that girlfriend of yours alone with Marcos." Then, she went back to her ranting and raving. "And what is going on with Katiana anyway? Either she is sleeping or standing in the bathroom all day. What is she doing in there? I have to use the kitchen sink to brush my teeth 'cause she's always in there. I took grandma's mirror from her side of the room to my side, so I could do my makeup. I store all my stuff in my room too." Taking her compact out to view her face in the small, round mirror, she put on dark lipstick as she mumbled, "By the way, I heard that somethin' was going on at her old job with her boss, like he wasn't treating her right. I'm just telling you what I heard, Santi. That's all I heard, but hear what I'm sayin'?"

"No, Lita, I don't know what's going on in that thick head of yours, but Katiana would have told me if her old boss had not been treating her nicely. Plus, why would he have given her money before she left? I think he just wanted to help us out."

Lita tilted her head back to gulp her Coke, then looked beyond him to watch Katiana staring at herself in the mirror. Carmelita rolled her eyes. "Hell, believe what you want to believe 'cause I can't stand around here listening to your problems, Brother. I'm out of here. I'm goin' to Bianca's party down the street, so don't wait up." As quickly as she appeared, she disappeared, turning on her high-heeled shoes and flicking her long hair to make it swish as she vanished out the back door.

Santiago looked at Marcos, sitting in the family room, eating the Galletas he'd found in the cupboard. Santiago walked over to him, squatted down to his level, and asked, "*Mijo*, do you want *sopita*?" He knew Marcos liked soup and that it was easy enough for Santiago to heat up.

"*Por favor, Papá.*"

He sighed. He knew that Katiana had started sleeping a lot and lingered in the bathroom after she had been laid off from her second job. It was unusual behavior, but he just assumed she was bummed that she didn't have a job—although she didn't go out looking for another one either. He assured her that he could support the family, and she could just stay home and take care of Marcos and go out with her girlfriends again.

Eventually, Katiana came out of the bathroom and headed to bed. She didn't even look Santiago in the eye or kiss Marcos good night. She didn't even acknowledge that her son was sitting at the dining room table eating *sopita* and drinking from his purple sippy cup. Santiago didn't know why she was so tired, because for God's sake, she didn't do anything all day as far as he knew. He actually didn't know much about her at all these days. She wouldn't talk to him, and when he studied her face, she never responded to his stare. She seemed so distant, not completely engaged in the here and now.

It was late when his grandmother finally came home that night; Marcos was in bed, sleeping, and Santiago was watching MMA, resting in the easy chair given to them by an old neighbor before they had moved.

"Where were you, *Abuelita*?" Santiago inquired when she walked in the house looking tired and dazed.

"*Mi'jo.* I left for something, but then I couldn't remember what for, and then I couldn't remember how to get back home." Her hair was out of place, no longer in its neat curls. Her eyebrows were furrowed, like they were when she was frightened. "Rubén saw me on some corner, and I told him I couldn't remember how to get home, so he brought me here. We left my car there, somewhere…I don't remember where, but you can ask Rubén," Grandmother explained. "I'm just so tired and want to go to bed, Santi." She came over to him, touched his cheek lightly with the palm of her hand, and kissed the other cheek.

"Well, *Abuelita*, I'm just glad you got home safe," Santiago said, trying to mask his worry.

"Yes, safe. Night *Mijo*," she said drowsily.

A passing twinge of guilt assailed him that he hadn't gone out searching for her, but she had never been out so long before, and when she did go out, she always came back. He sighed and got up from the chair with the brown leather that stuck to his leg and that was cracking in the center. That is probably why his old neighbors gave it to them, he thought. He clicked off the TV with the remote and went to bed next to his girlfriend, who didn't talk to him much less let him touch her. Santiago felt like he was treading water, moving his limbs as fast as he could, but he was getting more exhausted every minute. It was in this exhaustion that, if his diligence slipped for just one second, he would drown.

The Decision
(Evelyn)

Lorena, Spencer's wife, agreed to meet Evelyn at Caffe Carpe Diem for lunch on a Saturday. They had never met just the two of them, and Evelyn was a bit fidgety.

Carpe Diem was located in Bankers Hill, just up the street from downtown and outside of Balboa Park. The café had an eclectic European flair and was decorated with bright colors, an elaborate chandelier, dark wood floors, a copper espresso machine, large art pieces hanging on every inch of wall space, an exposed ceiling, and a chalkboard wall with a list of specialty coffees and teas. The food was fresh, organic, and unique.

Evelyn had already had her Saturday workout and was famished. She sat at the marble-topped table waiting, studying the menu while downing a second glass of water.

Evelyn was born in Albany, Georgia, then spent her preschool years in Jacksonville, North Carolina, her first few years of elementary school in Yuma, Arizona—the sunniest place on earth—and then moved to Laurel, Maryland, where they experienced ice and snow, and then back to perpetual sun in San Diego, California, for her last years in elementary school. Her middle school years were spent in Okinawa, Japan, and then they moved back to the States, to the little town of Waynesville, Missouri. And then the US Marines did the unthinkable; they moved the Knipple family out of their comfortable home and away from all their friends and relocated them to Arlington, Virginia, the summer before Evelyn's senior year of high school.

As Evelyn discovered earlier in life, in her perspective, girls were more difficult to become friends with. They would sit in a huddle at lunchtime, talk nonstop nonsense, and Evelyn couldn't figure out how to break into their group; she didn't know how to talk girl talk, but she could talk sports and joke around with the guys easily, and once she got the boys' attention, the girls finally started talking to her too.

"*Hola, chica,*" Lorena said on this fine Saturday morning as the birds chirped on the banister outside the café window. She slid into the clunky wooden chair, and Evelyn smiled at hearing Spanish.

"*Hola,* Miss Lorena. How art thou this fine afternoon?"

"Just groovy. Glad it's Saturday and happy to be out of the classroom. I had the wildest group of kids yesterday, and this kid named Ed-ward"—Lorena lingered on the last syllable of his name—"is a crazy nut, and he brought in a homemade can of pepper spray! I don't think he was trying to be malicious or anything; he's just a funny kid, but his butt got suspended for it, for sure."

"Geez. Did he get reported for a weapon on campus?"

"Yes, there is a no-tolerance policy on campus, so he was suspended for a day. He crossed the line, and it was a misjudgment on his part. But anyway, enough about the crazy kids in my class, what's good on the menu? I've never been here before."

"Well, I love their salads. Their salad with cranberries, walnuts, and gorgonzola is super delish," Evelyn said as she closed the menu.

"Thanks, Ev, but salad doesn't fill me up. I'm going for the Panini."

Evelyn smiled at Lorena, thinking that Lorena just didn't concern herself with fresh or organic food, but she decided to not talk about food with her today—she knew they didn't agree, but she was pleased that Lorena was willing to try a new place. "So, while our boys are out mountain biking today, I thought it would be good for you and I to get together, since we really only get to talk when we're with the gang."

"Yeah, great idea." Lorena sat up in her chair and straightened her chambray skirt. She wore a tight blazer over a white tank top and low-heeled brown cowboy boots.

"So, I've never heard your story. Where did you grow up, and how did you get here to San Diego and marry our ol' buddy Mr. Spencer, the surfer dude?"

"Well, geez, where to start?" she said as she looked down at her ring—a ring with three different colored stones set in a thick display of silver. "Well, I was born in Encinitas, México. My dad is an architect, and my mom is a nurse. My mom's sisters, my aunties, had already crossed the border way back then and kept telling my mom to come live with them. My parents wanted my brother and me to get an education in the United States, so it was worth it to them to consider leaving Mexico." The waitress came by and dropped off two more glasses of water and some wheat bread with honey butter. After buttering her bread and taking a bite, Lorena continued, "Although my parents had middle-class jobs, the wealthy made a lot more money than we did, so we weren't really quite middle class and my parents still had a challenge making ends meet. And there was a water ration about then, and they had dreams of having something more for their kids. The area of town where my parents lived wasn't protected by Mexican police, and it was run by a local gang. They had some sort of agreement that the gang wouldn't trade in a certain part of town, the tourist part, and the police would leave them alone in their area of town." Lorena took a big gulp of water and carried on. "Now that was back when I was a little girl, so I'm not sure what it's like now. My mom—she was an RN at the time—wanted something more for my brother and me and was willing to take us over the border to San Diego. We left my papa there in México because he loved his México and didn't want to take the entrance exam. He also didn't want to learn English—he was set in his ways. So we came over the border no problem, didn't even need to show a passport, and we said we were just visiting relatives, which was partially true. We lived with one of my aunts for a couple years, and then she sponsored my mom." Lorena looked up, her bread in her hand. "Geez, I'm talking a lot. Do you want me to go on?"

Completely interested, Evelyn said, "Yes, please, go on."

"Well, then my mom took her entrance exam, and just like that, she became a US citizen. She has a dual citizenship. That was back in the day, when it was easier to become a citizen; now it's so difficult. I went to a private all-girl's Catholic school called Our Lady of Peace, and my brother went to an all-boy's Catholic school, Saint Augustine. There was a large Hispanic population at both schools, and many of them crossed the border on a daily basis. There are lots of kids who cross the border daily to go to school in Chula Vista and other border towns."

"Really? I had no idea that they could cross the border so easily. Is that why you don't have much of an accent, going to school here?"

"We were immersed in American culture. We spoke Spanish at home and English at school. My father still doesn't speak any English, but Spencer and I hope to have kids one day; I mean soon, actually, and hope they learn and feel comfortable in both languages."

The waitress came and set their iced teas down on their table.

"So what happened after you moved here? Your dad stayed in Mexico?" Evelyn asked.

"Yes, he did, and he's still there. My mom was a nurse, like I said, but she started cleaning houses when she came over, because she wasn't a citizen yet and the hospitals and doctor's offices didn't recognize her credentials. She cleaned houses for many years, but she saved money and got herself through school and received her RN degree here in the States. I'm so proud of my mom. She's now the head nurse at Scripps Hospital in Chula Vista. She worked from the ground up."

The waitress came by again and, this time, set their food down and asked if they needed anything else. They both looked at each other and shook their heads, not wanting their time to be interrupted. Evelyn munched on her salad while Lorena took big bites of her sandwich.

"So what happened to your brother?" Evelyn asked. "I know you both went on to college, right?"

"My brother lives in Boston. He studied molecular biology and does research at MIT. So proud of him. He isn't married yet, and we worry about it. He doesn't even date, actually, because he's so busy working. He comes back here regularly, and I talk to him every week. And yes, I went to SDSU and studied psychology. It wasn't till later that I figured out what I wanted to do: be a teacher. I love it. I know I complain about the kids, but I really enjoy teaching."

"So why didn't your dad come over?"

"He still doesn't want to take the citizen test. Seriously, that is the one thing, that and learning English, that keeps him in Mexico after all these years, well that and he loves his México," she tilted the palms of her hands up and shrugged slightly. "My mom crosses the border to México just about every weekend. They have a very nice house there in México, and I don't think they want to give that up. My dad comes over once in a while, but he just doesn't feel comfortable here. I think he breaks out in a cold sweat when he's forced to speak in English. He just won't do it."

Evelyn poked at her salad. "Interesting."

Lorena looked up and put her fork down. "Now did you really ask me to get together to find out my life history, or is something else going on? You were pretty drunk the other night. Hammered actually. I've never seen you like that. Is there something going on?"

Evelyn looked up, and their eyes locked, and she knew she was called out and needed to confess. "Yes, yes, something is up, but I haven't told Chad yet, so it needs to be of the utmost secrecy for right now. I've been meaning to tell him for some time, but the opportunity hasn't presented itself. I'm going to tell him soon."

Lorena tilted her head to the side. "I'm not sure I want to enter into any confidential agreement. I've been known to leak a secret, and I don't like to get between couples, but if you feel it's important, then maybe I can help."

"Um, well, I don't know how to start, but I fell in love with a boy."

Lorena didn't know how to react to the news and just squinted her eyes and pursed her lips. "What the hell are you talking about?"

"A little boy, about three years old. I met him in a parking lot and took him to the Polinsky Center because we couldn't find his parents. I've been visiting him ever since, and I have the opportunity to bring him home as a temporary guardian."

"Whoa. Slow down. You don't even like kids."

"Why does everyone say that?" She put her hand on her face, frustrated that people kept saying that to her. "I like kids. Chad and I had just decided not to have our own children, but I do like kids; besides, this one is different."

"What do you mean he's different? What's he like?"

Evelyn told Lorena of her recent adventures and how Marcos had wriggled himself into her heart. "I guess I just didn't know that kids could have so much personality, and I just love the way he looks at me, and I love his laugh—he has this real hearty, unique laugh that makes me laugh. I just want to help him. He's just so loveable and innocent, and, well, I just want to be there for him right now. I know it doesn't seem reasonable to bring him into our lives—we're always at work, and I travel a lot—but lately I've been able to stay in the area. It seems worth it to me that maybe I can invest in a person. Maybe it's my chance to make a real difference. I mean, I know I'm making a difference at work, but this investment is close by, and there's an immediate need for a real and tangible person. I don't know…that little boy has just challenged me to reexamine my priorities and maybe, just maybe I'm willing to make a change. But I don't think Chad is there, and I'm a bit apprehensive about sharing the news and also kind of hesitant, as I think he might say no," she said in a low voice. "I just don't know how to break the news to Chad—he may not feel the same way about Marcos that I do, but maybe he'll fall for him as quickly as I did. Plus, Marcos doesn't speak a lick of English."

Lorena smirked and put her napkin down on the table. "Well, now it's all starting to make sense. And that's why I am here today, right? Bullshit about getting together to get to know each other while our men are away."

"Well, I have wanted to get together with you for a while, but yes, you are a teacher, you love kids, you want to be a mom, and you happen to be Mexican. I could use your help."

"So what do you want me to do? How do you want me to help?"

"We-ll," Evelyn said, drawing the word out, "I was concerned about bringing a Mexican kid into my environment, and given your experience working with kids, I thought maybe you could offer advice."

"Take no offense, Evelyn, but I would be concerned for any kid coming into your environment, Mexican or not."

"What does that mean?" Evelyn asked, trying not sound defensive.

"Honey, you are not really kid material. You and Chad are gone all the time. You both work late, and he works weird hours, and you're always out running or something. You both are into expensive shit, like sailboats, the newest version of a mountain bike, clothes, and Chad and his surfboards. Plus, your house is not kid friendly at all. You would need to have locks installed on your drawers, get rid of the glass coffee table and white rug, and say good-bye to the anal cleanliness. Spencer and I have been trying to get pregnant for almost a year now. We've been trying to change our lifestyle, and I've decided to quit my job for a couple years, until our future kid is in kindergarten or something, and then I would go back to teaching. It's taking us a while to prepare ourselves and our lives for kids, and bam, you think you can bring a three-year-old into your life just like that?" Lorena paused, looking a bit upset. "Anyway, I didn't even know you liked kids."

"You see, Lorena, that's the thing. I feel something very real for this boy. I want to give him an environment where he feels cared for. I want him to forget about his troubles and forget he was abandoned. I want to give him a stable place to live while they search for his parents."

"Well, that's the thing, Evelyn…While I was visiting my relatives in Mexico City a couple months ago, they were telling me about *coyotaje*, otherwise known as "coyotes" or "*polleros*," who are people hired by migrants to smuggle them across the border in exchange for large sums of money, for outrageous amounts like fifteen hundred to two thousand dollars—a very profitable business. Once they get over here, they oftentimes abandoned children for a variety of reasons, such as the child's parents died in the desert while crossing. The terrain around the border in places like Arizona is difficult, harsh, and people don't always survive in the desert." Lorena wiped her face with her napkin and then set it carefully on the table. "You know, you've heard the stories. They can't carry enough water across in backpacks, not enough to get them across the desert, or they get lost. There are many people who die trying to cross into the United States. Or they cross and families get split up and the coyotes couldn't find the child's family on the US side, or maybe once they got to the other side, the family couldn't afford to pay the smuggling fee. There are many reasons that a child could be abandoned, and maybe a coyote is trying to find a parent for the child without getting caught themselves, because their reputation in Mexico is on the line. Maybe a smuggler was there at the Costco parking lot, looking for a white, wealthy woman to take that cute little boy in, and then you walk up with all your food and perfect-looking world." Lorena circled her hand to show she was talking about Evelyn. She paused and looked down at the corner of her sandwich still on the plate. "I'm just saying…well, I'm just saying that the adorable little boy's parents might not be coming by to pick him up."

Evelyn sat there, quiet, wringing her napkin, and looked almost distraught.

Lorena broke the silence. "And do you think you can care for him?"

Evelyn stopped and looked up. "I'm not so sure, but I do want to try. Marcos is so different, and I want to change things in my life for him."

"That's very nice and all, but I hate to inform you, your husband is going to flip. And frankly, you can't even bring yourself to tell him about Marcos. Sounds as if there's a lack of communication in your relationship, which is never good when you want to bring another human being into the situation. It's just not healthy. Plus, he hasn't been on the same journey you have, and you haven't shared it with him; he won't be all that understanding. And frankly, I'm not so convinced about you either. It probably felt good to rescue Marcos, but I'm not so sure you can keep it up for the long run. He needs to be in a home where the mommy and daddy communicate with each other."

A Change
of Life

The Nightmare
(Santiago)

Rubén and Santiago had joined the *La Eme*, the Mexican Mafia, as soldiers a couple of years ago and were collecting taxes from the clients and would deliver it to their contact, where they would return the "package." Right before Marcos was born, Santiago was promoted from solider to lieutenant; he ran a crew of three to four runners from a drop house in a dilapidated neighborhood, the area of town where many families had to move out due to the recession and their landlords were not able to pay their mortgages. The homes sat deserted, owned by the bank. Many forward thinking homeless folks quietly took up residence in these empty homes, staying out of sight in their abandoned homes. The house Santiago set up as his office was paid for through an accountant who was friends with their leader. The gang didn't want any authorities to come snooping around their place, so they kept it as discreet as they could. Santiago had pushed a table up, the very table with the Pooky Bear *Garfield* cartoon, against the front window, just left of the front door, where the dining room would have been. Bushes hugged the front of the house and kept those who came up to the window well hidden. His runners would rap on the window with their knuckles, and he would slide the glass up and do the exchange. The system seemed to work well, and the runners seemed to appreciate not having any exchanges in public. Santiago had started working late hours and meeting more people, gathering more runners and clientele; he was determined to be the most successful damn lieutenant in his area. He also taught his runners a birdcall to let him know they were approaching. Soon enough, he had five runners, each about fifteen years old, as he wouldn't accept kids not in high school.

Santiago had opened a savings account at the bank. As long as he kept his deposits small, no one would be suspicious, even if his deposits were always in cash. The rest of the money, he kept hidden away in the crawl space in the attic.

Now that Santiago had his new role, he was finally making enough money to support his family. Rubén worked at the border and was a loyal solider, making deliveries that were more dangerous and required longer hours.

Six weeks before the Costco incident, Santiago had come home hoping to find everyone peacefully sleeping in their beds. He had come home just before midnight, later than usual. Many of his runners hadn't arrived at their posts until after hours, as their delivery had been held up at the border, so it kept Santiago away from his family longer.

The porch light wasn't on when he arrived home, as his grandmother hadn't been switching it on for some time now. He walked in the house, and there was no lingering aroma of tortillas or beans. It was dark except for the dim light from the TV. There was a soft murmur coming from the speakers he had mounted on the wall. Some infomercial was playing about a vacuum cleaner that could get around corners without you pushing the machine back and forth.

There, next to the beat-up coffee table, on the woven circle rug in the family room, was Marcos, lying in a fetal position, hugging his Pooky Bear. Santiago was horrified that his Marcos had been forgotten and left alone to fall asleep in the middle of the room with no blanket or kiss good night. He was angry at his *Abuelita*, at Katiana, and Carmelita for not being there for Marcos. As far as he knew, none of them had jobs and could be available to care for Marcos while Santiago was out working and making money for the family. There was no need to leave Marcos alone or to have him fend for himself at such a young age. He wanted Marcos to feel well cared for and to not have a care in the world; he wanted him to feel secure with his family and in his environment.

Santiago stared at his boy's sweet face, so peaceful in slumber. Santiago bent down next to him, rubbed his coarse red hair down, and kissed him repeatedly on his cheek. He knew he took the chance of waking him, but he wanted Marcos to know he was not forgotten.

"Oh, my Lucky Marcos, sweet dreams, my boy," Santiago whispered in his ear as he gently picked him up. Marcos instinctively put his head on his papa's shoulder, wrapping his arms around his father's neck.

"*Buenos noches, Papá*," Marcos mumbled, half-asleep.

Walking through the small, dark house, he put Marcos in the little junior bed they had in the room Santiago shared with Katiana. Santiago quickly scanned their queen-sized bed in the center of the room to see if Katiana was there sleeping, but it was empty. He walked down the short hallway to the kitchen, quietly calling out for someone in the house. "*Abuelita*? Katiana? Carmelita?" No response. He walked across the kitchen, to the room his grandma and Carmelita shared, and knocked on their door. No response. He checked all the rooms and walked outside to check out back, but no one was home. Suddenly, he felt intense despair that his three-year-old son had been all alone for the entire evening. No one had been home. Marcos had fallen asleep uncared for, and possibly without dinner.

He then noticed the bathroom door was closed, but the light was not on. He held his ear close to the door, and he could hear water dripping into what sounded like a pool of water. He knocked on the door. "Kat? *Querido, cariña*? Are you in there?" No response. He knocked louder and called out, "Katiana?" He opened the door to darkness. "Katiana?" He switched on the light.

The light revealed a horrific scene. There in the bathtub, under the red water, lay Katiana. One arm was still over the side of the bathtub with blood that had spilled from her wrists to the floor. Her other arm was in the water and her head completely submerged, her long black hair stretched across the water, over her face, and resting on her chest. Her feet were floating on top, her body, completely naked, barely fit in the tub. Water still dripped from the faucet. She must have slit her wrists while it was still daylight. With her last breath, she must have sunk underneath the water as she lost all strength. She must have done this while Marcos was in the other room, watching *Dora the Explorer* or whatever was on. He probably thought he was all alone in the house, or maybe he thought his mama was taking a nap and he didn't want to bother her. Santiago sank to the floor and put his head in his hands.

Intense anger rippled through his body. How dare she do this to their son? What if Marcos had come in and found her? He groaned and wanted to yell in rage. How could this have happened? *How could she do this to herself? How could she do this to us? What was so bad about our life?* Santiago had tried so hard to provide for the family and keep her happy, like she had been when they first met. He was bringing in enough money; they didn't need her grocery-store income. What brought her to despair? Santiago got on his knees and peered into the water to study her beautiful face. He moved her long thick black hair—the hair she had finally decided not to cut—away from her features, so he could really look at her. They had had some good times; he really felt as if he could love her forever. He and Katiana shared a son together, for heaven's sake. How could she leave them?

He stared at her now with her eyes closed and noticed her long, dark eyelashes, her curved black brows that she used to continually pluck to perfection, and her full lips that had been naturally red but were now colorless. Her cheekbones were high, and she still had smile marks in the creases of her mouth. He took her cold, lifeless hand and touched his cheek to it. His tears flowed down her fingers, and he kissed each one. "*Nunca te olvidaré, mi amor.*" He slipped the gold bracelet off her wrist, the one he'd noticed when he first met her. He studied the cursive words on the bangle: "Be true to yourself."

He didn't know how long he sat studying her face and remembering their good times together—reflecting on how he would watch her pile the fruit so high in the grocery store and how her smile was so infectious and how it would make him feel so warm inside. As he stood up from the side of the bathtub, he realized he needed to do something with her body. "*Oh Virgen de Guadalupe, por favor ayúdame,*" he prayed in desperation.

He couldn't call the police; he was wanted for the marijuana possession and skipping the court date, and he didn't want to bring attention to himself in case they started looking into his business. *Dammit, where is Carmelita? Bianca's house?* he thought to himself. Carmelita had been hanging out with her quite a bit lately. He closed the door to Marcos's room and propped a chair up so Marcos couldn't leave his room. He then hurried out the front, down the street four blocks to Bianca's house, and pounded on the door. "Carmelita!" he yelled. "Bianca!" He was pounding the door when it opened.

It was Bianca's brother. "What the hell?" Then, he recognized Santiago. "Man, what the hell, you causing such a ruckus, man. We thought somethin' bad was happenin', homes."

"Frankie, I need Carmelita right now. Is she here?" Santiago was still gasping, trying to catch his breath from the run and still in shock over what had happened.

"Man, take a chill, man. She's here, but I don't think she's ready to go," Frankie said slowly.

Santiago walked inside the house. The light was dim. "*Un Minuto*" was playing in the background, young people were smoking weed and snorting drugs, milling around the room. Carmelita was sitting on the couch with Bianca and a guy Santiago didn't know. They were all dazed, and didn't even notice Santiago until he was in front of them.

"Carmelita," he said urgently, "you need to get up and get home right now."

"You're not the boss of me, Brother. I'm the boss of me, not you," she said slowly, lazily pointing at him and then at herself.

"Okay, I see that. Do you think you're doing a good job taking care of yourself, Sister, eh?" he said harshly. "It's not about you right now, Carmelita. You need to get home. *Abuela* is still gone, out in the night, lost, and something else happened, and you need to get home right now." He took her hands and lifted her up. She was rather easy to lift, and surprisingly, she let him. Santiago knew that Carmelita actually really did care for *Abuelita*; he knew she must have been concerned as she was willing to leave the party and didn't protest as Santiago led her toward the door.

"You take me home, then. Bianca, girl, I see ya later. You save some of that stuff for me, you hear, girl?" Santiago recognized Carmelita's purse next to the couch and handed it to her.

Her friend mumbled something inaudible, and Santiago led his sister back to the house. As he tried to hurry her down the street, he explained what needed to happen. "Listen to me, Katiana hurt herself very badly, and I need you to call for help, but I can't be there, you hear me? Just say you came home, found her in the dark and under the water."

"*Ay dios*," she gasped, raising her hand to her mouth in shock and stopping in her staggered walk. "What happened?"

"Just do as I say, Lita. Just do as I say. First, let's get you some coffee and wash your face."

When they got back to the house, she gulped down some lukewarm instant coffee, and as Santiago put a cold rag on her face, he forcefully said, "Listen, Lita, call the police and then take Marcos to Rubén's house. I'll call Rubén to help me find *Abuelita*, and then I'll come back when the ambulance leaves and get you and Marcos, so we can all come home."

"You're going to leave me by myself?" she said childlike, scared.

"I thought you said you could take care of yourself. You just got to do what I say. Now hand me your phone."

She dug through her purse and pulled out her cell; he dialed 911 and handed it to her.

"Now you follow through, do as I said, and I'll be back." He left her in the kitchen, looking a bit scared. "And, Lita, take care of Marcos while I'm gone. Make sure you get him out of here before the police get here." And then he was gone, speeding to Rubén's house in his Impala.

The Confession

(Evelyn)

Evelyn called her boss, Irene, to let her know that she wouldn't be coming into work. Irene mumbled, "Okay," quickly said good-bye, and hung up the phone. Evelyn tied the laces on her running shoes, grabbed her water bottle, jumped into her Mini Cooper, and headed to the hills of Torrey Pines to run. She used to go to those trails more frequently; however, since she'd met Marcos, she'd had less time. She ran under the pine trees, around sage bushes, jumped over rocks, ran up and down hills on narrow dirt pathways, and ran right out of the park, down to the beach. She stood at the edge of the waves, turned toward the horizon, and set off at a fast pace. As she ran, she picked up speed; her bent arms, shifting back and forth, her legs effortlessly alternated from one to another as she ran, and she no longer felt the sand beneath her feet. She heard herself breathing rapidly; she felt the sweat fall on her eyebrows and slowly trickle down her chin; she felt the wind go past her, but the only thing she heard was the air rush in and out of her lungs.

Running always made her feel as if she was in control of her body, her life, and her future. As she pushed herself to run longer, faster, and harder, she felt accomplished in many areas, as if she could and would succeed. Running was also a complete experience for her as she would also make sure she went out of her way to see nature's beauty, the hills, the beach, or an island. It was a means of escape, a way to stay out of touch with a moment in life; she created her own reality when running. Although, today her mind kept racing to areas in her life she wasn't in control of, and she tried to make sense of the confusion.

As she ran, she questioned how she could take care of a child. How would Chad react when she finally told him about Marcos? How would he respond when she said she was thinking about taking Marcos in while the authorities searched for his parents? What if his family never came to pick him up, as Lorena suggested? What if they did come to pick him up, but she didn't want to let Marcos go? What would Emily and Brian and the rest of their family think of them? Would they think them crazy for taking in a child when they didn't even have time to come over and visit their nieces and nephews? What would her friends think? Would Monica think Evelyn had lost her marbles, and would Addy stop being her friend? Was Lorena right about what it meant for her relationship that she hadn't even told her husband about Marcos yet? How could a woman who strived to succeed in her job, to be in her boss's position by the end of next year, to keep her body in top physical condition, and to travel the world by the time she was forty possibly be thinking of taking a child into her home? It would be a setback to some personal goals. People at work wouldn't give her the challenging projects. She would have to leave early to take him to appointments, and then people in the office would look at her and question her ability and dedication. She wouldn't have time to exercise five times a week. She would get fat. In the end, did those goals really matter, or were they valid fears? Deep down inside, were those really her personal goals? Couldn't she have a goal of living a fulfilling life that didn't involve looks, career success, or a timeframe? Ultimately, the big question of the day was: Would Chad like him?

She always believed that taking care of a child wouldn't create happiness; she'd always thought a successful career would. She wasn't mommy material; why was she even considering taking Marcos into her home and life? What was it about Marcos that even made her consider changing her lifestyle? What was it about Marcos that made her feel so comfortable, while other kids convinced her she would never have kids? What was it about Marcos that made her think about him all the time? These were the questions that raced through Evelyn's mind as she ran alongside the crashing waves. She didn't know the answers, and she didn't know if she would ever know how to proceed, but her heart was overpowering her mind's logic. Love seemed to supersede the practical, but in her upbringing, feelings were not allowed to influence decisions.

Evelyn thought back to an eye-opening experience she'd had on a train trip to her old school. Her high school years in Missouri where the best school days she'd ever had. She had some faithful guy friends and was actually making some friends with the girls—they were the girlfriends of her guy friends, but she was fine with that. She also was doing well on the swim and track teams and getting invited to parties. When she received the news that the marines were moving her family out of Missouri her senior year, she was devastated. She had worked for two and a half years on finally being accepted into a group, and she just didn't want to start over her senior year; she liked her friends, and she was tired of trying to make new ones all the time, especially when she was dreadful at it. Plus, most kids were already established in their friendships by their last year of high school and were not looking to make new pals. Everyone was just looking forward to getting out of school and going to college.

It was October when her school in Missouri had their fall dance, and Evelyn didn't want to miss it. She was part of the swim team at her new school, but she still didn't have an after-school set of friends. She was determined to attend the dance at her old school and asked her mom if she could go. "Absolutely not" was her mom's reply. Evelyn asked again, and her mother made the same response, adding, "We couldn't possibly get you out there for a weekend. You need to start making friends in your new school. Don't go crawling back to old friends. You just have to move on."

Evelyn was seventeen years old and felt mature enough to make her own decisions; she didn't need her mother to tell her what she could and couldn't do, because wasn't it enough that they kept carting her from city to city, state to state, school to school, and uprooting her from what it had taken her years to establish? While her mother was busy setting up furniture, emptying out boxes, and establishing their new house, and her dad was busy making a name for himself with his new crew of marines, Evelyn bought a bus ticket to Missouri. She decided she wouldn't tell her parents until she got to Missouri, so they couldn't make her come home. She had a hundred and fifty dollars from her lifeguarding money, and she made sure all the bills were facing one direction as she placed them in her wallet, and then in her purse as she slung the strap across her chest. The trip would take one day, six hours, and fifty-five minutes and had four transfers. She couldn't imagine that anything could go wrong on a train trip halfway across the country. It was 1996, and people were not carrying cell phones. No one would be able to find her or get ahold of her, and she felt so free when she stepped onto the bus at Arlington Cemetery Metro Station at 2:49 p.m. on a Thursday. She was ditching school on Friday, would go to the dance at her old school on Saturday, and would miss school Monday but be back home that afternoon. She would call her parents when she arrived in Missouri, to let them know there was nothing to worry about and that she would be home soon.

It was an hour and fifty-six minutes to Washington Union Station, and she transferred twice and walked ten minutes from one stop to another, transferring from the Met to the DC Circulator. She boarded Amtrak at 4:03 p.m. and sat in a comfortable seat in a relatively empty car. She watched a variety of people walk past her and find seats in the back or in adjacent cars. Then, as she was looking down at her ticket to see how long it would take to get to the next stop, someone was asking if anyone was sitting next to her. "No, no one," she replied.

"Can I sit here?" the man asked.

"Yes, sure." She moved her carry-on bag out of the way and put it in the stowaway area underneath the chair in front of her.

"I'm Ralph," he said, extending his hand in greeting.

She shook his hand and introduced herself. As he sat down, she took a look at him putting his bag away. He appeared to be, she would guess, in his early forties. His hair was brown and straggly, his face looked worn, and his clothes looked drab. There was nothing impressive about him, and she wondered why he would sit next to her when there were plenty of other seats in the car, and, she was sure, there were several cars available as well.

He asked where she was going, and she was feeling giddy and free, and responded, "I'm going to Missouri. My parents don't know that I left or where I'm going. I'm kind of a runaway, of sorts, just for the weekend, but I'll be back on Monday night," she said proudly, as if she was trying out her newfound freedom and relishing her rebellion. "Where are you going?"

"I'm going to Chicago. Back home. I just got out of the DC jail today. I've been away for six years."

His words hung there like dirty clothes hanging on a line, dangling in the stagnant air, and then, suddenly, she realized she had just told him that no one knew where she was at that moment. She gulped and tried to stay composed, "Oh, really? Um, it must feel good to be going home," she stammered.

She looked down at her ticket again. It was seventeen hours and forty minutes, and fifteen stops to Chicago Union Station. She might have to sit with him for seventeen hours until he finally got off. Suddenly, she was breathing shallow, and the palms of her hands started sweating.

In the seventeen hours and forty minutes on the train ride, she found out that Ralph went to prison because he'd assaulted an officer. He couldn't remember the details, as he was drunk at the time, but eyewitnesses said that Ralph was being obnoxious in the bar, and the owner called the police to ask him to leave his pub, as he was disturbing the other customers. When the police arrived, they asked Ralph to leave, touching him on the arm, when Ralph reacted instinctively by punching the officer in the jaw—not just one punch. He kept punching him. The policeman was able to grab his arm and put it behind his back when the other police officer was coming up behind him, and Ralph kicked backward and hit the officer in the crotch. The two police officers managed to get Ralph on the ground and into the police car, but they were wounded and mad. Ralph had taken karate for years and was a black belt, and he thought the back kick was a karate instinct; he must have felt attacked and didn't register that they were policemen.

Evelyn sat there in the train seat, next to the window, feeling trapped next to a man who had just gotten out of prison on assault, who had been a black belt, and who hadn't seen a woman in a long time. She was thinking that it was just his luck that she was a young girl who'd run away. Suddenly, she wished she'd told her parents where she was going and how she was getting there. She held her purse tighter and moved a little closer to the window. As time ticked by, Evelyn needed to use the restroom but didn't want to leave her stuff with Ralph. She tried to hold it as long as possible, but there was still twelve more hours, and she knew she had to get up and excuse herself. She brought her purse with her, freshened up in the bathroom, got a muffin and a water at the snack bar, and then came back to find Ralph still sitting there, her bag still under the chair, apparently untouched.

As they continued to talk, she noticed that Ralph had hazel eyes, a cleft chin, and wore no rings or jewelry. His hair was slicked back, and his face was freshly shaven, but it looked raw, as if it hadn't been shaven in a long time. He smelled fresh, and she suspected that he was wearing his "Sunday best" on his first day out from behind the prison walls. She learned that he had moved to Washington, DC, for a girl. He had been working at the hospital and studying to be a nurse, and his girlfriend had been working at a government job, hoping to work at the White House one day. He said there was a big influx of men as nurses, and it was relatively easy to get a job, even though there were so many weird connotations that a nurse was a women's job. He loved helping others who were sick, though, and felt like such a part of a team when he worked with doctors and other nurses to help a patient get better. In prison, they'd found out his medical abilities, and he had been allowed to work in the infirmary, which he was thankful for, as the work kept his mind off of other things; he had something to do that still made him feel useful, even behind bars.

He and his girlfriend knew each other from Chicago, but moved out to DC in hopes that she could pursue her dream job. The two had been living together in a condo and spent their weekends visiting the free museums, the National Mall, and the numerous ethnic restaurants in the area. He'd also just figured out the layout of the city. It took a while for him to figure out how the streets were laid out, and soon they were able to navigate the city and could gauge how much farther they needed to go and where they were in relation to the White House.

Then, over time, his girlfriend had been coming home later and going into "work" a lot more on weekends. Ralph had made air quotes when he said it. She'd told him she was working more hours to get ahead and get noticed, which was why they were in Washington, DC, so he'd encouraged her. Then, out of the blue, she'd told him she'd been seeing someone and she was no longer in love with Ralph—she was in love with this other guy, and could Ralph move out this weekend?

She had been so charming and kind when he'd met her, Ralph was saying. Such a Midwestern girl suddenly influenced by the "chew 'em up and spit 'em out" mentality of the city. He was so irate, confused, and mad that night that he'd gone to the local bar to drown his sorrows and gotten completely carried away. Ralph claimed he wasn't much of a drinker and the alcohol must have really had an effect on him; he was actually a coffeehouse connoisseur, which made Evelyn raise her eyebrows in disbelief, as he didn't look like a coffee connoisseur, but he continued on about how he must have been feeling numb after his drinks and was slowly forgetting his troubles when the policeman touched him on his arm. It was a reaction, Ralph said, and he turned around and decked the police officer across his face and the big guy fell to the ground. His family and friends were shocked when they'd learned he was sentenced to six years in prison.

He had been thirty-one at the time of the bar incident, and he wasn't sure if he would be able to find a job when he got back home. His friend who was meeting him at the train station said that Ralph might be able to get a job at the hospital, but they would do a background check, and he might have start in a position away from patients, maybe doing laundry or something else, since he had a criminal record.

Evelyn caught him up on what had happened in the world while he was gone: the TV shows, the news, the latest fashion trends, the record-breaking sports scores, while he taught her how to play a card game, canasta. She finally won a game and hoped she would remember how to play so she could teach her friends. He said the first thing he was going to do when he finally made it home, after he saw all his family, was go to the library and check out *Time* magazine and *World News* and catch up on the news and check out the movies that were released while he was locked up, behind walls that hid him from what was happening in the world around him. He was also anticipating, with "salivating taste buds," his mother's home-cooked meals and hoped his family would accept him back into their lives, that life would continue on as if nothing—except some bad luck—had ever happened.

Evelyn sat and listened to him politely. As the hours ticked on, he never tried to touch her, never eyed her purse, was always respectful, and didn't appear to sit next to her because he was interested in her for any sexual reasons. He didn't even ask her any personal questions, although he was always attentive when she spoke. But at the end of seventeen hours and fifty-five minutes, she'd realized that he sat next to her because he was lonely and wanted someone to talk to. Maybe, she considered at the time, she looked like safe company for his train ride home.

They arrived at the Chicago Union Station and parted with a handshake. He thanked her for listening to his story. As he was just about to leave, he turned back around and said, "Hey, Evelyn, maybe you should call your parents to let them know that you're fine. If I were your father, I would be worried sick about you." He turned and left, and she watched him weave through the crowd and disappear into the distance. Later in life, she would wonder about him and hope he was doing well and that he had a new, faithful love in his life. She had hoped the best for him, and from that experience, she'd learned not to be so quick to judge the cover but to find out a person's backstory. People might have rough edges, but they might be really good-hearted people. Ralph unintentionally taught Evelyn a lesson she would reflect on the rest of her life.

After watching him disappear in the crowd, Evelyn had turned to look for a pay phone to call her parents. She was expecting them to be angry with her when she called, but they actually knew she was on her way to Missouri, and family friends would be there to greet her. They said they were sure she'd learned her lesson, so she wasn't grounded—"Just get home safely and don't do it again."

Evelyn had an enjoyable time at the dance with her friends, and her train trip back to Virginia was uneventful. When she finally made it home, her dad just slapped her back and, with a big grin, said, "Way to go. My little girl is ready for the big world out there."

Maybe she had learned something that day on the train that would affect her on this day many years later. She had an image of a person that had turned out to be completely wrong.

She was also sure her parents were going to ground her for the rest of her senior year, but all she had received was a congratulatory slap on the back. Maybe her conflict with bringing Marcos home and fearing the response of Chad was really just making the situation out to be bigger than it really was. Maybe it would all turn out perfectly, and everyone would walk away peacefully; maybe the situation would work itself out on its own. Maybe Chad was ready to have children and neither one of them wanted to be the first to admit it.

That day at Torrey Pines State Beach, she ran back up the side of the hill at a slower pace and started her cool down, walking at a fast pace, then a little slower, then in circles in the shade. She stretched out her hamstrings and got her heart rate down, then sat on a boulder under a tree overlooking the crashing waves, lost in her thoughts about what people would think of Marcos.

Although she had an iPod at home, she never brought it on her runs. She felt it distracted her from noticing the world around her. She loved running in nature; it made her feel closer to the Creator, even if she wasn't familiar with Him. Nature and exercise helped her think. She had solved work dilemmas running among the pine trees, made the decision to move to San Diego jogging the eleven-mile Golden Gate Bridge Run; she'd made up her mind about which job to accept while running the Silver Strand half marathon; she'd come up with a slogan for their company product on the Mud Run at Camp Pendleton, and she'd agreed to marry Chad during the Rock 'n' Roll marathon, but her run between the trees and the ocean on this particular day just confused her.

She rarely listened to her heart, yet she felt a heartfelt tug to bring Marcos home…but her mind usually won, and it said this would never work. She considered that maybe Lorena was right: it wasn't a good fit, a driven woman who hungered for power, prestigious, and position and who had no experience with children bringing a homeless three-year-old into her house. Evelyn and Chad's household included tight schedules, an overflow of sporting goods, and furniture that had never met a dirty hand. Their lives weren't set up for a kid, and their future plans would be thwarted if she had to include a child's needs. Evelyn felt the coolness of the boulder beneath her legs where she sat, heard the wind blowing through the pine trees and the waves hitting the sand, and in her stillness, she felt her heart beat a little faster at the very thought of a charming Marcos in her life.

She had been nervous to tell Chad about Marcos, but after searching deep down and admitting that she could give up her time and rewrite some of her goals, she'd decided that her immediate ambitions could be postponed; she had a new interest and a complete change of heart concerning her views on having kids. Marcos had changed everything in her life. With that personal acknowledgement, she was sure she was now ready to tell Chad.

Evelyn had been gone several hours by the time she arrived home. Chad's car was in the garage, and she called out to him when she walked in, so as not to scare him. His briefcase was hung on the designated hook by the door, his keys were in the bowl by his cell phone on the kitchen counter, his scrubs were laid carefully next to the laundry door, and she heard him whistling in the shower.

As she was taking off her shoes and the band out of her hair, Chad came out of the bathroom.

"Holy shit, what are you doing here?" Chad said, startled, his green towel wrapped around his waist as he rubbed his hair dry with a hand towel. "What the hell? Why aren't you at work?" It was cursing that made her stop and reconsider bringing a child into their environment; they had a habit of blurting out expletives that were inappropriate for kid's ears.

"I took the day off," she said calmly and tried to sit down slowly and purposefully on the corner of the bed.

"Whatever for? What's gotten into you? Are you back into training again? You've been running quite a bit lately, but Addy mentioned you're missing your yoga classes. How many miles have you run this week?" He put on his boxers and a gray V-neck T-shirt.

"Well…" she stammered and reconsidered saying anything. But then she thought of Marcos's face as he sang "Itsy Bitsy Spider" and how he'd laughed when he'd offered her his oatmeal. She had to confront her fears for his sake. "Honey, I haven't been completely honest with you," she said as she twisted her hands and took a deep breath. "What are you doing here? Don't you have patients to see and rounds to make today?"

"Crazy thing. I had a prostate surgery scheduled for today, but this is the second time we had to reschedule for this guy. He's not supposed to eat before surgery, and he ate breakfast again. And not a light breakfast, mind you, but he had biscuits, gravy, and sausage, as well as two cups of coffee. This guy is over three hundred pounds, and let me just say, he is not a tall guy." He stopped running his hands through his brown, curly hair, and he sat next to her and put his arm around her shoulder. "Listen, I would just love to hear your thoughts, but, seriously, speaking of breakfast, I am so hungry and haven't eaten for hours, feels like days. Do you mind if I make myself a breakfast…or is it lunch now? I might not have eaten dinner either…Oh well, do you mind if we take this down to the kitchen?"

"No problem. That's fine." Evelyn's fear was giving way to annoyance. She had just told her husband of four years that she had been deceiving him, and his response was to tell her that he was hungry? Maybe Lorena was right: they had a serious communication problem, or maybe Chad knew he just couldn't actively listen to her until he filled his stomach with food.

He ran down the stairs to the kitchen, all the while continuing his monologue. "You won't believe who I saw today. Crap, I can't even believe it myself. This guy I know from water polo in high school, and we usually played opposite each other, same position, great swimmer—geez, I tell you, it was tough, but I had to tell him some bad news. Most of the time, I like what I do, but, Ev, when I have to tell someone bad news, I can't stand my job. Although I think we can really help him." He opened the refrigerator and started pulling out food. Evelyn watched him as he made a lemongrass tofu bánh mì with toasted baguette, extra-firm tofu, fresh lemongrass, thinly sliced radish, fresh cilantro, and cucumber. Chad enjoyed exploring new ways to combine healthy foods, and Evelyn enjoyed whatever he came up with.

"Oh, hon, I'm sorry to hear that. Cancer doesn't discriminate. It must have been difficult to tell your friend bad news. I hope you can help him."

"Yes, I think we can help him. It's just going to be a difficult and long road ahead. But, yes, I think we can definitely help him."

She paused and studied his face for a bit then turned and pulled out a storage baggie from the cupboard. "Try these. They're kale chips I made."

"Kale? No joke? Wow! You made these?"

"Yes, I…" She was just going to start in about the entire process of making kale chips, but then remembered why she was standing in their kitchen in the early afternoon when she could have been having a Skype conversation with Dr. Goodwin in Haiti. "Oh, I'll tell you about the kale chips later."

Chad looked over at her curiously. "So tell me, what's on your mind." He began eating his lunch at the kitchen bar.

"Well, I met a boy," Evelyn muttered as she nervously twirled her hair with her finger, watching Chad carefully. "He's three years old. I met him in the parking lot, we couldn't find his parents, so we called the police, and I followed them over to the center for children." She knew she was talking fast so she took a deep breath and tried to slow down "His name is Marcos. I stayed there with him at the center while his social worker filled out the paper work."

"When did all this happen?"

"The day before your birthday party."

Chad looked irritated, as his birthday had been a while ago. He set the plate down, leaned against the kitchen counter, and placed his hands behind him on the edge.

"We sat there at the center and sang 'Itsy Bitsy Spider' together and had a touching moment. Then I visited him the next day during his breakfast and he made me laugh so hard while he was eating his oatmeal. I've been visiting him ever since and I feel so comfortable around him."

Chad just stared at her, puzzled, and his eyes had slowly seemed to go out of focus; it looked as if he were going into some sort of coma.

"The police and social services have been looking for his family and they can't be found. They can't find any of Marcos' relatives. We don't know where he came from and why he was left at the Costco parking lot wandering around." Evelyn paused for a moment and watched Chad, as he seemed to be fixated on a tile on their kitchen floor. "Well, Marcos can't stay at the center anymore, as they only keep kids there at their facility temporarily. So his social worker asked if we could be his temporary guardians while they continue to look for his family. That Marcos could come here and live with us for a while." Evelyn held her breath as she finished her last line. She so hoped Chad would want to help Marcos, as she knew he was compassionate and she wanted him so badly to be moved from just her story alone.

His eyebrows furrowed, and he walked into the living room, paced around the couch, and then suddenly began taking two steps at a time up the stairs.

"Chad? Honey? Where the hell are you going?" Evelyn stood there in the kitchen, glaring up the stairs. She couldn't understand why he would walk away. Chad liked to confront problems head-on, and she was confused at his desertion. She followed him up the stairs to the bedroom, where he was drawing the curtains closed. "Why did you do that? Why did you walk away?"

"You know, I'm just tired, and I'm going to bed."

"I was hoping that we could go to the center and you could meet Marcos today. It wasn't easy to tell you all that, you know."

"Obviously."

"What do you mean 'obviously'?" She stood with her hands on her hips as she watched him fold down the covers of the bed. Chad would never just pull them down with abandon.

"Obviously because it took you an entire month, or however long it's been, to finally tell me why you've been sneaking around and vanishing for hours."

"What are you talking about? You've been at work."

"Oh, I see, you try to go when you think I won't know that you're missing. What the hell, Evie? He's an unknown kid from somewhere. How do you think he could ever fit in around here? I don't even know what I'm talking about; we can't even have a kid around here. We're never home. We hardly ever see each other. I'm gone for hours. You're gone for hours, sometimes days. The only reason we're seeing each other right now is because this guy ate breakfast when he wasn't supposed to and you unexpectedly took the day off! Sometimes you skip off for weeks overseas. How could we possibly take care of a kid?" He stood at the side of the bed with his shirt off as his face turned the shade of a pomegranate.

"I know you're right, Chad. I know you're right, but there's something about this kid that makes me want to take him home and care for him."

"What?" he demanded. "What is it about this kid that would make you want to do that?"

"He's just the most adorable kid ever, he makes me smile, and he's gentle, and he has red hair and freckles, and this deep, guttural laugh, and I just want to squeeze his cheeks and eat him up."

Chad looked at her in bewilderment. He had never heard her talk that way about a kid—about anyone or anything for that matter. Her voice had changed while she spoke, and he rarely saw her softer side—the side that could warm up to a child.

"You should meet him."

"I'm going to bed." He slipped under the covers quickly and punched his pillow.

Her voice softened. "Chad, hon. Please. Come with me to the center today and meet Marcos."

"I'm going to sleep, and I'll talk to you when I talk to you. So good night. Please close the door behind you."

The Matchbox

(Santiago)

It was getting late, and Santiago shifted his feet as he leaned up against the wall, pulling at his ear in worry. He hadn't sold his entire allotment of heroin and didn't make enough money for the taxes he owed the gang, much less enough to pay for rent that was due the next day. His eyes scanned the streets as he looked for Tony and Julio and some other soldiers who hadn't come around to pick up their stashes. How much longer should he wait? As soon as he left, he was sure the druggies would come around, and if he wasn't there for them, then they would go to Roberto down the street and buy from him in their impatience. He knew he had to go home and check on his *abuela* and see how Marcos was doing. It had only been four weeks since his beloved Katiana had died. They gave her a small funeral and buried her in plot in the local cemetery surrounded by no one who she would have known. Marcos brought a stuff teddy bear, as he felt his momma needed a stuffed animal just like he did, and placed it next to her grave as his gift to his mom. It took Santiago all afternoon to find the bear, as Marcos had given him specific instructions to find a Pooky Bear just like his, but Santiago couldn't find one so had to get an ordinary bear wearing a pink T-shirt with a red heart in the middle, as it reminded him of the pink and red-hearted shirt Katiana wore when she used to work at the grocery store when she was only fourteen years old. Marcos was very disappointed that he couldn't give his momma a Pooky Bear to take to heaven, and he had a little fit about it and sniffled and said maybe she was supposed to just take her own special bear with her. Santiago brought his gift and stuck a pinwheel next to the flat grave plaque, so it would twirl in the breeze; he wanted the continual movement to be a reminder of his enduring affection for his dearest. His *Abuelita* laid down a bunch of Katiana's favorite flower, the Gerber daisy, on the gravesite, and Carmelita brought a brush and a mirror and dropped them in the grave before the diggers tossed the dirt on the coffin. The four of them walked away from the grave and decided no one wanted to go home and face their house, where Katiana spent so much time, so they stayed at the park for the rest of the day and ate *guisado* tacos at Tacos Ricos food truck. As Santiago watched Marcos go down the slide, his *Abuelita* pushed him in the swing and later Carmelita played a game of tag with Marcos, giggling the whole time; Santiago was heartbroken that Katiana couldn't be there to see them all together, to watch Marcos grow up, to be Santiago's partner in parenting, and his friend and companion for life. He thought about his beautiful girlfriend and was thankful he had the time he had had with her and that she'd left this world having given him a beautiful son who lit up his life and gave him purpose to press on. He sat there on the park bench with a leaf in his hand and thought that Katiana would have enjoyed their day at the park together.

☙

A month after Santiago buried his girlfriend, La Eme's leaders promoted someone new to the rank of "key holder," who would oversee drug sales in gang territories in San Diego His name was El Serpiente. He was in his early thirties, and he was known for making the most money dealing narcotics in the city. He was promoted to underboss not only for his knowledge and profitability, but also for his charisma. He was well liked, and he had a way of making a lieutenant feel as if he was the best lieutenant in Southern California, but just as soon as the lieutenant was standing on a pedestal, the legs could be kicked out from under him. El Serpiente was a big talker, a motivator, and he didn't tolerate anything less than the best. He was coined El Serpiente before he had a tattoo made on his skull. The serpent tattoo was unforgettable as its tail started on the nape of his neck, and the body of the snake traveled up the back of El Serpiente's head, and the red, forked tongue spit out just at the tip of his forehead. He usually had his hair buzzed, so the snake's body could only faintly be seen, but Santiago had heard that when El Serpiente got mad, the serpent's tongue started glowing, and those who had witnessed his anger were sure the tail started rattling. Santiago knew that as the new key holder, El Serpiente would be coming around to the neighborhood, demanding the taxes and not tolerating any infractions. Santiago always honored La Eme and was thankful for his Mexican brothers and for the income, their commitment to protecting one another, and having a place he felt as if he belonged. Santiago had worked his way up to lieutenant by doing what had been asked of him—petty theft at a young age, shedding some blood in a few fistfights, but mostly by putting one hundred percent into proving he was a good worker and could sell more than his allotment in half the time of the other lieutenants. But four weeks after his girlfriend died, he didn't have the support at home for Marcos. It felt as if his world was falling apart and all he had was his son—he would do anything to make sure Marcos was secure and felt loved. He'd started taking his son to his great-aunt's house during the day; his sister hadn't been around the house at all and rumor had it she was in communication with their mother in Mexico, and his grandma needed constant surveillance at an old folks home and had been slipping into what they told him was Alzheimer's disease. With all of that going on in his home life, Santiago was distracted. His homeys around him understood—Tony, Pedro, and Rubén understood—but how long would they pick up the slack for him? How long would it be before El Serpiente found out he wasn't paying his taxes to La Eme?

Santiago stuffed his hands in his pockets and fiddled with a worn-out matchbox his friend had given him.

He had known his friend Hector since second grade, when they had played fútbol out in the open field. They even had class together; Hector was always turning in his homework on time and only missed school if he was actually sick. Hector's mom would come in one day a week to help the teacher with art projects, or she would animatedly read stories to the kids. She was the only mom in the class that would come in and help the teacher at the holiday parties. Hector wasn't nerdy, as he could hang with best of them, but he was actually self-confident and didn't conform to what others around him were doing. In high school, he hung out at the rec center, but he never exchanged drugs, smoked, or drank in excess, and he would walk away if a fight broke out. He rode in lowriders with friends, but he had them stop the car so he could get out if there was any talk of violence or he saw someone had a handgun on them. He wasn't like the rest of them, but everyone seemed to like him. Even if he had wanted to, nobody would have let him in their gang, because they believed in him and had high hopes for him succeeding outside of their neighborhood.

A year ago, Hector had pulled Santiago aside. "Hey, *güey*, you goin' to get yourself in the slammer if you continue down that route."

"Man, what you talkin' 'bout, man?"

"You know, *pinche*. I know you're man of the house and all, but I'm tellin' you, I can help you."

"How can you help me, *ese*?"

He had pulled a matchbook from his father's garage out of his shirt pocket and written down his phone number on the inside flap. "My dad, man, he owns his own garage, ya know, and you can work there on cars, man, if you want to. I saw what you did to your car, *güey*. I think the garage could really use a *chido* like you."

"Man, they're not going to hire me like this." He opened his jacket and showed him his tats and clothes.

"Sure, man, why not? I know you won't make as much money working on cars as you're making now, but it's sure better than sweating bullets when the cops come 'round, or being in the pokey, or getting an assignment for a drive-by to prove your loyalty, or being dead somewhere and there being no one to provide for your family, man."

Thinking back to that time Hector had given him the matches, Santiago fiddled with the book again. He'd never used any of the matches, but every morning, he would stuff those matches in his pocket, and every night, he would take out the matchbook and put it in the top drawer of the dark-green dresser he'd had since he was little boy.

He knew there must be a way out of dealing drugs and into working at the garage; he just wasn't sure how to take the next step. He'd made an unspoken vow to the gang to be loyal to them for life. The opportunity of working with Hector's father made him think that maybe he wasn't in a hopeless situation. He knew that his loyalty to his gang was till death, but maybe he could help the gang in other ways.

He had driven by Hector's father's garage several times and stopped to study it once just after Marcos was born. González Garage was a little outside of University Heights and had a glass and an ornamental iron shop on either side of it. The garage had three bays, and the large doors had been open, revealing cars up on the racks and guys in work overalls in the pits or half under the hoods of cars. The garage was well kept, all the tools not in use put neatly away. But there was an atmosphere of grease and sweat, and a variety of cars that Santiago loved. He knew he could feel at home in a place like that.

He moved away from his spot against the wall where he had been impatiently waiting for his runners and walked down the street to his car a couple blocks down and tucked away in an alley. As he walked the quiet street and listened to the hum of the cars and the click of the turning traffic lights, he saw a woman standing on the corner holding up a sign as she rocked back and forth, her hand rubbing the back of her head; her hair was nappy from negligence. Her clothes were tattered and colorless, and what moved Santiago enough to make him stop and stare was that she wore no shoes. He neared her corner and peered at her sign, written with crayon on a piece of cardboard. It said, "Laid off 9 months ago. Have 2 small children. Please help." The number of months had been crossed out several times, and the nine was darkened over the crossed out ones. He looked up from her sign, trying to look into her face as she held it close to her chest. Her face was unclear, hazy, and worried. He stopped in his tracks when he saw that she was quietly sobbing. He walked closer and dropped money into her bucket.

He walked quietly back to his car and drove to his great-aunt's house to pick up Marcos. He was grateful that his auntie was willing to take in Marcos while he was at work. She'd seemed hesitant when he'd asked her, but after a pause, she'd exclaimed, "Of course I'll take in little Marcos." Her house was in City Heights, a neighborhood close to theirs. He approached the house, which had five cars parked out front: two on the lawn and three parked bumper-to-bumper in the driveway, the third one blocking the sidewalk and sticking out into the street. He parked along the road just down the way. When he got out of his Impala, he heard loud, vibrating music, and when he walked closer to the house, he realized it was coming from his auntie's great-grandson's room. His aunt was usually waiting for him outside while Marcos played in the front yard, but today the cars blocked the patches of grass. He walked up to the house and found the front door wide open. As he walked in, another guy came in behind him, walked right past Santiago, took a right down the hallway, and opened the door to his cousin's room, releasing the blaring music. Santiago felt the deep bass vibrate his bones and heard it rattle the little chandelier that hung over the dining room table. Immediately, he got a good whiff of the marijuana smoke as it danced down the hall.

Santiago walked further into the house, to the family room, where he saw his great-uncle asleep in his La-Z-Boy. His great-uncle was Caucasian, born and raised in L.A., and had met his great-aunt in the city before they'd moved down to San Diego, where his great-uncle took a job at the shipyard. Santiago didn't know his great-uncle very well, as he rarely came to any family events. He stood before his great-uncle to see if he was okay, as his head was tilted back with his mouth wide open. His arms were hanging over the armrests, and one leg was hanging off the side of the chair. He noticed that there was a pile a beer cans just right of the chair. His great-uncle was in a drunken stupor. The TV was humming in the background as a *Wheel of Fortune* rerun played. He noticed some burger wrappings on the ground and torn pieces of paper. Next to the couch, on the side table, was a white substance. Suddenly Santiago's blood started to boil. He put his finger in the substance and then tasted it. Cocaine. There, on the table, was cocaine, lying around where his son could also stick his fingers into it and lick it. Santiago was irate and started urgently calling out to his aunt. He opened the sliding glass door and noticed the light in the backyard was, and it was slowly getting dark. The backyard was on a slope, and Santiago walked down farther and heard giggling. His auntie was sitting on the ground next to Marcos, and they were piercing leaves onto the ends of sticks and took their two hands around the sticks and were twirling their creations around. Marcos thought it was funny. He looked at his aunt, who looked up to see who was approaching, and then what looked like a flush of embarrassment washed over her as she quickly looked down at the stick she was twirling.

Santiago sat next to Marcos, who shouted, "Papa! Look, look at my kite!" He proudly showed his dad his makeshift "kite," and gleefully started running around as if he was flying a kite.

Santiago wasn't mad anymore; he looked into his aunt's eyes. "You should have told me." He had compassion for his aunt. He had no idea what was going on in the house, he just knew that she made really good tamales, which she brought over every Christmas. He knew that his uncle wasn't too involve in the family, but he never knew he got drunk out of his mind every day, nor that his cousin to be as selfish as he is bringing in his friends to get high in her own house. He felt frustrated for his aunt. He wish he could help her, but he really need to figure out how to care for Marcos first.

"I know I should have never let you bring Marcos over, but I wanted to hear him laugh and take my mind off of what was going on around here."

"What if you came over to my house and took care of him there?"

"I can do it for a while, while you look for someone else to take care of Marcos, but I really can't leave your uncle and your cousin alone in the house; they could kill each other or blow up the house. I'm not sure what could happen."

"He doesn't hurt you, does he, Auntie?" The corner of her mouth went up in a rueful smirk and she shrugged. "I can take care of myself. I'm more worried about those two." She pointed up at the house. "I've loved taking care of Marcos the last couple days, but I just don't feel you should bring him back."

"Yes, I agree."

"Santi, I'll give you two weeks to find someone else to take care of Marcos."

"Yes, okay. Thanks, Auntie, for giving me some time. I'm sorry to hear of your situation."

The two of them got up, gathered Marcos and his "kite," and Santiago hurried him through the house and out to the car. He was sad for his aunt; he knew his cousin was wild, but he hadn't known his great-uncle's condition. His aunt was his last sane relative; he had high hopes for her to be the one to take care of Marcos while he was at work.

Marcos hugged his bear in the backseat and told his dad about his day: he had been watching TV when the house started getting stinky, so he and his aunt went outside. As they continued down the street, Santiago turned the radio off and listened to Marcos sing to his bear. As they approached their house, Santiago saw the lights on in the front room. He wondered if Lita had finally decided to come home and if she'd invited friends over. As he drove closer to the house, he saw El Serpiente's car parked at the front curb. He turned the ignition off and sat in the car for a bit to think about what to do next when Marcos said in Spanish, "You okay, Papa?"

"Yes, my lucky boy. It just looks as if we have some visitors in the house, so I'm wondering"—Santiago turned around in his seat to look at Marcos—"if you could be a big boy for me and walk through the back door quietly, like a little mouse, go to your room, and you can stay up and play games on my phone until our company leaves. Then maybe we can go get some ice cream." Santiago rubbed his hands and licked his lips.

Marcos licked his lips too. "Ice scream!" He raised his hands and his bear over his head. "Ice scream, ice scream, ice scream!"

"Now, Marcos, you have to be real quiet, so we don't disturb our guests, okay?" Santiago put his finger to his lips.

"Okay, real quiet."

Santiago texted Rubén to see if he could come by and pick up Marcos and have him climb out through the side window. Rubén texted back, "Roger." Santiago turned down the volume on his phone and gave it to Marcos. "Here is my phone so you can play games. Uncle Rubén is going to come by to pick you up. Can you leave my phone under your pillow?"

"Okay," Marcos said very seriously as he reached out to accept the phone. Then, he looked up and smiled. "I'll be real good, Papa."

"I know, my lucky boy; you are the best boy ever."

Santiago had Marcos crawl up to the front of the car to get out through the driver's seat, so El Serpiente would only hear one car door shut. Marcos turned around to his dad, blew a kiss to him, and tiptoed and hunched down, creeping quietly to the backyard. Santiago walked up the walkway and then opened the front door wide. "Well, *amigos*, what brings you gentlemen to *mi casa* on this fine evening?"

As he walked in, he saw El Serpiente pacing the living room, swinging his brass knuckles. Julio was sitting leisurely in the old La-Z-Boy, playing *Call of Duty* on the Xbox, and Pedro was in the refrigerator, reaching for a beer.

"Santi!" Pedro cried out. "What the hell, *güey*? What do you have to eat around here? Where are your grandma's tortillas? Shit, there is no good food in here." Then he saw Marcos's Pancrema cookies. "This will do."

"You made it home, Santi. What took you so long, *pinche*?"

"Ah, well, El Serpiente, I had work to do, hard work. What brings you to my humble *abode*?"

El Serpiente put his brass knuckles in his pocket, but continued to pace the floor. "We just wanted to see how our homey was doing, you know how we take care of one another, eh. We wanted to see for ourselves what was going on around here. But when we got here"—he blew on the palm of his hand—"it was a deserted desert, like tumbleweeds blowing out front and crickets chirping. Crickets, Santi. No one here? Where is your family, *ese*?"

"Ah, El Serpiente, you are here to pay me a visit." Santiago put his hand on his chest and put his chin up, to appear proud he had company.

"Ah, yes, Santi, of course. We take care of each other, no? You scratch my back, and I'll scratch your back, eh. Your family well?"

Julio continued to play the Xbox and Pedro resorted to drinking his beer and eating cookies on the couch, watching. "Yes, well. They're all gone tonight, I guess. All doing whatever they do. I just never know if they're going to be home when I get here. They're so independent, out and about."

"Ah, well I guess everyone is different. I know exactly where my women are at all times, and I also know what all my family are doing, you know my big extended family, my brothers. My *güey*." He held out his hands and laughed, Pedro and Julio laughed, and Santiago joined them and laughed and nodded. "And, Santi." El Serpiente was still smiling and put his arm around Santiago's shoulders. "You are our brother, and, brother, I'm wondering what's been going on, homey. Are you still sad about your woman? Are you having a hard time focusing?" He pulled away, leaned up against the wall, and stared into Santiago's eyes. "I'm wondering if everything is okay, 'cause you've been promoted to lieutenant, and you were doing so well, homey, and then such sad news about your girl, and we gave you time, but it's been so much time, and I'm wondering if you can handle your job."

"Yes, yes, I can handle my job. I'm back. I'm back working hard and will surprise you." Santi smiled coolly. "I'll surprise you, El Serpiente."

He smiled. "Yes, please surprise me. Santi, I hate to tell you, but you were down one thousand denaro. I let you be for a while, but now it's two hundred thousand. Santi, I have people to pay, I need to move that money along, and I don't want to owe my brothers money, so I need my *pesos*. Understand, brother?"

"Yes, I understand, and thank you for letting me take care of my family stuff, but I'm back. I'll get you that money."

"Santi, I need that money by the end of the day tomorrow."

"Tomorrow?"

"You heard me, end of day. *¿Lo entiendes?*"

"*Comprendo.*"

"Good, *hermano*. I knew you were back. Yes, *hermanos*?" He turned to Pedro and Julio and then jerked his head toward the door.

"Yes, yes, we knew Santi would be back," Pedro said.

"Good to see you, *hermano*," Julio said as he bumped fists with Santi as they passed.

"Thanks, for coming over, brothers. Yes, *mi casa* is *su casa*," Santiago said as they walked out the front door.

A Breaking Point
(Santiago)

Santiago sighed in relief when El Serpiente left his house. The threesome left without too much drama. No one had gotten hurt, and Marcos had never felt threatened or scared. Only a warning was given, but it felt too much like a threat. Santiago sat on the brown chair with the ripped leather and ran his hands through his hair, trying to get his thoughts in order. The Medinas family's lives seemed to be unraveling, and he wanted to do everything he could do to keep them together and safe; he needed to start them down a different path. First, he had to get the money for El Serpiente, then make a clean break from the gang and move his family away from the pressures of the gang life. Maybe he could take a job at the garage or see if his father's old company had a place for him; even though he'd heard you had to be at least twenty-one, maybe they would make an exception for him. He still had an immediate problem; he didn't know where he was going to get the money, especially by the end of tomorrow. *Two hundred thousand dollars* kept echoing in Santiago's mind. He could buy a rundown house in East County for that amount—or a Tesla and drive Marcos and himself far away from here. It wasn't as if he could rob the local 7-Eleven or resell flat screen TVs for that kind of dough. It would take him at least two weeks to make that kind of take-home pay. How could he do it in one day? He had seventeen hours to get two hundred thousand dollars. His hands were shaking as he brought them to his face. He had to keep himself together; he couldn't lose it. He had to stay strong and focused—he owed that much to his son. He had to get them out of this situation.

He texted Rubén to ask if it was okay if Marcos stayed over and if Rubén could bring Marcos back in the morning to meet his aunt.

Sure. No problemo. Whts up?

Tell you later. Tx for taking Marcos. He's my everything, Santiago texted, a bit emotional. He told himself he needed to pull himself together and think of a way out of this situation. He didn't like the idea of Marcos staying over at Rubén's, because Santiago didn't trust Rubén's drunken father who was sometimes nocturnal, pacing the house at night and sleeping the day away, but Santiago trusted Rubén. Marcos had never stayed over at Rubén's place, but it was the best solution in the situation, and it would be the only time it would happen.

Now that that was settled, Santiago had to figure how to make money fast. Marijuana was the fastest sell. It had to be someone who trusted him and he trusted, so that it could all be transferred seamlessly. He picked up his cell phone and started calling around. Even at the late hour, he was able to get in touch with an old contact. Omar answered his phone on the second ring and said he didn't have that kind of dope right now, but recommend calling Felix. Felix said he'd heard that a girl named Breezy could get him the dope and already had a buyer. *Breezy? Who the hell?* He didn't know a Breezy. He learned that she was down in Arizona and required a 25 percent markup. Felix would arrange the meeting. What time? In six hours, enough time for him to drive over to his office, to get the money he had stashed in his attic, and then drive over to Phoenix.

Santiago grabbed fifty thousand dollars of the sixty-four thousand he had stored in his attic; trying not to draw attention to the house, he didn't turn on the lights and crawled up to the attic with guidance from the soft glow of a little flashlight he'd found in his glove compartment. After he locked up the deserted house and crept through the backyard, he got back in his car and started driving toward Arizona to meet up with Breezy. Breezy, the girl who supposedly knew where to get the dope and where to sell; he just had to do the delivery and get the cash. He didn't know her, but he knew and trusted Felix, so he decided it was worth trusting a woman he didn't even know. It wasn't how he usually worked, but the stakes were high, and he was doing everything with Marcos's safety in mind. He wanted to get the dope, then cash, and get it to El Serpiente so he could get out of the gang and not have to risk so much again. It wasn't the lifestyle he wanted now that it was just him and Marcos.

Basically, he needed to get his hands on eighty pounds of marijuana for seventy-eight bucks an ounce and sell it for two hundred dollars an ounce. Breezy had the other fifty thousand dollars to cover the street value, and they would make 256,000 dollars, market value. *It sounds a little too perfect*, he thought as he drove through desert, where the air was stale and the stars flickered brightly in the.

It was three in the morning; he still had three more hours to drive. He pulled over at a gas station in the middle of nowhere and filled his car up and got himself an energy drink and a Mountain Dew to keep him awake.

At five forty-five, he drove into a town just outside of Phoenix and followed the GPS directions to where he would find Breezy at a Denny's off the main street. He texted her when he arrived and she said she was sitting at the back corner table. He found her eating a Grand Slam—eating ferociously, as if she hadn't eaten for days. She had her nose almost to her plate, and she barely glanced up when he walked to the table.

"Sit down," Breezy said with food in her mouth, motioning her left hand to the bench across from her; her right hand still held a fork. "You might want to order something."

"Yeah sure," he said and opened the menu.

The first thing Santiago noticed about Breezy was that she was Caucasian. He didn't usually do deals with anyone outside of his circle of approved dealers and all of them were of Mexican descent. She had flyaway brown hair—so unlike Katiana's black silky smooth hair, which would slip easily through his fingers. Breezy was petite—she looked barely over a hundred pounds, although the way she was eating, it appeared it was her first full meal in a long time.

"So, you know Felix."

"Well, I know of Felix. I've never met him. I actually know Omar, who knows Felix."

Her eyebrows went up, and she continued eating. "Then how do I know I can trust you?"

"I have a three-year-old kid. I'm not going to do anything to fuck it up."

She stopped eating, looked up from her plate, and smiled. "Good one." She paused for a second. "This is kind of a tough business to be in when you have a kid." She paused again and leaned back in her chair. "I was pregnant once, but lost it."

She shrugged. "Just as well. I don't think I could have taken care of a kid. I mean, hell, what job could I do? I'm good at this one so I guess it was for the best." She gulped the rest of her orange juice, and let out a loud sigh when she was done. "Hell, that was a good breakfast. I needed that." She wiped her face with a napkin, set it down on the table, and looked squarely in Santiago's eyes. "Okay, I'm convinced. I've got eighty pounds and a drop-off. Are you in?"

"Yes."

"Yes, eh? All right, but I get twenty-five percent."

Her price was fair, but he had the fifty thousand dollars of his own stash to go toward the street value, and a twenty-five percent markup wouldn't give him enough to give to El Serpiente. He had fourteen thousand left of his own money that he could throw in, but that was all he had, and he needed money to cover his *abuela*'s new care center and his own rent and other recurring bills. "How about fifteen percent?"

"What the hell, man? No way." Breezy was quiet, spinning the spoon in her hand. "How about twenty percent? You wouldn't have nothin' without me."

"Yeah, okay."

"Yeah, okay," she said, mocking him, and tilted her head from side to side. "Yeah, okay, then here's the address to pick up the stash at eight," she said as she dug into the pocket of her blue jean jacket and pulled out a scrap of paper that looked as if it had been wadded up.

Santiago looked at the paper. "This is the place?" he said with concern in his voice as he wanted to make sure she was not sending him on some wild goose chase.

"What the hell, man? Of course that's the place. Half the money for the street value is in the backpack at your feet, dude." She said through her teeth then watched him as he bent down to touch the backpack. She then stood up from the table and bent down close to his ear. "You got my phone number, so call me when you get the dope or Felix will track you down, dude." And with that, Breezy dropped a twenty-dollar bill on the table. "Keep the change," she said as she waltzed out of Denny's, her hair flying behind her as though she was in a windstorm.

Santiago looked down at the address and typed it into maps on his phone. The location was twenty minutes away. He had some time, so he ordered a cup of coffee and eggs and sausage. He felt people staring at him as he sat and ate quietly and alone. He knew he wasn't really the Denny's type of customer, so he ate quickly, paid the bill, and added in a 20 percent tip. He grabbed the backpack, stood up from the table, and left in a hurry. He stopped by the restroom, so he could verify the amount in the backpack. It was as she said it would be.

He drove over to the address early, to scope out the area. It was in a poor Arizona ghetto, surrounded by dilapidating houses and no landscaped front yards. He parked a few houses down from the nondescript tan, one-story house with a single bare tree in the middle of the dead lawn. He knocked on the door. There was no answer. He knocked again, and then tried the doorknob. The door opened easily. He walked in cautiously. The place was nearly bare, with only a few furniture pieces sparsely scattered throughout the house, but that didn't alarm him, as that was common for a drop-off house. There was a kitchen table with a single chair, and when he walked through the house, he saw there were no beds in the two bedrooms, but a long table in the center of the room with no chairs around it. As he examined the place and got to the back of the house, a guy showed up through the back door. He was over six feet, a gringo with dark, curly hair and dark rimmed glasses, and skinny as a rail. He seemed to be amped up on something. Immediately, Santiago was suspicious and sized him up. He was outside his territory, and here, in this ludicrous situation, he was working with someone who he didn't know—another gringo at that.

"Let's see what ya got," Santiago said with a nod.

"Let's see what you got, yo."

"I need to see the weed before I give you the money."

"I need to see the money before I show you the weed."

Santiago wanted to hit this guy, but did his best to stay calm. "I'll get the money from my car and the scale. And you, dude, can go get the merchandise."

"Yeah, okay, just don't take long." They both turned to go get their stuff.

Santiago went out to his car and got his fifty thousand dollars and included Breezy's money to the stack, stuck it in a green zipper pouch with the Benjamin Franklins facing up, separated into hundreds, and slipped neatly in the backpack. Santiago always presented the money respectfully and professionally. He grabbed the backpack by the top handle and he felt his heart beating. He was very suspicious of this entire situation and he normally would have backed out of such a sketchy deal, but he wanted to make sure he got the money to El Serpiente in time as he didn't want any trouble for him and Marcos from here on out. He told himself that it was all for Marcos and he needed to follow through. He tried to walk casually to the open front door.

The curly-haired dude had gone out through the backdoor and came back dragging in two big boxes with the marijuana packs.

"Let's see the green stuff, yo." The gringo said as he picked up one of the wrapped packages.

Santiago reached into the backpack and pulled out the green pouch, unzipped it and showed him the green bills from a distance. He then stuffed the pouch in the back of his pants and pulled his shirt over it.

Tall, skinny guy pulled out one of the boxes that was wrapped in green cellophane and he slowly pulled the covering from the package to reveal the leaves. He stretched out his arm to let Santiago smell it.

In past transactions, Santiago would have rolled it and taken a puff, but he had been doing these exchanges long enough to just smell it to know what was good. He took a deep whiff and could tell it was quality. Santiago nodded, impressed. "Not bad, not bad at all."

Santiago backed away from the marijuana so that he could pull out his scale to make sure it was the correct quantity. He set the scale on the table and motioned the other guy to set the package on the scale. As he was peering down at the weight. from the corner of his eye, he saw a shadow of a gun which looked as if it was pointing right at Santiago

"Put your hands up," a guy said in a deep voice, "and turn around slowly."

Santiago watched as the curly-haired dude raised his hands, and Santiago turned slowly and saw a man wearing a police uniform, pointing a shiny .38 at him.

The man was average size and nondescript—no tattoos; straight, dishwater-blond hair; an all-around ordinary-looking dude. He pulled out a badge from the right front pocket of his blue shirt with his left hand while he continued to hold the gun steady at them with the other hand.

Santiago immediately noticed that this cop's uniform seemed rumpled and he had observed in the past that the police seemed to dress neatly. This guy looked disheveled and Santiago wondered if he was really a policeman, but reconsidered when he dangled handcuffs from his hand.

"*¡No Mames!* Who the hell are you?" Santiago was growing frustrated and just wanted the day to end, get back in his car, drive to San Diego, pick up Marcos and then just go home. At that minute of time, Santiago just wanted out of the business. Nothing had gone right in the last ten hours, nothing.

"Oh, hey, *chicano*, there's no need for such an attitude. I just want your money, so hand it over, and no one's going to get hurt."

Someone must have tipped this guy off—must have leaked the place and time of the exchange to this make-believe cop, because the timing was impeccable. Santiago was rather certain that it was Breezy who tipped him off. The pseudo-policeman pulled out two handcuffs from his back pocket and dangled them in front of the two men.

"Yes, boys, it's time to turn around and put your hands behind your back." Cop man walked over to the curly-haired dude and handcuffed him to the table as he kept his eye on Santiago. After skinny guy was securely fastened, the pseudo policeman stood in front of Santiago, pointing the gun at him as he firmly said, looking straight into his eyes, "Hand over the money, *Chicano*."

"What are you talking about?"

"I know what's going on here, Chicano. It's time to hand over your green backs. I know you have it."

Mr. Policeman must have seen Santiago go out to the car and stuff the money bag in his backpack. He stared at the so-called-policeman for a few seconds, considering if there was a way out of the situation. He thought maybe he could try and talk himself out of the situation, kick the gun out of the guy's hand, or throw the backpack in the cop's face as it was close enough to grab it and distract him momentarily. He continued to stare at the guy as Santiago considered all of his options, but he didn't want any more trouble than he was already in. he just wanted to abandon the mission and leave it all behind. There must be another way to get the money back, but at this point he just gave up on being resourceful and pulled the money out of his pants and handed it over the fake cop. He didn't have enough fight in him to get out of the situation and wanted to make sure he was in one piece for his Marcos.

Beside the fourteen thousand he left hidden in the attic of his office, the pouch in his and Breezy's money was the last to pay for any type of merchandise trade.

"That's right, Chicano. We don't want to keep the policeman waiting. I've got places to go and people to arrest. Now hand over your cell phone."

"My cell phone? Whatever for?"

"Evidence. Now hand it over, cause I'm getting very impatient."

Santiago knew the phone was locked down and password protected, but it was just a matter of time until they tapped into his connections. Santiago pulled it out of back pocket and set it on the floor in front of them. He watched the self-proclaiming policeman slip it into his front shirt pocket

"Now sit down." The fake policeman barked and then nodded towards the single chair standing in the room and then tossed the money pouch on the table. The policeman then handcuffed Santiago to the leg of the chair. As he turned to leave, the pseudo cop grabbed the money off the table, waved it in front of them, and said with a nod, "Taking this it for evidence too." Then he turned and walked out the front door, leaving the marijuana sitting there.

Santiago noticed curly-haired dude staring at him.

"That's no policeman I just wanted a fair exchange and to get the hell out of this hellhole. Have you seen that guy before? Do you know who he is?

"No."

"Are you working with Breezy?"

"Who the hell is Breezy?"

"You don't even know who Breezy is? Who are you? Do you know Omar or Felix?"

"I don't know those guys."

Santiago watched curly-haired dude as he lifted the table up, by getting under it and lifting it with his back, and slid the handcuffs from under it. Now free from the table, but his hands were still clamped together with the handcuffs, he clambered towards the back door. Santiago turned to watch him as he turned his back on the door and rotated the knob to go back out the windowed door. Santiago heard him run away. "Get out of here, you loser! I'm telling everyone not to do deals with you." Of course, Santiago didn't even know his name or who he really worked for.

"Screwed," he murmured. He knew he had to calm down and get himself out of there. He was just so angry with the sequence of events and frustrated with the situation. As he was kicking the table in front of him in frustration, he looked over and noticed the marijuana in the middle of the room, still untouched. Why did both guys leave without the merchandise? He felt a pang of hope that maybe he could sell the dope after all, but then he realized that someone was going to come back for it. He thought of Marcos and how he needed to get the money tonight so he could save his family and possibly his own head. After some kicks to the table and more cussing, Santiago calmed down. He knew he needed to act fast and get out of that house before someone came back for the dope. He tipped the chair over, and slid his handcuffs from the leg. Somehow he needed to hide the marijuana so he could come back for it.it once he got his handcuffs off. To move the boxes around, he had to shove it with his foot and was thankful that they seemed unusually light. He pushed both boxes to the back door then went outside to start investigating the area. Instead of putting the boxes in the bushes of the back yard, he looked around the house and found an opening under the foundation of the house. He pulled the crates back that were hiding the exposed underbelly of the house and managed to push the boxes under the house.

With the boxes well hidden, it was time for him to find a phone or someone who might call Rubén for him so he could come and pick him up all the way in Arizona. He didn't want to bring any attention to himself, especially as he was handcuffed behind his back, so he jumped over fences, dodging bushes and little dogs yapping. He was running along when he saw a park about a hundred yards away. He cut across the park and jumped in a ditch just south of it, and laid there for a bit, catching his breath, hoping no one had seen him—some Mexican guy running feverishly from behind bushes with his hands cuffed behind his back. He propped himself up to evaluate what was going on around him. There were some middle school–aged kids playing soccer nearby. There was one standing a bit off to the side, scrolling through his phone. Santiago whistled slightly, to try and get the boy's attention. The boy turned.

He was a thin kid, maybe of Asian descent, his black hair flopping over one eye. He looked over to the ditch, but didn't see Santiago at first. "Over here kid," Santiago whispered. The kid walked over cautiously and stood a distance away, not saying anything.

"Hey, kid, I left my phone in my car. Can you call *mi amigo* for me?"

"*Hindi ko alam kung Ingles.*"

"No English? *Español?*"

The kid shook his head.

"How about one, two, three? You know your numbers?"

The boy gave him a gentle nod.

"Okay, good. It's a start. Can you call my *amigo*? Ring ring?"

The boy did another slight nod.

"Here is his number, six-one-nine," Santiago said slowly as the boy took out his cell phone and punched the numbers in. "Five-five-six." He paused. "Two-five-two-four."

The boy held up his cell phone, nodded, and then walked away.

"Shit," Santiago mumbled. He watched the kid carefully as the young guy walked over to another boy who looked similar and showed him his phone. The kid never motioned to him but handed the phone to his friend, who took it, put it up to his ear, and soon seemed to be talking to someone. For all Santiago knew, the guy was calling the cops on him. He didn't know if he could trust these kids. Adrenaline started pumping, and Santiago became very anxious. He didn't know what he should do. Should he run, so the cops couldn't find him lying in the ditch, or should he trust the kid? He watched the boy with the hair over his one eye join in on the soccer game, and saw him dribble and then kick the ball in for a goal.

Santiago slid back down into the ditch and decided he had to trust this kid. He was sulking and stayed angry at the situation as he settled down on the cement, angry at the cop imposter, Breezy, and the curly-haired dude—who knew where he went to or how he got his handcuffs off. He sulked in the ditch while the Arizona sun rose higher in the sky. Had the boy sympathized with him and called his *amigo*, or had he just called for lunch or a friend, and just forgotten about him all together? He was afraid someone would see him with handcuffs, hiding in the ditch.

He thought about Marcos and was hoping he was okay after his night at Rubén's house. He thought about what he'd done wrong and how he'd gotten into this situation, and decided he would make things right. The sun continued to move across the sky and Santiago heard kids playing baseball—the crack of the bat, the cheering from the sidelines. He heard kids laughing and chasing one another and dogs barking. Hours went by, but he continued to trust the boy and just waited. The longer he waited, though, the more nervous he became. The later it got, the harder it would be for him to get his money back and to get El Serpiente his portion. He was getting hungry and thirsty, and his hands were starting to pulsate from the handcuffs being too tight. The Mountain Dew and the energy drink had worn off, and he was starting to get drowsy. Still, he continued to wait.

It was several hours later when he heard someone calling his name. "What the hell?" Santiago mumbled. He peeked over the ditch, and sure enough, there were Julio and Rubén, banging on doors as Pedro drove the car about ten miles per hour, with both back doors open, down the residential road. Santiago climbed out of the cement ditch and made a mad dash across the field. As he got closer to the road, he heard his friends say, "There he is." Santiago caught up to the car and dove in through the open back door. Rubén and Julio jumped, and they sped out of the neighborhood, leaving the residents to scratch their heads and wonder what was going on.

Everyone in the car started speaking rapidly about how they needed to get the handcuffs off. Santiago sat there relieved and thankful for the kid who had come through after all. He had known he could trust him.

Julio shouted, "I know someone, *ese*! I know who can take the handcuffs off."

"Homes, you know someone in Arizona who can take the handcuffs off?"

"Yes, I'll call him and tell him we're coming. Go that way, Pedro," Julio said, pointing to the left and getting out his cell phone, ready to call his friend.

Santiago looked to Rubén. "Thanks, man."

Rubén smiled. "Sure, *ese*, you my main man. We're here for you."

"How's Marcos?"

"Marcos is cool, *ese*. He's at my girlfriend's mom's house."

"What?"

"Yeah, your auntie never showed up at your house, so I took him over to Juanita's mom's. She's nice, *orale*. She was happy to watch him today. She was going to make empanadas with him."

Santiago fidgeted in his seat and tried twisting his hands in the cuffs, but they were locked tightly; there was no room to shift his wrists. He didn't feel good about Marcos being at someone else's house, especially someone he didn't know. He trusted Rubén, but he didn't trust Rubén's dad or Rubén's girlfriend, but he was hoping his girlfriend's mom was a lot nicer than her self-centered daughter.

"Well, you think she's taking good care of him?"

"Yeah, yeah, homes, he's in good care. She's nice, and cleans big, fancy homes, but didn't have to go in today. Not sure why, just worked out she could watch Marcos."

They'd only driven about five blocks when Julio shouted, "There it is! There's the house."

Pedro swerved recklessly and parked carelessly across the driveway.

The four of them walked up to the front door, and a burly man with tattoos up and down his arms and his neck, long hair, and a beard came out to greet them. He took them to the backyard, where he and his Hell's Angel–type friends were all talking and drinking as if it was any ordinary day; they barely glanced over to see the four Mexican dudes walk up. Big Burley Dude offered them hot dogs off the barbecue and beers. They weren't into hot dogs, but they all took one except for Julio, who only wanted the beer, and Santiago whose hands were still tied behind his back. They were all sitting on work crates when Big Burley Dude came back with bolt cutters and a hacksaw. He used the bolt cutters to cut the chain in half, and the hacksaw to take the cuffs off of each individual wrist. It seemed as if Big Burley Dude had taken off handcuffs before, but nobody asked him if he had.

Julio handed him a wad of cash to thank him for his services, and they piled back into Pedro's car.

Santiago had to figure out how to get back to the house where his car was still parked and where the marijuana was hidden. He still had the wadded-up paper Breezy had given him so he tried maneuvering his arms to dig into his back pocket and pull it out. Julio put the address in his phone's GPS.

Santiago's car was still parked down the street from the non-descript house, and they watched the place for a bit to see if there was anyone around before going through the side gate, to the backyard. Santiago told the guys where he hid the pot and they pulled it out from underneath the house. They wondered if anyone had come back for it, went searching for it on not to be able to find it. They pulled the brown boxes out and opened the box flaps pulling out a pack of dope that Santiago had sniffed, then they started to pull out the rest of the green cellophane packages.

"What the hell, man. These packages are full of straw!" Pedro exclaimed.

"What *ese*? No way. Pull them all out."

"What are you talking about?" Santiago's heart sank. This could not be happening, he thought.

It turned out that it wasn't the eighty pounds of marijuana Breezy had promised, nor what Santiago had hoped was his way out of the business and start something new. They had been duped.

"*Pinche*, we need to take that *loco* cop out. He can't do that. We got to find him." Pedro was ramped up and ready to tear out of there and search the streets of this unfamiliar to him city to find the man

"He's got your cell phone we can track him." Julio was usually coming up with their plans, so they all agreed to find Psycho Cop.

Santiago picked up the brick of marijuana that he'd smelled earlier, put it in his shirt, and this time, left through the front door; at this point, they didn't care who saw them come and go from that drab and depressing house. Rubén and Santiago got into Santiago's car, which was still where he parked it last. Since Breezy's phone number was in Santiago's phone, which was more than likely still deep in the crazy cop's pocket, Rubén pulled out his phone and called Omar who called Felix who then called Breezy. It wasn't two minutes after he hung up the phone when Breezy called and they all went over to her house.

When they got to Breezy's house, she looked nervous. When they told her the complete story, she acted surprised, as though she didn't know the imposter cop and she didn't know anything about the tall, curly-haired dude. She insisted they had both been framed. Santiago rubbed his forehead and muttered, "I'm screwed."

Breezy knew she needed to make it up to Santiago or the guys would talk about it with their gang brothers, and the news would get back to her dealers; it was important for her to keep her good reputation. She made a few calls and found out about the guy who would burst into a drug exchange posing as a police officer and then run out with the money. He had never been caught. The story started to get around about what happened to Santiago, and after several phone calls, and after trying to track Santiago's phone, Breezy discovered that Mr. Cop Imposter was sipping beers at a local bar.

Julio, Pedro, and Rubén were all enraged. One thing about the business is, if one doesn't play by the rules, then you don't get to play at all. "*Güey*, we'll do whatever you want us to do. You want us to go in and take him out, we'll do it," Pedro told Santiago as they all sat around Breezy's dented-wooden kitchen table. Rubén was pacing, and Julio was sitting at the table, nodding in agreement, chewing a straw. Both Pedro and Julio had brought their guns with them and had them tucked into their waistbands.

Pedro was known as El Serpiente's main man, and everyone knew he would take anyone out if the Serp asked him to. Julio was always the one strategizing the event, watching Pedro's back, and picking up the pieces for him. They were a team, and no one wanted to mess with them.

"We got your back, homes. That guy did you wrong. You're out of money and pot. We can take him out."

Santiago had never had a drug deal that went sour. And, in all his drug trades, he never needed to flash a gun around to get another's attention or too let them know he was serious. The system worked fine if they all played by the rules. Here, in his moment of decision, when his three friends and Breezy were staring at him and waiting to hear his direction, Santiago thought of his son and realized that risking their lives wasn't worth the revenge. He still owed El Serpiente money, and he needed to figure how to get it. He didn't have revenge in his heart, nor desire to prove a point. He just wanted to go home with his son.

"No, *hermanos*, no need to find that imposter. Let's just get the money and go home."

They all stared at him and were quiet. They fidgeted in their seats, exchanged glances with one another, and paced up and down Breezy's dining room. Pedro looked disappointed and Jose put his gun away.

"OK, Santiago, if that's what you want to do, then that's what we'll do. Let's figure out how to get that money for you." Rubén said as he sat down at the table and actually looked calm, which was unusual for Rubén as he was always fidgeting or pulling on his shirt sleeve or taking his hat on and off.

They all sat down at the table, and made a plan to get the money to El Serp. They had six more hours before midnight, six more hours to get the money, sell some merchandise, and drive back to San Diego to hand El Serp over the money Santiago owed him.

It was a code among brothers to help each other out, and Pedro, Rubén, and Julio chipped in twenty-one thousand each. Then Breezy got on the phone with Felix and they were able to call some of their contacts and find fifty pounds of marijuana with the money Santiago's three friends willingly donated. Omar was also helping them out over the phone calling his people and he found a buyer in North County who would buy it for two hundred dollars an ounce. That was one thousand and sixty thousand to Santiago; Breezy took a 15 percent markup and gave Felix five percent. It seemed that everyone was going to walk away from the situation unscathed and that Breezy would actually have saved her reputation to come out trustworthy in the end. Santiago owed Felix eighty thousand dollars for the street value of the previous weed lot, which Felix gave Santiago a week to pay back.

That night, Rubén and Santiago drove over to El Serpiente's at 11:45pm and delivered the money. He didn't say anything; he just waved them off with a nod. That was it. The whole crazy ordeal, and they were just acknowledged with a nod. Santiago shook the disappointment, the adrenaline rush, and the anger off. All he could think of was Marcos.

It felt as if it had been ages since Santiago had seen Marcos. Rubén brought him over that night, and Marcos snuggled in his daddy's arms with his Pooky Bear, and Santiago just held him while he fell asleep. As Marcos slept, Santiago realized that getting the money had been worth it. He would do anything to keep Marcos safe.

For the next couple of weeks, Santiago felt uneasy about the situation in Arizona. El Serpiente rarely spoke to him now, and when he did, he quickly turned away. Maybe he was still upset about the situation. Maybe he was angry at Santiago for dealing outside of their approved soldiers; maybe he was angry at the police imposter for doing them wrong. Maybe he believed that Santiago was too much of a wimp to take out the fake cop out when he had a chance; maybe it was because the entire incident made their gang look bad, as the drug deal had fallen through because Santiago hadn't checked his sources and their creditability; maybe El Serpiente didn't think Santiago was actually going to come up with the money in a day and it really was a setup to put an end to Santiago.

He wasn't sure of the reasons El Serpiente was giving him a cold shoulder, but Santiago didn't like it and knew that it wasn't over.

A week later, Santiago got a text from Breezy with a link to a newspaper article. The headline read, "Arizona police impersonator, shot in face." There was a photo of the plain-looking imposter on the top of the page—the very one who had stolen Santiago's money.

The Transition
(Evelyn)

The social worker took Evelyn's and Chad's fingerprints, did background checks, and then came to their house to see if their knives were out of reach, their cabinets were childproofed, there were smoke alarms on every floor, no accessible guns, and if there was a gate on the pool…if they had a pool, of course.

Chad went along at first, but he had yet to meet Marcos—he never had gone down to the center. One evening, when Evelyn came home from buying bedding at Bed Bath & Beyond for Marcos's new bed, Chad finally spoke to her about the whole ordeal and bringing Marcos to live with them.

She opened the door from the garage and saw Chad sitting on their lemon-colored couch, staring off into the darkness through the corner window. The TV wasn't on, and he didn't have his iPhone in hand. He got up quickly when Evelyn walked in.

"Listen, Evelyn, I've been thinking about this entire deal with that little boy staying here."

Evelyn walked across the living room to the dining room and set her bags down on the table. "Oh good, good." She almost did a little dance. "I'm so glad you've been thinking about it, Chad, and I'm so glad you brought it up."

"Well, it's all happened so fast, and I really haven't been involved in this whole decision making."

"I know, I know, Chad," she interrupted, "but I think if you came down to the center and met him, you would be certain we're doing the right thing."

Chad walked over to Evelyn, took her hands, and said, "Evelyn, it might be the right thing for you, but it's not the right thing for me. We had a pact before we got married. You knew I didn't want kids around." He dropped her hands and stepped back. "You've had a change of heart, but I haven't. I'm not a kid person. I don't want to change my lifestyle. I like that we're free to go where we want to go; I want to advance in my career and not feel guilty about not being home or not doing my share of the work raising a kid. I don't want to bring another person into our lives. I don't want to bring in someone I don't know." He looked at her intently, sternly, right into her eyes, and then turned away and started pacing around the couch again. "I'm going to let you think about it, but this child thing is not what I signed up for. Now if you want to bring him in temporarily, while they're trying to find his parents, fine, but according to Lorena, his parents are more than likely on the other side of the border and can't be found." He stopped, ran his hand through his hair like he always did when he was tense, walked over to her, and touched her shoulders. "Look, I'll meet him. You can bring him in temporally, until they find somewhere else for him to live, but he is not staying here any longer than that. It's not a forever thing. It's temporary, Evelyn, and if you decide it's not temporary, I'm not staying around for that. I didn't sign up for it. I haven't changed in that way in the last four years. I still don't want kids. I had hoped you were still with me on that, but for me, it's not going to change."

Evelyn had thought the conversation was going to in an entirely different direction. She was hoping he would come around to her side and have a change of heart, and this would be the moment he would say that he was in; instead, she was left with her mouth gaping open in disbelief. She didn't really know what to say. She stared at him, studying his face, until she couldn't be strong any longer. Tears started streaming down her face. She understood at that moment the ramifications of keeping Marcos in their house, but she also still firmly believed that once Chad met Marcos, everything would change.

She stood there in the dining room, in the same spot where she'd just done a happy dance five minutes ago, dumbstruck and tongue-tied by his monologue.

Chad walked over to Evelyn, bent down every so lightly, and kissed a tear that had landed on her cheekbone. He kissed it, turned, walked away briskly, almost in a trot, to the stairs, taking the steps up two at a time.

She stood there, where she'd laid down her purchase, and looked at the astronomy sheet set she'd bought for Marcos's bed. She pulled out a chair from the dining table, sat down, put her head in her hands, and did something she hadn't done in a long time: cried uncontrollably.

A week later, Jessica called to check in, to make sure everything was going as planned and to see if Evelyn was still good with the court date and time. Evelyn was. Continue as planned. She believed that Chad would have a change of heart as soon as he met Marcos.

Evelyn ended up going to court alone, and her social worker spoke for her. Jessica and the judge deemed Chad and Evelyn fit to bring Marcos into their home as a dependent, as they continued to look for Marcos's parents. His case was deemed child abuse due to neglect.

She brought Marcos home on a Monday. Chad met him in the afternoon. He gave him a high five and ruffled up Marcos's coarse locks when he got home from work, and then he walked upstairs and went to bed. He didn't help put Marcos to bed or encourage him to feel comfortable about being in a new place. "What did I expect anyway?" Evelyn asked herself. Chad didn't wait up for her, to talk about the new transition. He was fast asleep when she climbed their steps to their room. She still believed he would change his mind, and she proceeded as planned. He knew the transition was hard on everyone, and she wanted to wait it out. She just felt as if they were all going to get along together one day.

Evelyn had taken a two-week vacation and used that time to get to know Marcos, help him adapt to his new surroundings, fix up their spare bedroom as a cute boy's room, check out the parks nearby, and put his name on the waiting list at her company's day care. She found that once she opened up and told Irene about Marcos—about how they were still looking for his parents and how she was taking in Marcos temporarily—Irene was surprisingly supportive and helpful. It turned out that she had two young stepchildren who came every other weekend to her house, and she never knew what to do with them and had done some research of about events in the community. She sent Evelyn link after link of fun resources around the city for parents and caregivers of young kids.

Evelyn and Marcos went to the zoo, the beach, the wading pool, the local park, and, of course, Sea World. She bought kid-proof dishes and a dinosaur sippy cup, a scooter with a helmet, so he could join her on a slow-paced run on the boardwalk, and purchased several books, which of course included *The Itsy Bitsy Spider*. They went to Pepper Grove Playground at Balboa Park with the cushioned flooring and the bell tower in the background. She even let him keep his toys in a basket down in the living room, where he could easily reach for them while watching *Sesame Street*.

She started researching kid-friendly foods and made him some homemade macaroni and cheese casserole with wheat pasta and mozzarella cheese. He ate Greek yogurt with homemade granola sprinkled on top for an afternoon snack, and even tasted the kale chips when she offered it to him, but he didn't reach for another one. But when she took him to Taco Surf at the beach, he effortlessly scarfed down three street tacos.

Chad would come home from work and see the two of them playing Go Fish or pushing little cars around on the floor or trying to figure out how to assemble a LEGO Bionicle that Monica had given to Marcos. Chad would watch their activities, then head to the kitchen and make himself a smoothie or a sandwich, not asking if anyone else wanted a sip or a bite, and then he'd head up to bed or out to the gym to lift weights with Charlie. Evelyn and Chad's conversations were limited to what time he was coming home or where he was going next. He didn't tell her about his day, and he didn't ask her about hers. They continued to sleep in the same bed, but he would turn toward the wall. She would scoot close to him, so their skin was touching, and she was thankful that he wouldn't move away, but he would lay there motionless. He didn't complain about the toys in the living room or the ABC song playing on *Sesame Street*, but he didn't comment on it either. The lack of conversation and not knowing what Chad was thinking made Evelyn concerned. She hoped that Marcos would grow on Chad, and that Chad would become very fond of him. As Evelyn and Marcos continued to play and giggle, she hoped Chad would see everything Evelyn's way, have a change of heart, and be convinced that the two of them were supposed to take care of him until they found one of his relatives—or stayed with them the rest of his life, which Evelyn was secretly hoping. But in fact, Chad wasn't having a change of heart at all, and he seemed to become more nervous around Marcos. He was pulling away from her, and she started to think that maybe he would really stand firm that he wasn't going to stick around if there was a child involved. He remained stoic and appeared to be heartless, but Evelyn kept believing that once he got to know Marcos, he would change his mind. Despite his silence on the matter, Evelyn remained hopeful.

Two weeks went by, and still they didn't talk about the change in the household dynamics or their relationship.

Monica came over one afternoon on a Saturday. She walked in cautiously. "So, where is that kiddo of yours?" She laughed. "Oh, that sounds weird,"

"He's taking a nap," Evelyn responded cheerfully.

"Well, how's it going? Work is the worst without you."

"We're having so much fun together. Too much fun, I think. Marcos doesn't cause any trouble or talk back or say no." She chuckled. "Kind of weird. Seems like something should happen, like crying or a tantrum, or something. He seems to really like it here, although I find he chews the collar of his T-shirts and gets them all wet. He might do it when he's nervous. I can't figure that out yet."

"Oh, well that's good. Sounds like he's adapting—a little collar chewing never hurt anyone. So, does he understand you? Is he catching on to English and all?"

"Faster than I'm learning Spanish, that's for sure. He knows *cup*, *outside*, *playground*, and about twenty other words, but he still says *perro* for dog when we see them at the park or on our walks."

"So, here you are, in your blue jeans," Monica said as she motioned up and down at Evelyn's tattered jeans, see-through white T-shirt that revealed her aqua-colored bra underneath. Monica also noticed Evelyn wore flip-flops, not her usual ultra-high heels or her running shoes—the only two types of shoes Monica had ever seen her wear.

"Yes, yes, here I am in my full glory. I haven't been paying attention to my clothes much lately, just kind of taking a shower and grabbing whatever is near. I haven't even run all week. I'm feeling a bit sluggish lately." Evelyn fidgeted with her hair and pulled her shirt over her hips as she spoke.

Before she left, Monica crept upstairs and peeked in on the napping Marcos, who was completely zonked out on his stomach, taking up the entire bed with arms and legs flung wide.

"How is Chad taking all of this?" Monica whispered and waved her hand toward Marcos and his room.

"Not at all, actually. He's not reacting to it at all. He isn't mad; he isn't sad; he isn't anything but distant. I keep giving him more time, letting him be, but he still hasn't come around. I don't want to press the issue if he isn't ready to talk, but I hope he'll come to me when he's ready. Not sure what he is thinking." Evelyn was aware that she wasn't being completely honest with Monica, not mentioning that Chad had reminded her of their childless pact and still stood firm on his side of the deal.

"You probably should say something, ask him how it's going and if you can do anything to make the process a little easier on him."

"Yes, I should probably say something. I think I'll say something tonight."

Evelyn thought that maybe what needed to happen was that Marcos and Chad could spend some alone time together, so she decided to ask Chad if he would be willing to watch Marcos for a few hours and give them an opportunity to bond a little— would he take care of Marcos while she went for a run? To her surprise, he said he would. She asked him again the following week if he could watch him while she went to her yoga class, and once again he was okay with it. On another occasion, when she got back from a late-afternoon run, she found both them asleep on the couch in front of the television. It was evident that Chad had fallen asleep while sitting up, but had fallen over, and Marcos must have taken the opportunity to snuggle up to Chad, Pooky Bear lying on Marcos's chest. The scene touched Evelyn, and she thought there might be hope for them. The hockey game, Minnesota against Chicago, continued to battle it in hushed tones on the TV.

That night, their friends were going to meet up at a downtown restaurant for drinks. Evelyn wasn't attending because she hadn't had time to find a babysitter—she wasn't even sure how to find one—and she hoped that she and Chad could use time over the weekend to talk honestly to each other and reconnect. Chad was dressed up a little nicer than usual to go out with his friends, which Evelyn found odd, since he dressed more casually than her when they went out together and he would be the one to suggest to her to dress-down a bit more; and without commenting that it was too bad that they couldn't find a babysitter, Chad left with a simple "good-bye," no farewell kiss for Evelyn and no ruffle of Marcos's hair. He just slipped out the side door as if he was in a hurry, as if he was eager to escape. She thought that maybe Chad was just anxious to get out of the house and forgot himself for a bit, as he did sometimes when he was stressed or tense. She didn't think much more of it that night, and she kissed and cuddled up close to him when he came to bed that night and asked if he had a good time—yes, yes he had. Nothing more was said, and he didn't reciprocate the intimacy.

The next weekend, when Evelyn and Marcos came home on a Sunday afternoon from the park, she noticed two suitcases lined up by the door to the garage. Evelyn tried to stay calm.

She positioned Marcos and Pooky Bear in front of the TV to watch *Bob the Builder*, a distraction from anything whatever was going to happen in the other room. She climbed up the stairs to find Chad packing some of his books in a box.

"So"—she tried to bite back any accusatory comments, doing her best to stay as in control of her emotions as she could manage—"what's going on with the packing?"

"I'm going to stay on Charlie's yacht while he's down in Puerto Rico." Chad didn't look up and just continued packing.

"Are you coming home when he gets back?"

"Probably just stay there until he kicks me out."

She looked out the window, down at her hands, and back at Chad. "Are you leaving me?" she said in a shaky voice, trying to bite back tears. "I thought you were starting to like Marcos."

"Evie, this is not what I signed up for," he said, looking down as he continued to pack his clock and other items from his bedside table.

His response raised anger in Evelyn. "Oh, and what did you sign up for? Happily ever after just so long as I support you coming and going as you please, to have a completely independent life from your spouse, to enjoy freedom forever?"

"That is not fair, and you know it. I didn't sign up for a two-year-old—"

"Three-year-old."

"Okay, three-year-old, coming and living with us and our whole life changing. We can't come and go as we please, and we have to check on nap times and toys all over and sticky tables and peanut butter on my keys."

"Peanut butter on your keys?"

"Yes, peanut butter on my keys! When I pulled out my stethoscope that had peanut butter on it too."

"That's it? That's your breaking point. That's what did it for you? That's what's driving you away from our commitment?"

He whirled around and came right in front of her, and Evelyn saw the blood rise to his face and his eyes start to bulge as he constrained himself from gripping her arms. "You brought this child into our house without my consent. You were secretly visiting him. You were deceiving me and betraying our trust on a daily basis for weeks! Did you think it was okay to be sneaking around? Did you think I was going to be okay with you bringing home a child, that I was instantly ready for our lives to change? You were ready, maybe, but I wasn't. There weren't two consenting adults on this decision when there definitely should have been. You don't get to make all the decisions around here and just assume I'll go along with them. You weren't thinking or considering the other part of your commitment—me." He jabbed his finger into his chest and then turned to finish packing.

"That is not how it went, Chad."

"Oh, really? Well, I wouldn't know how it went, because frankly, I wasn't consulted. I was not a part of this whole experience of falling for a child. Where was I? At work? Sleeping in our bed? Eating breakfast with you? It wasn't like I was that hard to get a hold of. An email, a call, a text message, a note on the refrigerator, a smoke signal—anything would have worked."

"Shhh. He'll hear you."

"Oh don't worry. I'll be leaving now, so no need to worry."

"Can't we just talk about it?"

"Oh, I get it, we talk about it when you want to talk about it, is that how it works? Well, sorry, that window is closed. You had your chance to include me, and you chose not to, so I'll leave you two be." And with that, he headed downstairs. She heard him open the door to the garage and she heard him say, "Bye, little man." Maybe he patted him on his head. Maybe he gave Marcos a high five. She wasn't sure, and she was a bit surprised he even said good-bye to him.

She sat there on the corner of their bed and stared out into the emptiness, numb to what had just happened. Was he gone? Like, really gone? She sat there longer, looking around the room. His alarm clock was gone, his medal he won from the San Dieguito Half Marathon was gone; the frame with his doctorate degree he was planning on taking to his office anyway was gone. It suddenly looked empty without his things in the room.

Could he really be gone?

"*Mammi? Mammi?*" she heard Marcos call for her.

Tears started to slowly roll down her cheeks and felt her bottom lip start to tremble. Then, suddenly, she just couldn't control it. She ran into the bathroom, so Marcos wouldn't see her, and there, she let herself cry.

The Confession
(Santiago)

They sat in Santiago's car, waiting for their drug shipment, and looked out into the darkness for José, one of Santiago's runners, to run up with their stash. They usually sat together once a week, waiting for Julio in Santiago's Impala. Rubén loved Santiago's car and Santiago knew it. Rubén had an old car he hadn't bothered to fix up, so Santiago didn't mind sitting in his own car while Rubén babbled on.

"Man, she is such a bitch. You won't believe what she did yesterday. I came home late, and there she was, waiting for me on the doorstep. I just wanted to go to bed, *esé*. Just long day, but there she is, all worked up about somethin'. Shit, I don't even know what I said yesterday. How am I supposed to take it back, man? There she is, going on and on, and I just want to go in the house." He took a breath and then continued, "Man, shit, I tell you, that girl asks so much of me. She keeps nagging me about my friends, not you, man, not you, but you know, Julio, and Pedro, and you know, that bunch. They're fine, but she says they are bad news. I tell you, I don't know how much longer I can take her. She says I should stop running drugs, but, man, you know she likes the money. Every time we go out, I pay and I got her a damn Dooney and…shit, I don't know, some sort of fancy bag and a sexy dress." He curved his hands down to define an hourglass figure and lifts his eyebrows. "She carries that purse around and shows it off to her girlfriends." In a high voice, he imitated her with hand motions. "Look, girls, at my purse. Rubén got it for me. Ain't he the nicest boyfriend? Yeah, I love it. Don't you just love my new purse?" He switched to his normal, scratchy voice. "She's always showing it off. So if I stop selling drugs, homes, she is going to start complaining about no money, man, I know she will. I think she is getting serious and wants to get married. Man, no way. I can't get tied down to no woman. I don't know." He shook his head as if he was bewildered.

Rubén had been dating his girlfriend for three years, and he was always complaining about her, but he never left her, and he answered her phone calls immediately (always complaining, "She's calling again, calling me all the time," before he answered, but never let it go past the first ring). He was always there for her. Everybody wanted him to leave her, so he would stop complaining, but he didn't, and they were all sure he wasn't going to. He was intensely loyal, and frankly, Santiago thought, Rubén just didn't want to be alone, since he really didn't have a family around. Plus, Jaunita, his girlfriend, had a close family with a *mami* and *papa*, an older brother and younger sister. They ate dinner together and played games every Sunday evening.

"Homes, we should get together sometime and play *Grand Theft Auto*. I beat you to a pulp last time, *esé*. To a pulp." Rubén would have gone on for who knows how long, from one subject to the next, but then he stopped. "Homes, where have you been lately? Julio was looking for you the other day, and you were not at your post. I tell you, you got to be careful, man, or El Serpiente will have you taken out, and Julio would be the man to do it for him; his loyalties lie with the gang and El Serp. Somethin's going on, *ése*. They're suspicious and been askin' about you. Be careful, *amigo*. Don't lose him mo' money, or he'll have no sympathy. I know it's been tough, with Katiana and all with that Arizona deal. I'm just sayin', you better be careful and get your shit together."

Santiago gripped the steering wheel and fidgeted in his seat, contemplating if he should tell Rubén what he did.

"I can't believe Katiana. I know she was in a crazy state of mind, man, but I don't know how she can leave your *chico*. Man, that kid I tell you—she just was not thinking. I hear decisions made in depression just make no sense. Like, if she was thinking, she never would have done that, man."

"Yeah, maybe." Still fidgeting, he decided to tell him. "Things ain't going too great at home lately."

"Dude, I know it's been tough," Rubén said sincerely.

"Well, not only because of Katiana, but of course that's big, but you know *mi abuelita* has gotten worse and is in a care house that I've been paying for. She just wasn't able to take care of Marcos anymore. She kept forgetting a lot. Dude, every time I came home, she asked me where the garbage disposal switch was. Then she just started asking me, 'Where's that thing?'" He motioned up and down. "Rubén, *Abuelita* couldn't even remember where she put her toothbrush much less where she last saw Marcos, so I found a place for her to stay that will take good care of her. And Lita only cares about herself, and I actually haven't seen her for a while, and I have my suspicions that she's been talking to our mom and is planning to go back down to Mexico, carting dope like a mule, man. Like, my mom thinks that is okay for her daughter to do, eh? There for a while, I would come home and find Marcos all by himself. And as you know, I asked my great-aunt if she would watch Marcos, but her grandson is living with her and is giving her so much shit, getting in fights in their front yard, and the cops get called, and her husband is of no help. And I think something bad is going to happen to me—I just have that feeling, man. El Serpiente is not happy. He looks at me, like, in disgust, where he used to be so proud of me. Somethin' bad is going to happen, man, I just know it, and I had to do something drastic to make sure Marcos was going to be taken care of." He gave no time for Rubén to respond and just told him, frankly, "Rubén, I gave Marcos to a really nice lady. He has a new family."

Rubén turned to him. His face was a mix of confusion and rage. "What the hell are you saying?"

"He has no mother, a great grandmother who forgets where she is much less where he is, an aunt who is too busy with herself, and a father who is always out hustling, trying to make money…and I think I'm not going to be around much longer. I want him to enjoy being a kid and not feel forced to trade drugs to make money. I don't want him to go through what I went through. I don't want him to feel lonely or desperate enough to get into this business. I don't want him to see his aunt Carmelita come home drunk out of her mind or start stashing stuff in our house. I don't want people from the gang coming over to our house, waving guns around. I don't want him to fear for his life," Santiago reasoned. "He needs a family, a place to grow up where he's safe, people who will pay attention to him. I can't do that for him. He needs more, and I just can't provide it. I want him to complete school and maybe go to college. He might just have a chance to be all that without me."

"What the hell!" Rubén's anger was rising quickly as he processed what Santiago was saying. His face turned red, as he sat on the edge of his seat; his hands came to his chest in fists, and his jaw muscles bulged.

"Why didn't you come to me? I'm his family too," Rubén said with force as he jabbed a finger into Santiago's chest. "I'm his godfather. I could take care of him."

"What, are you saying you can do better than me? How? Your old man is drunk every day by ten in the morning, and who knows what he would do to Marcos? You're gone more than me, man, far away at the border. No way, man. This is a good decision. He'll have a family who will look after him all day, a family who will take care of him and send him to college. A family who will not demand or force him into a life with the gang or one out on the streets."

"Where is he, man? Where is he?" he yelled with urgency.

"He was at the Polinsky Center, but this woman—she lives in a place downtown on Ash Street in these gray-blue condos that are all lined up together—she's taking care of him right now. She looks real nice, man, like a real nice person."

"*Tú imbécil*. We could figure it out, man. We could have figured it out!" he said as he waved his open hands over his head in complete frustration.

"No, homey, you just don't get it. He's at a better place."

"Man, but there is nothing like family, no matter how messed up they are."

Rubén's enraged eyes pierced Santiago's until he couldn't stand it any longer. "Get out of the car, man. I don't know what I was thinking, telling you." Santiago got out, went to the other side of the car, jerked open the door, and motioned

Rubén out. "Get out, man. Get out." He pointed with his thumb to the edge of the road.

Rubén was still in a fury. "What are you going to do, homey, push us all away? You can't live your life all by yourself, man. We want to help. Juanita can help; her mom can help. We can help," he continued as he stubbornly got out of the car.

"I don't even know those people; they're not family to me." Santiago jumped back into the car, slammed the door, and sped off into the night.

"Then who's that girl on Ash Street who looks real nice? Who is she to you, homey? No one, that's who," Rubén yelled as loudly as he could as Santiago raced away, not caring if he woke the neighbors up. The dogs started barking and lights switched on in the little beat-up homes. Then, quietly, Rubén said to himself, "Who the hell is she? Nobody. Nobody to our Marcos."

The Moment

(Evelyn)

Evelyn had texted her sister earlier in the week and asked if Emily's kids, Annabelle and Brady, could come over that Saturday to spend some of the day with her and Marcos. Emily could drop them off early and start her Christmas shopping the weekend before Black Friday. Her sister took a while to respond, maybe unsure of the sincerity of the offer. She texted back: *Really? U would really do that? R you sure u would be okay with 3 kids all on your own? More than an hour?*

I can handle it. Do you want to meet Marcos? Here he is, Evelyn typed as Marcos sat on her lap playing with a yo-yo she'd found at the 99 Cents Only Store. She gave him her phone, and he knew exactly what to do: *ikllkjkllkki*. Marcos punched the keys several times on her phone, and then Evelyn reached over to click the send button.

Nice 2 meet u, Marcos, Emily responded. Evelyn smiled to herself as she knew that Emily still didn't have a smart phone with the automatic spelling fill-in features and was still texting off her flip phone

hfdkfjsofdjkfkdfsk. Marcos pretended to be busy texting an important message.

Evelyn gently traded her phone for the yo-yo. *Marcos would love to have some friends over. Please come*, she texted back.

So it was settled. Emily was all smiles and almost giddy when she had come by that morning, bearing bagels with cream cheese for the kids and a green tea latte for Evelyn. Emily had turned quickly after she set the goodies down on the kitchen counter and waved as she headed back to her car. "Thanks, Evie, I'll see you early afternoon. I promise I'll be back, hopefully, before you go crazy." She knew her sister was feeling a little sense of freedom.

At first, Annabelle and Brady had just stared at Evelyn. They'd looked up at her as if to say, "Now what?"

"Well, Marcos isn't up yet, because he is quite the little sleeper, so we'll let him sleep while we dig into those bagels and have some orange juice, and maybe you can catch me up on what you two have been up to lately."

She'd learned that Annabelle was still taking tap dance and was now in fourth grade, which Evelyn could barely believe—hadn't Evelyn just gone to her first birthday party? Annabelle asked if her Aunt Evelyn could come to her dance performance. And Brady was playing basketball and in second grade. They both liked their teachers and were tired of living so far away from their friends, since they were located on the outskirts of town, on a small farm tucked away from the main road. She'd asked if either knew how to surf, and both had said no. "Well, I can take you out sometime," she'd said with a slight sadness, as it would have been fun to take them out with Chad, who loved to surf. "Or maybe we could just take the kayaks out for starters." They'd both nodded at that.

Marcos had lazily walked around the corner, into the kitchen, as he rubbed his eyes with one hand and held tightly to his Pooky with the other. "*Buenos* morn," he'd said. Marcos tried his best to practice his English, but was still working on it.

"*Buenos dias*, my sweet Marcos," Evelyn had said, as she bent down to kiss him on his cheek and lift him up onto her hip. "Look who we have here today, Annabelle"—Evelyn had held out her other hand to present her niece—"and Brady, who brought a soccer ball with him."

Brady held up his ball, and Marcos had exclaimed, as he pointed to it, "Fútbol!"

"You like that, Marcos?" she'd said as she turned to him. "You want to play some football, you big sleepy head?"

He'd smiled ear to ear, turned to Evelyn, and exclaimed louder than before, more excitedly, with his arm up in the air, "Fútbol!"

Annabelle and Brady had laughed at that, and Evelyn had been thankful that Marcos had broken the ice.

After breakfast, they'd headed out in the sixty-eight-degree San Diego November air, to a park near her house, nestled among the office buildings and condos. They'd played soccer, slid down the red slide, pushed Marcos high in the swing—and he'd giggled each time he'd swooped down and Evelyn tickled his feet. They'd played tag and capture the flag. Marcos had been on Evelyn's team each time, and he'd giggled as Evelyn raced after her niece and nephew while he rode on her back.

Annabelle skipped along the grass, her ponytail flinging back and forth, and called out, "Thanks so much for inviting us to the park, Aunt Evelyn!"

"Thank you, Miss Belle, for coming down and bringing your brother with you. Marcos had such a great time with you and Brady. You should come back again to play."

"Oh, that would be so great. We would really like that. Marcos is so cute. I think he had fun too. He laughed a lot."

"Yes, he did," Evelyn said as she bent down to tickle Marcos's tummy. He squealed and caught her finger.

Evelyn, her niece, nephew, and Marcos were walking across the park, back to Evelyn's place. Marcos held Evelyn's left hand and waved a butterfly catcher in the other, hoping to capture a butterfly even though there were none flitting about. Annabelle skipped along on Evelyn's right, looking as if she was happy to be spending time with more than just her brother and thankful to get out of doing chores. Brady was ahead, kicking a rock along, trying to see if he could guide it all the way back to Evelyn's condo.

The kids were exhausted at the end of the day, and Evelyn felt satisfied that she'd tired them out. When they arrived back at her condo from the park, Evelyn made them lunch, and they settled on the Angora area rug and played Chutes and Ladders and Candyland, games she'd recently picked up at the thrift store. Marcos didn't quite understand the game but knew enough to know that the goal was to pass the Ice Cream Sea and get to the Candy Castle to win. He was lucky rolling the dice; he rolled more sixes than any of them. Evelyn figured he was one lucky boy.

After board games, they got into a tickle fest, and Evelyn picked up Marcos, then Brady caught her leg, and Annabelle jumped on her back, and they were trying to take her down to the ground. She was surprised that the kids took to her so quickly and felt comfortable enough to hang on her. Suddenly, she was glad she was strong enough to carry all three of them; her weight lifting time had paid off. They all ended up on the ground laughing.

When Emily arrived late in the afternoon, she smirked when she found her kids in front of the TV, watching some sort of cartoon.

"Honestly, Emily," Evelyn felt the need to explain, "I seriously wore them out."

"Oh, is that what that is?" Emily said with a smile. "I'm sure you did. Honestly, I'm fine with them watching TV. I got so much done! It was nice going into Best Buy without the crowds and without the kids. I'm almost done with my Christmas shopping! Plus, I met a girlfriend for lunch." Emily shook her head. "And I can't tell you how nice it was not worrying about a spilled drink or to hear bickering or whining while trying to have a conversation over a meal and to actually enjoy my food without having to cut, roll, or portion out some else's food."

"My niece and nephew whine and bicker? I can't believe that," Evelyn said with a smile. "No seriously, we had so much fun, and we laughed a lot. Please bring them back again soon."

Emily gave Evelyn an "it's about time" look, addressing the fact that Evelyn had never invited her kids before. "I will," she said firmly.

Her sister gathered their jackets and flip-flops—only in San Diego could one wear the two comfortably—and placed them in her Land's End oversized tote with her initials on it.

"Thank you so much, Emily, for coming down this way with Annabelle and Brady," Evelyn said as Emily turned off the TV and got her kids ready to go. "I think Marcos had so much fun with them." She gave her a kiss on the cheek and a hug, and then to her niece and nephew.

"It was our pleasure. Seriously, it was. We just never see you. And please, keep the bag of toys. I brought them down not just for today, but for Marcos."

"Thank you, sweet Sister. You are too kind."

They said their good-byes to Marcos. Annabelle even gave him a kiss on the cheek. He waved good-bye to them at the door. The sky was growing dark, and when Evelyn closed the door, Marcos looked up at her and said, "Play Shoot 'n' Lad?"

For bedtime, Evelyn sat with Marcos in his twin-size bed, a bit big for him but fit both of them perfectly, and she read him Dr. Seuss's *One Fish, Two Fish, Red Fish, Blue Fish*. As she read the book, Marcos looked up at her with droopy, tired eyes and smiled. She closed the book and took his hand, looking at the dimples for his knuckles, turning his pudgy hand over to look at the faint creases in his palm and his pink fingertips. She put his hand in hers; it fit in her palm. Marcos pulled his Pooky Bear from under the covers and put it up to her face. "Kiss?" Evelyn took Pooky and looked at him, that brown bear with the round pink paws, pink stitching in his ears, black nose, and round, black eyes. "Good night, Pooky." Then Evelyn kissed the bear and handed him over to Marcos, who gave Pooky a big hug and kiss too.

Evelyn got up, bent down, and kissed Marcos's cheek. "Night, night, sweet Marcos. It's so good to have you here."

Marcos smiled up at her and said, "*Buenos noches, Mami.*"

Although Marcos had been calling Evelyn "*mami*" since the first day she'd met him, him saying it today somehow affected her, and she dabbed the corners of her eyes to stop the tears from falling.

The dragon nightlight came on as she switched off the overhead light, and then she just stood there at the door, watching him as he cuddled up to Pooky and closed his eyes.

She watched as his face became more relaxed; he fell asleep quickly and looked so peaceful.

He seemed happy in his new home. He seemed as if he liked his blue room and as if he had chosen her to be the "*mami*" in his life. She noticed, and was surprised to see, how he had adjusted to his environment so quickly, as if he had been waiting for someone to care for him. Evelyn walked back into the room, drew the curtains next to his bed, and looked down at him again. "It's so nice to have you here, sweet boy. It's so very nice," she said to him, fingering his curly hair. She kissed her finger, then pressed it onto his cheek. "Good night," she said again to the sleeping boy and walked quietly out, leaving the door to his room open and the light in the hallway on. Knowing he was sleeping in his bed in her house gave Evelyn so much comfort and, foreign to her, contentment.

She walked downstairs, sat on the couch, and listened to the buzz of the cars and the chatter of the passerby outside. She sat there silently, not switching on the TV or reaching for her phone to check messages or her laptop to finish up some work. At that moment, she wasn't curious about the national news or what was trending on Twitter or her friends' status updates on Facebook or who was asking her for the next press release. She sat there with her arms resting on her legs, images flashing in her mind of Annabelle and Brady laughing, Marcos gleefully playing soccer, and Emily almost skipping to her car when she had a few hours of freedom. Marcos looked so happy and comfortable with the kids, in her house, and with her. She could almost feel his soft, chubby hand in hers at that moment. She wouldn't change Marcos being there with her, not for the world, but she missed Chad. She wished she had handled the situation with him differently. She wished he would change his mind and come back to her, to them—her and Marcos. She looked out the window at the one lone tree swaying in the moonlight. She leaned back, hugging the single decorative pillow on the couch, and she couldn't get past it—she missed Chad and wished he were sharing the moment with her.

The End of the Beginning
(Santiago)

The ants marched along in a convoluted pathway that only an ant could follow: across the droplets of water, over the Pepsi can, and through a straw to a half-eaten bag of Doritos. They marched without stopping. They had a mission with an unknown destination.

Santiago looked up from the clutter on the ground and saw people scattering along the street this way and that, seeming to twitch and speak with fear.

He looked down the street—the very street he would shuffle along, kicking up dirt as he dribbled a pebble as far along as he could to his house. When he was a kid and got home after school, his grandmother wouldn't let him in the house looking so dirty after playing *fútbol* in the open field all afternoon, so he would go around the back, bang his shoes together, then proceed to dust off his pants. He would come into the house and Santiago would hear his grandmother mutter to herself, "Why is Santi always so filthy?"

He saw Señor Alfonzo dart into his market, which was located on the east corner, the very place Santi used to rush to in the morning for *pandulce*, a piece of sweet bread, and a bottle of yogurt to drink as he ran off to school.

The buildings along the street were painted vibrant colors, and bright banners gently waved in the slight breeze. He remembered when they painted the *carnicero tienda*, the butcher's store, red. José's sister painted pigs and chickens on the storefront's window, but someone threw water on it, and the paint dripped down to the sidewalk, leaving streaks on the glass.

Some Saturday afternoons, he would take his sister to the *Mercados Públicos*, the public market that took up most of the block, where they would get a combination of beet, carrots, and cucumber juice at one of his favorite vendor booths.

There was the Tacos Ricos food truck on the north corner that Señorita Maria owned. She opened her truck early and kept the window up until the sun went down as she made tortillas all day and every day. She would always wink at Santiago when he wandered by, and she would give him a warm *atole* in exchange for him taking out the trash.

The gas station on the west corner hadn't always been there. It used to be an open lot, where he and his friends would play fútbol. Today, he recognized Pedro's car parked in front of the drugstore; Santiago wondered what he was buying. He remembered seeing him earlier, darting behind buildings, probably doing some of El Serp's dirty work, taking someone out— Julio probably wasn't far behind. Were they looking for him? Santiago wondered. Were they lurking about to kill him? His friends, his *comprandres*—how could they help him out of bad situation in Arizona only to kill him when El Serpiente felt as if it was his time to go? According to El Serp, Santiago wasn't needed in the gang anymore, not as important as he once was—a blemish on their reputation.

Santiago had heard footsteps behind him as he walked over to the market to get some fresh tortillas for his *Abuelita*, who had asked him to bring some the next time he visited. He was going to see her that afternoon.

Suddenly, he heard a gunshot and felt incredible pain—was that Pedro who killed him? He'd shot him in the back? How could his friend shoot him in the back? How could Pedro do such a thing? His very friend who was willing to fight for him, a friend who was willing to stand by his side in a time of need. The very friend who more than likely couldn't face looking Santiago in his eyes as he pointed a gun at him so choose to shoot him in his back instead. Pedro was doing El Serp's dirty work again, but this time it involved Santiago.

He was only short some money, and he was going to make it up to El Serp soon. He had paid Felix back his money in a week's time, as promised. Santiago was a loyal servant and a hard-working lieutenant. Things were going better for him. He was going to get the money; there was no reason to take him out of this world.

As Santiago lay there in the gutter, a car drove by. Water touched his face and his cheek twitched. Warm liquid dripped off his chin, and he noticed red water expand around him, disrupting the ant's march, but they dutifully continued, only slightly altering their route.

His mind slowly cleared, and he tried to find himself in reality, but he couldn't seem to move. He actually didn't want to. He felt restful. He wasn't angry—not at El Serp or Julio or Pedro for not standing up for him. He didn't hold their actions against them. At that moment, he didn't care.

The cars, people, and activity around him sounded muffled and far away. The sun seemed to shine its golden rays right on his face, and he looked up into the light. He thought about his life, how his dad would put him on his shoulders and purposefully go under a tree, so the leaves would tickle Santi's neck and make him giggle. He remembered how his dad would take him to the park and push him in the swing and rush down the slide with him. He thought about his girlfriend, Kat, with her long, beautiful black hair that was so silky that it would fall through his hands, and how her eyes sparkled when she smiled. His nose twitched, and he thought he smelled his *Abuela's* tortillas and was sure she was near, humming her sweet songs to him like she would when she patted the tortillas. He thought of Marcos throwing out his arms when Santiago came home, jumping up to give him a big hug with all his little might, and saying into his ear, "*Te quiero, Papá.*" He thought he felt Marcos still sleeping in his arms—his Marcos, who was his everything, who drove him to be a better person, who motivated him to work hard to provide for the family, who brought light into his dark life. His Marcos whom he would love till his last breath, his last heartbeat, who was now in the arms of another mother. He remembered when he came into the house one late afternoon to see Marcos asleep in Katiana's arms, the sun caressing their peaceful faces.

He heard a muffled noise, a faint siren, and he noticed feet and hands surrounding him, but his mind settled on the beautiful people he loved, and he smiled. He wondered if a guy like him—someone who dealt drugs, committed petty theft, and put others' lives in jeopardy—would go to heaven. Would he meet Jesus there?

He felt so warm inside, and it was as if the sun reached down its rays and touched his face, and suddenly, he rested peacefully; he breathed his last breath, and his heart beat for the last time.

The Endless Day
(Evelyn)

It was Friday night and Evelyn, Marcos, and Monica went on an evening out to "Holiday Nights" at Balboa Park, the location of the first World's Fair, with 1,200 acres of rolling hills overlooking the twinkling lights of downtown San Diego. The park had extensive landscaping and a street lined with museums, which were originally constructed for the celebration of the 1915 Panama Exposition. Annually, on the first weekend of December, every museum opened their doors and offered free admission for the entire weekend. There were also cottages nestled in an area that offered food from all over the world. People from the far corners of San Diego would come to the event each year and the park was packed with people.

On this night, Evelyn was determined to take Marcos out on a big outing complete with crowds of people, bright colors, variety of music, and Christmas lights galore. They ate international foods, such as bratwurst, Lumpia, and Swedish meatballs. They took train rides, watched dancers, listened to carolers, and enjoyed the free museums: the Model Railroad Museum, with miniature engines pulling ten to thirty cars behind it, and the Natural History Museum, with the huge dinosaur skeletons staring down at their frightened observer. Marcos's eyes were as big as saucers as he took in the sights. At his age, he was captivated by the world revolving around him. There were bright lights, a cacophony of noises, people everywhere, and lots of walking. Marcos ended up riding on Evelyn's back for the end of the evening. Evelyn was so thankful that Monica came with them and appreciated her more than ever; she'd realized that Monica could talk business with any executive, enjoy concerts with her indie friends, appreciate a good cup of coffee at hole-in-the-wall café, and then romp around with a friend and a three-year old with full vigor. Monica laughed easily and had seemed to enjoy the festivities of the evening just as much as Marcos. At the end of their night, they'd walked past the merry-go-round and the squawking birds from the nearby world-famous zoo, and trooped out to the parking lot.

"Are you happy?" Monica asked Evelyn.

"I'm happy, so happy with Marcos." Then she'd paused and tilted her head in thought as she walked along with Marcos asleep on her back. "I'm happy, but I'm not complete without Chad. He's missing out. Honestly, kids used to scare me. They always seemed so rude or loud. They got in the way when they would race around in the grocery store, and I just never knew what to say to little kids. I wouldn't even take the time to understand them, but I'm just so comfortable with Marcos, and he seems so happy here with me."

"He is such a good kid. He did great tonight. When I told my friends I was coming with you tonight with a three-year-old, and that we weren't going to bring a stroller because it is too crowded to push a stroller through, they thought I was crazy. They said no way a three-year-old would make it. I think he just loved it tonight. He really liked the trains at the museum. Maybe you should go find him some toy trains."

"Yes, good idea. I'll look for some—not sure where to start, but I'm sure someone on Craigslist is selling an entire boxful in town."

Evelyn opened the back door of her car and placed the sleeping Marcos in the car seat she had bought for him at Toys "R" Us before she'd picked him up at the Polinsky Center. She stopped and looked at his peaceful face as he rested in a deep slumber. "Look at his face. Isn't he just an angel?"

"You know, Evelyn, I didn't understand your big switch from driven, prey-eating businesswoman to rescuer of a young child. It made no sense at all, but now that I see you and Marcos together, it seems as if there is some sort of connection. They say love changes everything, even the most ambitious."

"Who says that?"

"I don't know. 'They' do," Monica said with a smile as she made air quotes. "But about Chad. You've been married over four years now, and you had an agreement that you weren't going to include children in your lives. He gave you an ultimatum, and now you've chosen Marcos over him."

"I don't really see it that way. Yes, I can honestly say when I agreed on our pact all those years ago, when life was grand fling with him and we were enjoying our freedom, I didn't want anything to do with kids. We had big career ambitions and enjoyed our freedom to go out and run and travel, but life has just progressed for me. I wanted all that up until just a couple months ago, but now it's all changed. I just want to give Chad more time. He must see it. He must want to be together with me more than romping around here and there. There must be some turning point for him, and I just want to give him time. I have to believe that there must have been some sort of connection between him and Marcos and that his mind is just on his job right now, and he'll think differently when his thoughts clear."

"Evelyn, you know kids are not for everyone, and Chad may not come around. You two had an agreement, and you changed that. He wasn't ready yet."

"Yes, that's true, but Marcos was. And I was. I'm not going to let a child be sent back over the border to an unknown. You know about all those kids coming over the border from South America. I don't want him falling back into that system of immigration. It can take years in the system, and who knows where he would go? I think it's time for me to think about more than just myself. I enjoy my freedom, and I do love Chad, but I can't let Marcos just go back…back into what? An endless system where I can't help him? I think I did the right thing, Monica. I didn't choose Marcos over Chad—I think life choose me and him."

"Okay, be all philosophical and spiritual on me with all that gushy stuff. I get what you're saying. If you can be at peace with yourself—and I'm all about Marcos now—I'll support you on your newfound adventure, but I still think you should make some efforts to bring Chad back into your life. Remember, you made a commitment before Godand man."

"Yes, but I think he just needs a little more time and he'll come around."

They meandered through the traffic of the parking lot, driving up the hill, through the city nightlife to Monica's house, which was tucked among the craftsmen-style bungalows of yesteryear. They parted with a smile and deeper appreciation for each other.

"See ya at work Monday. Tell Marcos, when he wakes, thanks for hanging with me." Monica smiled and closed the car door, and Evelyn watched her walk, in her black, clunky boots, down the pathway to her quaint home.

Evelyn smiled as she shifted into first gear and drove slowly away from the curb. It had been a good evening. She would make this Christmas excursion a yearly event, the beginning of a tradition, and she was planning on many more to come.

☙

Saturday morning, the day after their night festivities, and Evelyn jumped out of bed at seven. She was ready to go for a run, but wanted to let Marcos sleep in longer. They had stayed out late the night before and she was sure he was going to sleep in late as well. He was a good sleeper and didn't get up at those godforsaken times in the morning, like her niece and nephew, who would get up at five in the morning, while it was still dark outside.

She opened Marcos's bedroom door slowly and peeked in on him. He looked as if he were still in the deep slumber that she'd left him in the night before. He wouldn't be waking for a while, she thought. Rubbing the sleep out of her own eyes, she made her way downstairs to make breakfast and start her Christmas shopping list.

As she passed through the living room, she cracked the window to let the air in. It was the first weekend in December, but the temperatures were still in the sixties during the day. She thought maybe they could go get a Christmas tree that afternoon and pull out the one box of Christmas decorations they had in the garage—maybe they could also pick out a stocking for Marcos.She sauntered into the kitchen and switched on the little TV on the counter to watch the last of the news before the cartoons came on. She boiled water and turned on her espresso machine, which made a loud whirring sound as she steamed milk for a chai latte. She poached an egg and ate it over dry wheat toast as she drank her fresh-squeezed orange juice. She made more for Marcos, so it would be ready when he woke. She sipped her latte loudly and sat down to check her messages on her laptop, tweeting, "Nothing smells like Christmas like the smell of chai tea in the morning." She opened up a Word document and started making her Christmas gift list.

Suddenly Evelyn looked up. She stopped her typing because she'd heard a noise. She listened to see if Marcos was already getting up. Maybe she woke him up? She sat there for a bit long, listening. She thought she heard sounds, albeit they were faint. Picking up her warm latte, she walked into the living room. It was unusually cold in the room after she had the window open for such a short time. The white, transparent curtains were billowing in the slight breeze. She stood in front of the windows and looked out. A green lowrider drove by her house. She'd seen it before but had thought nothing of it. Suddenly, her stomach felt heavy, her mouth went dry, and her throat felt as if it had a big lump stuck in it. Something was wrong. Something was very wrong.

She clunked her coffee mug down on the Plexiglas coffee table and knew it was a moment she had never prepared for. She ran up the stairs, not really seeing the steps or realizing how she managed to go up two flights in no time at all, and she reached Marcos's room, where the door was standing wide open. She fearfully looked in and, with panic in her voice, called out to Marcos. Her hand up to her mouth, she couldn't find her voice, and it felt as if her heart had stopped; the room spun as she looked down at his bed and found it empty. No sleeping Marcos spread out on the bed. No Pooky lying on his pillow. She weakly called out for him, hoping she was overreacting and that he was somewhere in the house. She called out quietly at first, then louder, then in desperation. She checked the bathroom, the closet, underneath his bed. Then she ran outside, felt the wind whipping her hair and the clouds move in heavily; once again, she tried to yell, but all that came out was a whisper. She feared the worst—Marcos was gone.

The police came in about twenty minutes—twenty minutes that felt like an eternity—after she'd punched 911 on her cell phone. Her neighbors came out. Cars stopped. People from across the street pointed. The world swirled around her; the chaos began to weigh on her, and suddenly she felt completely alone. She saw colors and shapes, heard the sound of voices, but it all seemed to be happening in a dream or to someone else. Everything seemed to be moving at an unnatural pace, and she stood still at the center, wondering what had happened to her reality. Uncertainty lurked. Her life seemed as if it were about to end—now she was without the man she loved, Chad, and the most adorable boy ever, Marcos.

Life Will Go On

The "Rescue"
(Rubén)

Rubén stayed late after work to spray paint the Impala black—he didn't understand why Santiago had painted it an unusual green anyway. It was too noticeable. Rubén had secretively loved Santiago's car, although he never would have confessed that to Santiago, and he decided he was going to take real good care of it now that Santiago was gone. He was sure Santiago would be proud of him taking such good care of his car. As Rubén was cleaning up the garage, Juanita drove up in the Mustang her papa had given her, to pick Rubén up, as he was leaving the Impala in the garage to let the paint dry overnight. She sauntered up wearing the dark purple dress that she wore real tight, kissing him at the corners of his mouth and shifting her hips in the flirtatious way she did.

"Nita, where is Marcos?" Rubén asked, noticing he wasn't in the car.

"Oh, I left him with Mami since he was still eating dinner. He eats dinner early, like he eats all day, really. Maybe that woman never fed him or something." She watched him put away the air compressor, paint sprayer, power sander, solvents, primer, and paint. "*Querida*, I think we did the right thing," she said, as if she was convincing herself. She tilted her head and wrapped her hair around her finger while smacking on a piece of gum.

"I know we did the right thing, *mi amos*. We so did the right thing," Rubén assured her. "We don't want Marcos growing up with some Caucasian *chica*, no? Growing up not knowing his culture and his family? He would just grow up wondering who he was and be lost in this world. We can be that family to him. We are the closest to family he's got. Course we did the right thing."

"Mamá and Papá took him in to their house without any questions, no question at all. They didn't say nothin'. She had a little bed already from my aunt. So weird how they weren't at home, then all of a sudden they showed up like right after us. So weird. I'm sure Mamá has no idea what really happened. I think they really believed our story, which is also true—his momma died; she killed herself, and may she rest in peace." She crossed herself quickly, touching her fingers to each shoulder and then kissing the tips. "His papa was shot to death, his *abuela* has gone senile—my word, Rubén, *senile*—and is now in a special home, and Marcos's aunt went down to Mexico, looking for her *mami* who left her when she was a child. Maybe Carmelita started carrying drugs across the border like her *mami* 'cause she couldn't figure out how to make money now without her brother, who paid for everything. She was spoiled, that girl. My mama totally believed Marcos had nowhere else to go but our house. Really, he doesn't have nowhere else to go."

"Yeah, that's right. We are it. We are all he's got," Rubén agreed.

Juanita continued with the story she told her mama: "We just found him at his home, alone, with no one to care for him, and now we have him."

Rubén was staring at her as she talked with a faint expression of disbelief on his face as she described Marcos's situation. She seemed a bit insensitive, but maybe he was wrong about that. She must care, he told himself. She must have done all that because she cared about Marcos, right?

It was true; Juanita's parents had taken Marcos right in. They brought in a little bed and clothes for him from the local Goodwill . Juanita's *mamá* was also willing to juggle her housekeeping jobs, so she could take care of Marcos when Rubén and Juanita were away. It all worked out way too easy, Rubén thought, and he just wanted to lay low and keep Marcos inside the house, in case there were cops still driving around looking for him. Pedro said a cop came around their neighborhood asking questions about a Mexican boy with red hair. Juanita's parents lived in a little nicer part of town than Santiago had, and he was hoping it was far enough away that the police wouldn't be snooping around their neighborhood. Marcos's characteristics were distinguishable, and any neighbor could blurt out that they had seen such a boy down the street. Juanita's *mami* was even okay keeping Marcos inside and occupied, even though he seemed anxious to go out and play fútbol. It made Rubén a bit suspicious about this family, a family he had known for three years, yet they were so different than his own—he just wasn't sure about them.

Juanita had convinced Rubén that if they did take Marcos in, he would have to stop selling drugs and get a "real" job. Rubén had heard Santiago talk about working at Gonzalez

Garage on the corner of Fifth and Broadway, as he had a friend who had offered him a position there, so Rubén thought maybe they would hire him instead. He knew he didn't have the mechanical skills like Santiago, but he was hopeful. He went into the garage to set up a time to meet with the owner, and he placed Rubén on painting and detailing the cars. The owner was even good with Rubén staying after to paint the Impala two weeks after he was hired; he said he needed practice, although the owner wagged a finger at Rubén and said, "No funny business. We run a clean garage, you hear?" The owner was coming back to lock everything up just as Rubén finished painting his car. He wanted to make sure the owner knew he was a hard worker. He was doing everything he could to leave the old life behind him. He told the guys in the gang that he was religious now and was turning his life over to Jesus. Rubén started going to Mass Sunday nights at St. Brigid's, down the street. The gang didn't mess with dudes who went the religious route. He was transferred off of his station near the border. Somehow El Serp believed that Rubén was going all religious on them and didn't want them bothering him anymore—or maybe El Serp regretted killing Santiago and knew that Rubén was now taking care of his family.

It was a new Rubén, going to Mass twice a week, and he was even trying to quit smoking, but smoking cigarettes helped to calm him down, and he was having a difficult time giving it up. Juanita's momma, Rosita, made him smoke outside, just like Santiago's *Abuelita* had made him, so it wouldn't make the house smoky, and she said it was not good for kids to be around secondhand smoke. For Marcos's sake, he tried to cut down on the smoking altogether, but it wasn't easy.

Juanita put a contingency on bringing Marcos into their home that her and Rubén had to get married. Her parents would want that, she said. So he agreed. What the heck? It was a new him, and Marcos needed a family. They had been together for so long, and if he could stand her that long, then maybe they would be okay married.

"Yes, we rescued him, and now he is safe with us and has a family," Rubén muttered under his breath as he picked up the respirator, dust masks, and goggles he'd used to paint Santiago's car.

"Mami and Papá didn't even blink an eye when we told them we were getting married. Oh, it was so pretty, *querido*, at the church. I just loved my *bellisima* wedding dress. Thank you, *miha*, only the best from you. I can't believe I found it at Rosanna's shop. It was all white and pretty, with all those sparkles all over it." Juanita flicked her finger in front of her body, indicating the sparkles, and she shimmered as if a spotlight were on her. Rubén had heard her go on and on about her beautiful weeding dress before. "You liked it, eh, *miha*? Oh, *miha*, let's go to the Cantina tonight? I think we should go out again. We've just been so cooped up in the house, keeping Marcos inside and all."

He didn't hear what she said. He was distracted by his thoughts, fidgeting with putting the cap back on the paint thinner. He suddenly got suspicious and stood up to look at her. Would Juanita really care for Marcos, or did she just go along with him because she wanted to get married? Would Juanita's *mami* really take care of him? Would Marcos be happy with them? Marcos seemed unusually attached to his bear and carried his Pooky Bear everywhere; he wouldn't even put him down at the dinner table, and he heard that the stuffed animal even sat on the faucet when Marcos took a bath. He was also always chewing on the collar of his shirts too.

Rubén just had to believe they did the right thing, that Marcos was in a better place around people who looked more like him and could teach him about his own Mexican culture, people who were there when he was born and were as close to family as he had now. "We did the right thing," he muttered under his breath, trying to convince himself it was true.

Life Without Her
(Chad)

Chad walked the aisles of the hospital in a daze, avoiding conversation with fellow doctors, nurses, and administration. He preferred his solace at work and wanted to be left to his thoughts. Chad didn't call Charlie, and he didn't meet up with friends at the gym. He called off their Friday night drinks. Spencer, his longtime friend who he knew from Santa Barbara High, was also a doctor at the same hospital, tried to catch his attention to talk, but Chad did his best to avoid his gaze.

Chad's life seemed convoluted and mixed up; he had withdrawn into himself, shut the world out, and refused to ponder his confusion for too long. He sat, lost in his muddled thoughts; his days were the same, the same demanding day as the day, and weeks, before.

His schedule was the same every day:

Up at 6:00 a.m., at the hospital at 7:00 a.m., made his rounds and visited his patients, then scrubbed in and ready for surgery at 8:00 a.m.

Every other Monday, Chad had clinic from eight to five, with a one-hour lunch, when he kept his head down and caught up on writing his notes on his patients and studies. He tried to bring his own meals, but now that he was living on Charlie's boat, he had started eating cafeteria food. There was a special room for doctors to sit, away from the community cafeteria, so the family members of patients wouldn't come up and ask questions while they were on their break. Sometimes, when the cafeteria was busy, Chad would steal away and eat down at La Jolla shores, a quick ten-minute drive and a refreshing reminder that he lived in Southern California and could breathe in the ocean air. Growing up in Santa Barbara, his days were mostly spent surfing; his soul just wanted to be out riding the waves and forgetting about his troubles. Also, the rhythmic sound of the waves calmed him and helped him center his mind, so he could go back to the fast-paced life of the hospital. It was nature that gave him back his sanity. It was something that he and Evelyn had shared; he had always felt there was more to life. His heart was still unfulfilled and uneasy.

On the other Mondays, Chad would usually have two big surgeries that took approximately four hours each. As a recent fellow, Chad was in the room retraining from the console (a robotic system which the doctors look through to enable them to operate), then assisting at the bedside to the attending surgeon, the boss of the case. On surgery days, Chad rarely had downtime and went through the entire day with only a kale and banana smoothie for breakfast.

Tuesdays were usually more open surgery, less robotics, or clinic again.

Wednesdays had the biggest case of the week, but at the end of the day, as they wrapped up long hours in surgery, the doctors would grab dinner at Roberto's Mexican Food, which, according to Chad, served the best fish burritos this side of highway 8. It was a hole-in-the-wall type of restaurant, but it was open twenty-four/seven, so it served its purpose. The front of the restaurant was ceiling-to-floor windows with red peppers flashing in a string of red lights that pierced the darkness. The joint was small, and the doctors awkwardly dragged the small, round tables to the front corner of the restaurant. They needed a skoch more room, but they made it work, stiffly sitting closely to one another. The one cook and one server were always welcoming of the doctors arriving late in the night. One week, Chad thought about ditching out on the Wednesday routine, as he had the prior couple of weeks, but a hearty meal was too tempting to pass up. Spencer finally met up with Chad there.

There, late at night, they stuffed themselves with carne asada tacos, filled with seasoned meat and topped with super-creamy avocados and tangy salsa served on warm tortillas. The doctors would fill their stomachs and collaborate and discuss research projects or tell surgery war stories. When the doctors were rubbing their bellies and standing up and scraping the wrought-iron chairs across the terracotta-tile floor with an irritating screech, on this particular Wednesday, Spencer touched Chad on the arm. It had been several weeks since they had all met up at Seersuckers and were introduced to Charlie's date, Veronica. Since then, Spencer and Lorena hadn't seen, nor heard from, their friends.

"Hey, I'll walk you out to your car."

"Sure, man, but I need to rush off to get some shut-eye."

Once out in the cool, late-night air, Spencer turned to him. "What the hell has happened to you? Dude, not only do you look like shit, you are a real asshole at work. We haven't seen or heard from you or Evelyn either. What's going on?"

"Shit, it's a long story, Spence, and I just don't have the time to tell it." Chad dragged his fingers through his hair.

"So who are you going to tell? Are you just going to be your own little island and handle it yourself?" Spencer looked at Chad with fiery eyes full of deep concern.

"Yup, pretty much."

The two of them stood in front of Chad's car, staring at each other. Chad fidgeted, shifting his weight from one leg to the other as he hoped to escape the strained and awkward conversation, while Spencer stood fast in his stance and stared. "So, there you have it. Man, you don't need to be all macho about it. You should tell someone; maybe it will help you get some perspective on the situation. I know Evelyn got pretty drunk that night we last saw you two and maybe there was something going on there that we didn't know about. Evelyn did have lunch with Lorena later, but Lorena didn't tell me any details of the conversation."

"Nope. I think I have a fine perspective on the situation—it's just fine."

Spencer paused briefly. "Well, no need to turn your back on your friends. When you're ready to talk about it, just let me know." Spencer's voice was suddenly calm as he seemed to switch over to his practiced, doctor's mannerisms—the mannerisms for when they were about to deliver bad news.

"Thanks, man, I appreciate that, but really, I'm okay."

"Well, great then. I'll see you around."

"Yeah, see ya around." As soon as Spencer took a step back, Chad jumped in his car and sped all the way back to the yacht. Driving the empty highway from the hills of La Jolla towards the lights of downtown and the waterfront, his mind turned off, all was numb. He didn't want to admit things were not going so great—he was confused and didn't know how to articulate his feelings about the situation, because he wasn't in touch with how he felt. He felt somewhat dead, as if he could hear and see but couldn't feel or move. Once he arrived at the dimly lit boat, he threw his scrubs in the corner, which he never would have done in the house, and fastidiously brushed his teeth. He quickly jumped into the stiff bed and fixed his eyes on the wood-paneled ceiling, the swaying of the boat finally putting him to sleep in the wee hours in the morning.

On Thursdays, Chad had smaller surgeries scheduled, maybe some clinic hours with procedures (cystoscopy, prostate biopsy, vasectomy, urodynamics, etc.). Research time and/or meetings for those into research—he used the time to do data entry with some statistical work. He would do animal research, which consisted of mouse surgery, as the team of urologists was working on making tumors glow during robotic surgery so the borders were easier to see.

Fridays consisted of more clinic hours and research in the afternoon. Dr. McCoy's research on pancreatic cancer was finally published, and a nurse came out on a Friday and popped a champagne bottle, the cork hitting the ceiling, and drinks were poured all around. Some of the urologists were going golfing and asked Chad to join them, but he claimed he wasn't feeling well, which was partially true, as he was having a difficult time sleeping and wasn't eating as well as he wanted to. He just wanted to lie on the stiff couch in the small main area on Charlie's yacht and stare mindlessly at the TV.

Chad had been spending his time away from the hospital on Charlie's boat. It was a seventy-foot yacht, built in

1959, and had a steel hull and beautiful wood appointments. It had taken Charlie three years to restore the old boat and bring the luster back to the wood, and he worked on it diligently, not only on weekends but during the week as only Charlie could, as he had such a flexible schedule. His work on the boat was evident, as the wood surfaces were magnificent, with glossy finish, so that it almost looked wet. The boat was Charlie's Lady Grace, and he also referred to her as "his Grace who saved him from land and disaster." She was Her Majesty, and no other woman could offer him the freedom he found in her. Her name had been given to her at her conception, with a champagne bottle broken on her hull, but after Charlie had bought the beauty, he had thought of a new name; he was told that it was bad luck to change the name of a boat and was disappointed at first, but now he couldn't think of her any other way—she was his Lady Grace.

The yacht wasn't typically decorated, as it was void of shells and anchor artifacts. One of his four-week girlfriends had been commissioned to decorate the historic yacht, and the boat had her signature touch throughout. The three staterooms had white bedding with accents of navy blue; vintage black-and-white wallpaper with an old fisherman smoking a pipe, the fumes circling his head, adorned a wall of the kitchen. The furniture was hidden under white slipcovers, and blue stripes—vertical, horizontal, and diagonal—could be found everywhere on the yacht, so much so that Chad felt as if he were going cross-eyed from all the stripes or suffering from a little seasickness. On the stern, there was a teak fold-down table and a shiny silver bell with "Lady Grace" in cursive lettering that clanked when the boat tossed back and forth. The yacht was full of enmities, such as two flat screen TVs, an extensive CD library, a four-by-twelve foot swim platform with swim ladder, a full wet bar, and board games and beach toys. The boat wasn't just recreational or a prize possession; it was Charlie's house when he wasn't traveling. It was also a prodigious meeting place, and Charlie enjoyed inviting one and all on board to share in a sunset and a drink.

Chad had done a lot of thinking on Charlie's yacht while his friend explored some exotic land, hiking some interesting mountain, or riding a taxi in some busy city in India. Chad rocked to and fro on the big boat, feeling sorry for himself, growing lazy, thumbing through surfing magazines and old textbooks he had grabbed from the house on his way out. He didn't know why he'd grabbed them; he just had. As he mindlessly thumbed through the magazine, he tried to figure out why he'd done what he had.

Chad couldn't figure out why he'd walked out on her. What was he running from? Did he really want to live his life away from Evelyn? He had known Evelyn for only six years but couldn't remember life without her. She was smart, kept him on his toes, conversed on just about any topic, and was enthusiastic and just as driven as him. He liked that she had five different athletic shoes, each with a different purpose. He liked that she would challenge him to a run on the beach and almost win. He appreciated that her job was important to her and that she wanted to grow and be a better employee and make a difference in the world. He loved taking care of her; even though she thought she was a tough girl who didn't need a protector, she often relinquished and let him pamper her. He marveled at her strength, both physically and in her opinions. Their conversations were always lively, never dull. Their ambitions in life were so similar that when she switched midfield and decided that those really weren't her life goals anymore, he just didn't know how to handle the change. Marcos came into their house so causally, as if he wasn't any big deal—the deal breaker in their marriage that he was. He watched Evelyn with Marcos, and she looked so relaxed, as if she had been around kids all her life. But he knew she was nervous with kids and fidgeted and laughed too loudly, and it was only in those instances that she looked awkward, out of place. If a kid couldn't talk about international world affairs, then she was put out, which of course had been every time until now. She loved a conversation that stimulated her mind and challenged her thinking—she couldn't do small talk. Her sneaking around, her deception in seeing Marcos behind his back, suddenly made him realize that there was a trust issue. He thought they could talk about anything and that they had open communication between them, but for some reason, she had seemed scared to admit what she was doing. She was trying to help another person, true, but having a life without him seemed unbearable to him. Marcos was a cute kid, but his and Evelyn's plans didn't include a child, much less a kid off the street with no adoption papers or known history. Maybe it was just him, maybe life was just happening too fast for Chad, and he was concentrating so much on his fellowship and work that he couldn't accept a change in plans. He didn't see himself as a kid person. His friend Charlie was. Chad didn't get down on his hands and knees and color or play trucks. He didn't know how to talk to a child. Why and how could Evelyn change in an instant? Had her desire for motherhood been lurking close to the surface, and she'd suppressed it because Chad didn't want that for them? Or had Marcos just brought it out in her?

Was he scared to go down that road of parenting? What if he took his eyes off his career and faltered? Was he really not ready to take in a child? Did Marcos really mess up his plans for the future, or was he really starting to care for Marcos? Did he fear his life would change? Didn't he and Evelyn have a good life the way it was? Why did she have to mess it up? Chad contemplated these things as he walked the aisles of the hospital, as he listened to patient's talk of their life-threatening illness, as he sat in Starbucks and drank his coffee alone, as he stared idly into the horizon where the ocean and sky met, as he lifted weights at the neighborhood gym, and as he lay on the couch on the boat, being lulled by the waves.

He thought about Lady Grace, and he realized that Evelyn was his Lady Grace—the person who rescued him from monotony, the doldrums of life. She brought fresh life to him, and he knew he didn't want to live apart from her—maybe he needed to accept that he needed to share her with someone else.

While he blended his fruits and vegetables into a smoothie after his Sunday morning workout, he thought about how he wanted to start going to church but didn't even know where to start. As he stood there downing his smoothie and contemplating church, he got a text from Monica: *Marcos was taken. Come and comfort Evelyn.* That's all she said. No elaboration, just to the point. He circled the tiny kitchen a few times, dragging his hand through his hair, and then situated himself on the hull of the boat, staring out into the distance, not seeing the moving boats and life around him. He was lost in his thoughts, sitting and staring for an unknown amount of time. And then, suddenly, as if a Tsunami hit the boat, he knew it was his time to go back to her.

After his time away from Evelyn, he realized he couldn't live life without her; he was sorry to hear about Marcos, and suddenly it was so clear to him what he needed to do.

He packed up his things and left Charlie's boat. He got in his car and hurried off to her. It was as if his heart was finally coming home; he had just needed some solitude to finally realize he already had something good.

A Moment Alone

(Evelyn)

Evelyn sat alone on her yellow couch, looking at her striped wall hanging and the tree swaying in the side yard. Her sister, Emily, had stayed with her for a while during the day but had to go back and take care of her kids. Evelyn continued to sit there in her house as the sun set, and she watched the colors of light change on the walls. It grew dark in the room, but she just sat there and couldn't move. Her cell phone sat on her lap, just in case the social worker or a police officer called to give her an update on the missing Marcos. Her legs were stretched out on the acrylic coffee table, and even though she was thirsty and needed a drink, she just couldn't move from the sofa. She was sitting there in the quiet, in her solitude, alone in her thoughts and her grief, when she heard quiet knocking on the door.

The wrapping continued quietly, and she heard a muffled voice say, "Evie, Evie, babe, it's me, Chad. I'm so sorry," he said gently from behind the wooden door, his mouth up to the crack of the doorjamb. "I'm so sorry I left, and I'm so sorry about Marcos. Oh, babe, I'm so sad to hear that…I never wished for that, I just wanted us to be together, but I realized later that I really did like Marcos and was scared about letting him in, but then I missed him, and then I really missed you. Just being without you has been so hard this past month. We belong together, you and I. We fit together perfectly—I just didn't realize it until I was away from you. I just wasn't ready for another person in our lives. I was so concentrated on getting that fellowship and thinking about us that I didn't consider another person with us. You have to admit, you did spring it on me, but I'll try to be a better listener and try and tell you things that I'm thinking and feeling. I just didn't know what I was thinking and feeling, so I retreated, confused, maybe just to get my thoughts in order. I'll try to be better. I just wasn't ready for this transition, and now I'm so sad that I'm coming in so late, so sorry to hear about Marcos. Evie, I just want to be with you. I'm so sorry." He was quiet for a bit, then, just a little quieter, he said, "Will you take me back?"

Chad's quiet knocks and whispers of apologies at her door continued and Evelyn was so touched by his words that she didn't realize she'd finally shed a tear. She had sat there on her couch for hours and hadn't cried, but now, tears started flowing and flowing, and she couldn't control them. She got up quickly, unlocked the door, swung it open, fell into Chad's arms, and sobbed uncontrollable gasps of air for she didn't know how long. She felt his strong arms, and it was if she was taken care of again and had a glimmer of hope that maybe things would be okay. She might be able to face the situation of a heart-wrenching loss now that he was back.

The first three days after Marcos's disappearance, the police called frequently to give Evelyn updates on their search. Then, the phone calls became less frequent. At first, there was an entire team on the search for Marcos, and then two detectives, and then it was down to one detective. Spencer, Charlie, and Chad scoured their areas with posters that Monica created, which read, "Missing Child, call the police if you see this child," with a photo of Marcos and a physical description. They handed out fliers to residents and posted the fliers in store windows.

Time went slowly in the following days. The police hadn't had any leads and the phone was quiet. Seconds, then minutes, then days since Marcos was taken from Evelyn, but she still struggled to regain normality in her life. At first, she lay on her couch for several days and then moved up to her bed. She started drinking cola and eating mocha almond ice cream at odd times of the day. She even ate fried chicken for dinner one night, because she didn't have the energy to go to the store and grill chicken. She wore her sweats and slippers all day. She watched mindless TV while eating buttery popcorn. She lost track of time.

She was forever grateful that Chad came back to her, as she couldn't imagine life without him. Chad took a few days off, and together they went on leisurely walks through Balboa Park, stopping in to visit a few of the museums, the harbor, and the boats coming and going, and they went to the beach and waded through the waves as they lapped up on the sand. They talked about what had happened, and they promised each other that they would do their best to be honest with one another, to try and not be quick to judge, and to make efforts to communicate their thoughts, feelings, and life happenings. They were determined to make a go of it together. Chad apologized for abandoning her at a great time of need, and she asked him to forgive her for being deceptive and not communicating upfront; they realized they had a bigger problem and needed to seek some counseling on how to communicate and be honest with each other.

It was two weeks later and Evelyn went back to work. At first she just stared at her screens, feeling empty and uninterested in the world around her, but a week later, she started to get back into the grove of her job. Things had changed. People understood her lack of motivation, and she started taking time to talk to people in the break room and jumped in on the girl talk about what their kids had recently accomplished, what they'd made for dinner using curry or whatever spice or ingredient, and where they had bought their latest shoes. She never would have had any patience for that type of talk in the past, but she was actually becoming interested in their lives. She was thankful that the executives gave her time and still believed in her ability, and soon she was back online tweeting, blogging, and keeping up with the political news. One blogger commented, "Welcome back. Sounds as if you came back with a heart." But she felt as if she lost some piece of her heart every day that there was no news on Marcos.

Chad and Evelyn spent a quiet Christmas with Evelyn's sister, Emily, and her family, and sat and enjoyed playing games with Annabelle and Brady, but there was an ache in Evelyn's heart for Marcos, and everyone wished he were there to share the day with them.

After the New Year, Evelyn and Chad invited their group of friends back to Friday night drinks, and as they tipped wine glasses and downed crab cakes and artichoke hearts, they told them the entire story and apologized for not coming to them from the beginning. They confessed that they hadn't been honest with themselves or each other at first, and found it difficult to articulate the problems well enough to tell their friends. They had been hiding in the shadows.

The Girls
(Evelyn)

Since Saturdays were one of the most difficult days for Evelyn, as that was the day she and Marcos would explore the world and take some local adventures to see the snakes at the zoo or Shamu at Sea World or the tide pools at the shores, Addy suggested they start teaching a "Boot Camp" together. So they embarked on teaching an hour-long exercise class that included stretching, a wide variety of interval training, and lifting weights interspersed with running, pulling rubber TRX straps for suspension training, push-ups, sit-ups, squats, burpees, and various types of intense, explosive routines, ending with some yoga.

They had reserved a patch of grass on Mission Bay for every Saturday, and most mornings it was wet with dew, and their clothes were usually soaked after they crawled up hills and under benches, but they were done by nine. They stored all their kettlebells, weights, bags, TRX straps, and other tools in the back of Addy's truck, and then they took a short ride back to Addy's house to shower and clean up before meeting Monica for lunch.

After their class one day, Evelyn looked around Addy's cottage while her friend took a shower. It was nestled among other quaint homes on a pedestrian lane that ran from the ocean to the bay on a thin stretch of land called Mission Beach, a unique place with a main street running through it filled with surf-and-turf type cafés serving fish tacos to people who wandered in with bare feet, women only wearing bikinis, and men without shirts. These flesh-baring people meandered the streets of Mission Beach just about year-round due to the area's fair weather. The main street was lined with breakfast cafés, seafood restaurants, plenty of bars, tourist trap stores filled with San Diego paraphernalia, surf shops, tattoo and piercing parlors, and bohemian boutiques. The homes faced each other, and each house was completely different from the other: one house might be a neglected, weathered little cottage while next door was a fancy vacation rental. It was mid-April and many Arizonians crossed the border to enjoy some sun and surf on their spring break. People in their cutoff blue jean shorts and bathing suit tops passed Addy's house to the bay or the other direction to the waves. There was a constant flow of people, and when there was a pause in the pedestrian traffic, she could hear the breeze blowing in the palm trees that peered over the cottages.

Addy lived closer to the bay side in a square house painted dark blue with white trim. Her house was filled with sporting goods and tables stacked high with sports and educational magazines. Her surfboard decorated the wall over her slip-covered couch, and the only photos in the house were propped up on a dresser with a mirror behind it. Evelyn touched the wooden elephant that Addy had brought back from Africa and then she picked up a family photo that sat in a turquoise etched frame. The photo was of Addy's family when she was a young girl; it was the last family photo taken before her mother died. Her dad still had his black hair, and he smiled broadly. Her two younger sisters stood proudly, one showing off her little beaded purse and the other her bellybutton. Her mother sat in a chair in the middle and looked wistfully into the lens. She looked as if she had something on her mind. Addy stood at the end; she had both arms down her side as she stood up straight, showing off her perfect posture.

The other photo on the dresser was in a smaller black frame and it was just of Addy's mother, taken on the day of her mother's college graduation. She looked genuinely happy, swinging her black robe and extending her arms out as she held up her diploma for all to see. Below, the photo read, "In loving memory of Addison Norma McCoy. November 27, 1991."

The day before Thanksgiving, twenty years ago, Addy's mother took her life. Addy was twelve years old, and her two sisters were eight and six. Their mother had been depressed and had been seeing a psychologist and taking medicine. She was briefly hospitalized, but on that Thanksgiving eve, she couldn't take the darkness that she walked in any longer. With all those people around her who loved and looked up to her, her mother still felt so alone and was determined to take her life. She swallowed the entire contents of a bottle of aspirin, one white pill after the other. The ambulance came while the girls were sleeping. Addy had gotten up because she was awoken by the commotion, and then she saw her mother laid out on the stretcher as they carried her down the hallway. Her younger sisters were in such a deep sleep that neither one were woken by the sirens. Evelyn guessed that scene still stayed in Addy's mind, yet she never spoke of her mother. Evelyn was a bit surprised that these memories of the mother Addy once knew sat on this dresser.

Evelyn was rather sure that Addy was fearful to feel, to discover the darkness her mother once knew, and that was why Addy kept her mind busy with an endless amount of magazines and newspapers, and CNN was always blaring in the background. She thought that exercise was Addy's escapism, a way to avoid life, a way to always feel strong and in control of her own life. Evelyn had encouraged Addy to see a counselor to talk about what happened so long ago, but Addy only scowled at her in response.

Addy came into the room wearing a short blue jean skirt that showed off her defined legs, a light pink tank top, and thick-soled flip-flops as she towel dried her wet hair. Evelyn was hoping Addy would comb her hair while it was still wet, but she kept rubbing her head with the towel and getting it into more of a tangle.

"How is your dad doing these days?" Evelyn asked. Addy's dad had taken care of Addy and her two sisters while growing up, and Addy's grandparents had moved in next door that December, on that steep hill in San Francisco, so Addy and her sisters could spent their afternoons after school next door until their dad got home after six each night.

"He's doing well. He just took a case that is getting some media attention, something about some city mogul who swindled money in some sort of pyramid scheme deal from middle-class folks. Ya know, the same ol' story. They're all up in arms about it, and he really wants to represent those families well, because he hates to see innocent people have to scrape for money while millionaires keep stuffing their pockets."

"Wow, so he is still an active lawyer. No talk of retirement?"

"None. He just wants to keep on going in hopes of 'justice for all.'"

Evelyn watched Addy as she hung up her towel and didn't touch her hair with a comb—her long, thick brunette hair was one tangled mess. She wanted to spray leave-in conditioner into Addy's hair, grab a brush, and work those tangles out, but she assumed there must be a reason her friend neglected her hair. Maybe she had fond memories of time she'd spent with her mom, as her mother braided her hair or wrapped ribbons around her ponytails. She knew Addy must think and feel something about her mom, but she never mentioned her, and Addy refused to ask anyone any personal questions either, saying, "It's none of my business." Since Addy never asked personal questions, Evelyn did her best to keep her questions light and unobtrusive as well. It wasn't until Marcos's disappearance that Evelyn realized how important it was to be around people who weren't scared to ask those challenging questions, which was why Evie kept inviting Monica to just about all of her nonexercising events.

Monica and Addy still didn't get along that well, and Evelyn wondered what the two would talk about if she weren't there. She was hoping that Monica's questions would help Addy see how people conversed in this world. Addy had had boyfriends, but the longest one she had was about four months, and it lasted that long only because they enjoyed going to the gym and surfing together. He even showed up at some of their yoga classes, but when it came to getting to know each other a bit more, Addy couldn't go there with him. The guy really liked her and wanted to make it work with her, but Addy called it off after deciding she wanted to be by herself again in her safe little world of magazines and exercise.

Evelyn had already taken her shower, and she wore a Valentina knit dress in crushed berry with sandals. "Are you ready to go?" she said as she picked up her purse near the front door and slung it over her shoulder.

"Yes, let's go." Addy grabbed her wallet, locked the door, and together they walked down the lane to meet Monica at one of their favorite local café's, The Olive, which sat under an oversized olive tree that dropped its black fruit down on the guests.

It was a normal sunny day in San Diego in April, with blue skies and a light, warm breeze blowing through the palm trees. Monica was sitting at a table under an umbrella, saving their seats for them. She greeted them warmly and gave Addy a hug, as always, even though Addy seemed to wiggle in uneasiness from the closeness.

Monica had already attended a grand opening of an art gallery downtown that morning and wore a vintage Forget-Me-Not ruffle dress in lilac and her Jenny Oxfords. She looked a bit out of place among the young people who passed them in their skimpy bikinis, board shorts, and flip-flops.

They ordered their lunch as they chatted about the gallery Monica had visited. Addy was actually engaged in the conversation and said she would like to visit the gallery sometime.

As they ordered their food, they heard the waves crashing and the loud speaker bellow out names and times as there was a surfing competition going on at the beach nearby.

"Good idea coming here. These girlies around here don't wear much clothing, eh? Are they all nineteen or something?" Monica said as she took the wrapper off her straw and stuck it into her Diet Coke.

"Basically, everyone around here is the same age. If you see a family, well they're not from around here," Addy replied. Although Addy was an engineer in a global company, she fit right in, in the area she lived in—she just didn't realize she did. She was too busy to notice she looked a lot like everyone else there because Addy was off boating, kayaking, paddling, surfing, cycling, and running and didn't stop to evaluate life. She'd moved down to the bay side because she loved the unlimited access to all that she loved: physical activity and the ocean.

"Sooo, Miss Evie, I was wondering how things were going for you lately?" Monica said not wasting any time in small talk, as she twirled a fry in her hand.

Evie gave her a slight smile and tilted her head. "Fine, fine. Did you mean work or what?"

"Not work. I see you at work, and I'm in your same department, so I kind of have an idea how that's going. Seems as if you and Irene are becoming friends."

"Ha, cause we went to lunch together the other day," Evelyn said as she squeezed a lemon into her water.

"Yes, actually, that's it. How did that come about?"

"Well, I was sitting at my desk one day, working, and I saw Irene staring at me from her office window, kind of like she was glaring at me or something. Not sure why she was staring at me, but I decided I really didn't need animosity in my life anymore, so I got up to ask her to lunch. I thought maybe that would warm up our relationship or something. I got up then and there, and walked over to her office. She kept staring at me as I came to her office door. She didn't say anything, and she looked really surprised when I walked over to her. I said, 'Irene, what do you think about going to lunch with me sometime?' and she said, 'Today?' and I said, 'Yeah, sure, today is fine.' And she said, 'Sure.'" Evelyn chuckled to herself as she wiped her mouth with a paper napkin. "And that was that. At noon she came over to my desk and said, 'Ready?' and we walked to the deli downstairs."

"Did you talk about the Nelson deal?" Addy asked.

"No, we didn't, actually. Right away I asked her what she did in her spare time and discovered that she hikes peaks."

"She hikes peaks?" Addy was suddenly curious.

"Yes, Mount Whitney, Mount Elbrus, one in Mongolia, the one in Nepal, one in Mexico, something like Pico de something, Kilimanjaro, and she wants to climb the Matterhorn, Patagonia, Mount McKinley, Mount Everest, and she's working her way to K2. The biggies. She is planning on taking three weeks off next summer to walk the John Muir trail from Whitney to Yosemite, something like 215 miles long. Crazy. Then she wondered if I wouldn't mind overseeing her responsibilities while she was gone. Can you believe that?"

"No joke?" Monica lowered her fork, surprised at how quickly Irene had warmed up to Evelyn.

"No joke. I should have asked her to lunch a long time ago. She was actually pleasant. I had no idea she and her husband were hikers. Rather impressive." All three of them had known Irene for years, the one who wore complete pant suits every day and talked to the bosses behind closed doors, but no one knew that she hiked massive peaks on her vacations.

"I saw Chad the other day at Whole Foods in Hillcrest. How are you two doing?" Monica said.

"We went to Balboa Park to check out some of the museums together. We're doing well. It's like it's a new marriage. He's being so sweet, and we've purposely been finding time to be together."

Evelyn was suddenly quiet, and on that sunny day at the Olive Café, as Evelyn sat at that table and heard the thumping of the olives as they dropped onto the umbrella they sat under, she put her hand down flat on the table and was overcome by sadness. "I miss Marcos so much," she said.

Addy and Monica were quiet; Evelyn felt their eyes on her, studying her for clues of what to do next.

"I miss him so much. I can't go in the spare room. His little bed is still sitting in the middle of the room. I didn't even pull up the covers to make the bed, but my housekeeper stripped the bed and washed the sheets and made it again. I miss *Sesame Street* on the TV. One morning, I put it on just because, just because I wanted to see who the special guest was that day. Sometimes I hear him humming, humming a song I don't recognize. I thumbed through the books I gave him and couldn't let go of *The Itsy Bitsy Spider*. My heart hurts, and sometimes I just find myself staring. Sometimes I just can't leave the house to go for a run, and I just stare out the window. It is as if I'm heart broken or something. There's been no word from the police or Jessica, his social worker. No one has a lead. No one knows where my sweet boy Marcos has gone." Evelyn stopped for a moment, caught her breath, put her hair behind her ears, and looked up. "He came into my life for such a short time, but he has changed my life forever."

Evelyn's friends stared at her, and when it appeared that Evelyn was done, Monica moved her chair close to Evelyn's, put her an arm around her shoulders, touched her head with hers, and tried to come up with some comforting words, but all she could say, "I'm so sorry, Evelyn." As the wind blew, the waves crashed, and the young people around them laughed, the three girls sat there in silence.

"Monica?" Evelyn said, realizing something and turned to her friend. "I haven't asked about you in such a long time. How have you been lately?"

Monica took her arm down and leaned back in her chair. "My dog died last week."

Evelyn turned to her friend and, with complete compassion, said, "I'm so sorry to hear that, Monica." She reached out to hold her friend's hand. She looked to the perch at the end of the café, where Monica would usually tie him up, but sure enough there was no Frodo.

"A sixteen-year-old ran into him with his car while Frodo was on a long leash in a parking lot. He just didn't see him. The boy didn't even have his license yet. He was just practicing in the parking lot."

Struggling for words, Evelyn put her arm around Monica. "I'm so sorry, Mon. We all liked him. I'm sure you miss him so much."

They hugged each other and sat with their arms around each other's shoulders. Addy cleared her throat, put out her chest, closed her eyes, and said, "I'm going on the Out of the Darkness walk next weekend. My sisters are coming down, and we're going to do it together. My youngest sister, Katy, got T-shirts for us to wear that say, 'In memory of my mother.'" And then she said no more.

Evelyn knew of the organization that brought awareness to the darkness of depression and how it took so many lives. She understood that Addy was taking a step in being vulnerable by acknowledging the memory of her mother. Evelyn extended her other hand and grabbed ahold of Addy's. She gripped it for a while, and then Addy let go. Monica extended her arm from around Evelyn and reached over to Addy, who screeched her chair over, and the three of them sat with their arms around each other there at the table under the umbrella. Three strong women in a moment of weakness, listening to the waves crashing and the chatter around them.

"Aren't we a hopeless mess here?" Evelyn summarized. "It is hard to grow in the midst of hurt. But, girls, we can do it. Yes, we can do it, and I'm so thankful for you two."

The Birthday

(Marcos)

They were not sure what day he had been born. They thought maybe it was in July, or maybe it was June, although they were sure it was in the summer and were pretty sure it was a month starting with *J*. Even though Rubén had gone to visit Marcos the day he was born, he couldn't remember what day it had been. Once they decided it was in July, they still had no idea which day. It never occurred to them to go down to the County Records in the federal building on Front Street and request a copy of his birth certificate or check online, but they never ventured down to that area of town or searched for it on the Internet, because, frankly, they didn't think it was really that necessary.

Not knowing which day Marcos was born, they threw out a few numbers until Rubén suggested, "How about the eleventh?" Since Rubén frequented the 7-Eleven on Home Street and Alameda, he thought it would be fun if they celebrated Marcos's birthday on July 11. This worked out rather well for Rubén, because every July 11, the 7-Eleven stores offer free Slurpees. Rubén would wake Marcos up the morning of his "birthday" and take him down to the store he frequented and got their free Slurpees. He would announce to the person behind the counter, usually it was Cairo, who was of Arab descent with a turban wrapped around his head, that it was Marcos's birthday. Cairo would always smile, hand over a small cup to fill up and, acting generous, chuckle and say, "Then a Slurpee for the birthday boy. On the house." Marcos always filled up his cup with the Blue Raspberry, while Rubén preferred his Wild Cherry, and they both walked around for most of the day with bright-colored tongues. One "birthday," they managed to go to seven different 7-Eleven stores and got a free Slurpee from each one.

Today was no exception, and once again, Rubén came into Marco's room as he was stretching and rubbing the sleep out of his eyes. Rubén peeked his head around the door and whispered as not to wake Santi as they shared a room, "Marcos, Marcos, come on, let's be the first ones to collect our free Slurpees." They both knew they wouldn't be the first, as many came to fill up their free Slurpee cups in the wee hours of the morning. Today, though, it was a little bit of a different routine. Rubén would usually call from the doorway or the hallway, but on this day, he came inside Marcos's room, and actually sat on his bed. "Happy birthday, *M'hijo*. I'm so proud of you."

"Thanks, Rubén," Marcos gurgled, still trying to find his morning voice.

He was smiling from ear to ear, and in an unusual moment, Rubén couldn't find the words to express himself. He just smiled, sitting there on the side of the bed with his legs hanging over the edge and his hands resting on his knees. He peered down at Marcos, looking very proud. His eyes were doing all the communicating, and it appeared as though he had lots of thoughts going through his mind, but no words came out of his mouth. He was speechless, which was rare for Rubén indeed.

Marcos smiled back at him, amused by his speechlessness. To break the awkward silence, Marcos spoke. "Come on, Rubén, what are we waiting for? Let's get those Slurpees and see how many 7-Elevens we can hit before the party. We got to beat seven stops this time."

As Rubén and Marcos walked into their first 7-Eleven for the day, just like on his past birthdays, Rubén announced to anyone who happened to be in the store, "Here is the birthday boy." He motioned to Marcos as if he were up on a stage. "Marcos is now eighteen!" he said, still beaming.

"For that," the owner said, "he can have two Slurpee cups."

Rubén and Juanita had been married one month after they moved Marcos into her parent's house. Rubén had wanted them to save up their own money before they had a baby, so while Juanita went to beauty school, they saved. Juanita was pregnant soon after she received her beautician degree and never did work in a salon. She would just cut and do up her friends' hair, but they would never paid her, just brought over beer or homemade bread.

Juanita was never mean to Marcos; but she didn't play any kind of mother role for him either. She just never paid much attention to him. Marcos had his own room that was fixed up nice enough; it was painted blue with a large poster of a fútbol player on the wall. Later, they moved out of Juanita's parents' house when Marcos turned six, and they rented an old house on the other side of the neighborhood. Juanita did what she could with their new place, painting it bright colors and putting big, handmade Mexican blankets down on the floor. They never had anyone over to their house, as they were always trekking over to Juanita's mom's house instead; Grandmamma Rosita's front door was always open. It always smelled like chili in her house. She made the hottest, most mouthwatering chili of any Mexican grandma. She loved guests and was always inviting people over. She was different than her daughter, who kept her front door closed all the time. Juanita didn't like cleaning up after people, whereas Grandmamma Rosita wore an apron all day, and cooked, cleaned, and welcomed anyone who walked through her front door.

Rubén did his best in raising Marcos, making sure he went to school, teaching him how to play fútbol, and attempting to keep him busy so as to keep Marcos out of trouble. He did a good job providing for Marcos and the rest of his family, making sure they had enough food in the house, a roof over their heads, and a safe car to drive. He also made sure the kids were active in at least in one sport at the local community recreation center, and his wife could go out with her girlfriends. He taught Marcos about the long-term effects of smoking marijuana, doing drugs, and over drinking alcohol. Ruben's friends had once said that they were sure that his old gang wouldn't appreciate him keeping business away from them, and Ruben would say, "Their business is not business when I'm in my own backyard."

Ruben stayed away from his old gang as much as he could, trying to stay busy with the Catholic Church, his family, and the garage.

He slowly advanced in pay and position at the garage, but he never advanced to the mechanic job he wanted—he just never developed the skills necessary for the position. He couldn't quite understand the engine well enough, so he became the detail specialist, turning any car into the meanest, shiniest-looking lowrider in San Diego. He took real pride in his job, and the family all knew his boss was impressed with his abilities and his friendliness and courteousness to the customers; he always treated them with great respect and tried to give them what they wanted.

Rubén and Juanita had two kids of their own, a boy and a girl, Santi and Rosa. Juanita was consumed with her *niños* well-being and appearance, especially her youngest, the girl, who she dressed up in big, frilly dresses and black, shiny shoes on any day and for any event. Marcos wondered if the poor girl minded all that pulling of hair and getting dolled up for every occasion. Rosa did cry and whine when her hair was brushed, but would proudly show off her dress and pretty hair and promenade around the house, acting like she was a princess. Rosa paid no attention to Marcos either; she had other things to do and other people to go to who acted as if she were royalty. Santi was six years younger than Marcos, and they had a good time playing soccer together. There was a brotherhood between the two of them, and Marcos knew Santi looked up to him; Marcos was going to miss Santi when he moved out of the house soon.

It was Juanita's mother, Rosita, who Marcos called Grandmamma and who was generous with her time and affection toward Marcos. She was kindhearted and filled the mother role in Marcos's life. She worked hard for the family. She cooked and did all the cleaning around the house, and she cleaned several other families' homes as well. She left early every morning, came home and started working on dinner, then went to bed as soon as she'd washed the dishes and picked up the house a bit; then, she'd start it all over again in the morning.

For all of the family's events, and there were quite a few of them, from fútbol games to holidays and Sunday afternoon carne asada, they all trooped over to Grandmamma's house, where she cooked and served them with no complaints. Juanita acted like she was a princess and would not help her mama; she avoided cooking, serving, and cleaning up. She let her mama do everything. The guys would put their feet up on the coffee table and open a can of beer and eat Grandmamma Rosita's salsa and tortilla chips while watching soccer. Sometimes Marcos would go into the kitchen to see if he could help, but she never allowed him to, so he would sit at the counter and ask her questions about life. When she was all done washing the dishes, she would take off her yellow dishwashing gloves and say, "Ah, *M'hijo*, you sneaky boy, making me talk and keeping me distracted. Ah, *M'hijo, itravieso!*" And then she would ruffle Marcos's hair and kiss him on his cheek. "Just for that, here is a cookie."

Today, there was a party at her house again. Rubén said it was Marcos's birthday party, as he always said when they had a *reus* in July, and though they invited all the neighbors, relatives, and friends, no one would mention Marcos's birthday. People were always surprised to find out it was his birthday. They never hired musicians or a clown or any other entertainer for his birthday parties; they did, however, have piñatas hanging from a limb of their oak tree. The piñatas were in the form of a donkey, a colorful star, a fútbul, or a parrot full of *rocletas, lucas pelucas, papitas, paletas vero, skwinklotes*, and other sweet and tart candy. For some reason, the guests just thought their family would always have a piñata at their summer *reus*. Marcos never felt neglected or forgotten, because his grandmamma would always bring out a special, homemade birthday cake for him at the end of the day.

At Marcos's eighth birthday party, a friend of Rubén's came over and was off in the corner of the backyard, with a group of cousins around him, when he mentioned something about Marcos's mom. Rubén overheard them. "What are you saying over there about my friend?" Rubén said loudly. Everyone turned to see what the commotion was about and saw

Rubén's face get red as the blood rushed to his head, his veins showing on his forehead. He didn't like anyone talking about Marcos's dad or mom. Rubén came over to the group, and the others backed away from the *comprandre* who had spoken ill of Marcos's mother. "What are you saying, friend, about my friend?"

"I was just telling your cousins that Katiana was a real looker and the big boss at that grocery store had something for her, *esé.*"

"What do you mean, he 'had something for her'?" Rubén said, sticking his face right up in the guy's, almost touching his nose.

"I mean he would take her into the closet at break time and do stuff to her."

"What are you sayin', *esé*?"

"You know what I'm sayin'. We could hear him muffle her screams and do stuff to her." No one at the party would ever know why the dimwit said that; he must have known what was coming next, but maybe he had wanted to hurt Rubén somehow before he went down.

And bam, Rubén threw a fist at this guy's jaw, and the guy's head hit the fence as he fell to the ground. Everyone watched Rubén throw another fist at him after he had pulled him off the ground and then knee him in the stomach and shout, "Then why didn't you do anything about it, you *puta*? You listened to that moron defile my friend! How could you do nothing and now come to me sayin' she was in trouble?"

Bent over, holding his stomach, the guy muttered something about the big boss having red hair, and Rubén looked a bit troubled by that bit of information, but then he continued. "Do you know what she did to herself and how that guy tormented her? You shit, get out of my house." Well, it wasn't his house, but they all understood him that he meant don't come around here again.

And that's how Marcos learned what had brought on his mother's depression. After that incident, her former boss was never heard from again. Most suspected that Rubén used some of his old connections find the guy—one could only imagine what they did to the old grocery store owner. No one ever saw Rubén's old friend again either. One of Rubén's cousins said he was living up in L.A.

Ten years later, at Grandmamma's house, under the oak tree, Marcos sat at a picnic table with a red-and-white checked plastic tablecloth, thinking about his newfound freedom and being eighteen years old. Rubén always said that until Marcos turned eighteen, he was under his rules, but when he turned eighteen, he could do what he wanted; if he wanted to move out, he couldn't do it until his eighteenth birthday. So Marcos always looked forward to this day; he wanted to go off to college and make his own decisions.

Marcos listened to the younger kids playing fútbol. A group of guys hovered around the TV inside, watching Brazil versus the Netherlands World Cup game, which would determine who got third place. They were all shouting at the players; the women at the dining table were gossiping and talking faster than should really be possible, some of the younger kids were singing along with a guitar, and music pulsated out of the neighbors' window such as *Me gusta la gasoline*, *Adrenalina-Wisin ft*. Jennifer Lopez and Ricky Martin.

Santi finished his carne asda tacos, got up from the table, and left Marcos sitting alone, listening to the activities around him and swirling his fork around his Fideo, a pasta dish with a type of noodle simmered in a tomato sauce seasoned with cumin and chili powder. His Grandmamma Rosita came and sat beside him.

"Happy birthday, Marcos," she said, hugging him and planting a kiss on each cheek. She looked at him lovingly and attempted to smooth down his unruly hair. She touched the tip of his nose, as she had when he was little, and gently tapped a few of the freckles on his cheeks.

Rosita had black, curly hair that never seemed to be in place. She was a bit overweight, but she always dressed in clean, flowery prints and wore an apron with a ruffle on the bottom. She had a very motherly look about her; she was like everyone's mama. She wanted to mother all the friends Marcos brought over to her house. It seemed to Marcos that her heart was so big, it ached to see so many broken homes and separated parents, and kids wandering the streets without parental supervision. It was if she wanted to collect all the kids and invite them all over to her house. Marcos loved her and admired her for how she cared for so many people; she even volunteered at community events, helping serve meals at Father Joe's homeless shelter.

"You know Jesus loves you," she would always say.

"I know," Marcos would mutter, not really knowing if he did know if Jesus loved him.

Rosita had started going to a Christian Community Church and not the Catholic Church that Rubén and Juanita dragged their kids to. She always invited Marcos to come with her, but Rubén would look at her disapprovingly. She never pressured Marcos, and one day he went to an event with her and liked it, and thought he might go back. He wasn't sure about all the spiritual stuff, but was open to listening and was also kind of confused about what Catholics believed and how a community church was different.

Rosita looked at Marcos, her eyes shiny, as if a tear would spill over onto her cheek. She took the palm of her hand and caressed his cheek. "You think you have a good life, *M'hijo?*" she asked sincerely.

"Sure," Marcos replied, not giving it much thought.

"*Sí, sí. Muy bien, m'hijo.*" She stopped, put both her hands in her lap, and looked at him again. "When you were little, and not with your papa or mama, do you remember another woman taking care of you. A gringo?"

No one had ever mentioned her, and Marcos was relieved someone finally had. "Yes, I think so." He sat back a little more. "I remember being in a room with the sun coming down on me; the space was so sunny, and I felt so much warmth inside. And I remember a lady with white skin hugging me and humming in my ear—a peaceful song I wasn't familiar with. I remember something about her, a feeling, but not what she looked like, just a very vague memory." Marcos suddenly turned to his grandmamma. "Grandmamma, why do you ask?"

"I know her," she said, looking Marcos square in the eye, searching his face for a reaction.

"You know her? How could you know her?"

"I clean her house," she said, pausing, still waiting for a reaction. "I should say, I cleaned her house for years, but I don't anymore." She sat up on the bench and continued. "Long time ago, when you were just little, I overheard Rubén and Juanita talking in their room about how they were going to pick you up from her house, so Grandpapa and I followed them to her house, and a week later, I went back to her place and asked her if she needed a housekeeper. I've cleaned her house every Friday since the day you came to live with us. I cleaned her house after she moved out of downtown, to her place in Coronado. I even made your bed at her house, after you came to live with us."

Marcos just stared at her, trying to soak the information in, not really knowing what it meant to him. "Why, Grandmamma, are you telling me this now? It was so long ago."

"Because, as of today, you are eighteen years old and can make your own decisions. Rubén didn't want you to know about her, and we were all forbidden from mentioning her to you—until you were eighteen years old. As of today, you are free to make your own decisions. I've been cleaning her house for the last fifteen years. I quit about a week ago. She still remembers you and still holds you in her heart." Then, without waiting for a reply and not searching for a reaction, she turned and looked out at the yard, at all the commotion around them, put her clasped hands up on the table, and, without looking at him, said, "You should go see her." She turned her head toward Marcos. "You are now eighteen years old and free to go. You should visit her. She may not mean a lot to you, as it was a long time ago and you were little, but you mean so much to her."

Marcos closed his eyes for a second and shook his head. "Grandmamma, I'm not so sure I should bring up old stuff. Why should I go visit her? I'm sure she would not remember me."

"*M'hijo*, she will never forget you. She must mean something in your journey through life. You must go—when you are ready."

Life Without Him
(Evelyn)

After Marcos's disappearance, Evelyn's and Chad's lives changed. The police looked everywhere for the redheaded boy who had thrown his arms out wide at the sound of his name, but the search never came to a positive conclusion. She often wondered, *How many red-haired, almost-four-year-old Mexican boys are there out there?*

The police interviewed people on the streets, mothers in their homes, employees in their shops, but no one seemed to know the sweet, freckled boy with a Pooky Bear tucked under his arm.

When Chad came back to Evelyn after Marcos was kidnapped, their relationship changed. After being away, he'd realized he was just running away from his feelings. Before, he hadn't wanted to care for anything more than his job and hadn't wanted to change his comfortable lifestyle with his one and only girl, Evelyn. He didn't want to share her with another person.

He wanted to be the one to take care of her. It was Marcos being in their lives that made Chad realize there was more to life than a comfortable lifestyle and a prestigious job. There was an unrequited love he hadn't experienced. It came out of nowhere, and there was no way to control it.

Evelyn and Chad waited for news about Marcos daily. They found themselves paralyzed and could barely drag themselves to work. Their weekends were quiet, and they resorted to reading on the little patio overlooking the bay or taking walks on the beach, holding hands.

Marcos had come into their lives and, in a few months, changed them completely. Evelyn learned she could love and that there was more to life than scoring her boss's job or traveling to Costa Rica or London whenever she wanted or maintaining her weight; she learned it wasn't the end of the world if she missed her morning run or had a little girth to her thighs. Together, Chad's and Evelyn's lives changed, and they let people in and allowed themselves to love and to experience more than just their personal goals. Evelyn started volunteering at the Polinsky Center, reading to kids or serving food in their cafeteria, and Chad took several weeks off to volunteer in Haiti with Doctors Without Borders, helping with prostate cancer screening and diagnosis.

As their lives slowed down and their priorities changed, Chad came to Evelyn and wanted to know if she would consider having a child with him; he was ready to care for another one. She took a deep breath and acknowledged that was what she wanted too; together, they were ready. She had been ready; she had just been waiting for him to say the word. They sold their townhome downtown and moved to Coronado—across the bay and over the bridge, a peninsula complete with waves crashing on quiet beaches—a place where they could have a small backyard to grow their own organic vegetables and ample access to spacious streets and pathways to run on; a place where they could attend art shows in the local park, participate in the community's holiday parades, and sit on the curb, watching familiar faces walk by; a place to enjoy the great outdoors together.

That spring, Evelyn discovered she was pregnant, and they rejoiced when their baby girl, Noelle, came on a chilly winter night two days before Christmas. Evelyn and Noelle were released from the hospital Christmas morning, and Chad and Evelyn both knew Noelle was the best Christmas gift they had ever received. They were ready to love unconditionally. Their second child, Elise, came in the spring and was easily entertained. Even as a baby, she laughed easily and slept hard and long. She brought the gift of laughter into their lives.

Her girls both brought new life not only to Evelyn, but also to her marriage. Those babies fulfilled a longing, a heart's desire she hadn't known she had, one that had surfaced through time but that she had shoved back down and repressed. She didn't care anymore what people thought of her. Essentially, she feared that she wouldn't be a good mother, that she couldn't express love to them, or that her girls would grow up thinking they'd had bad luck, getting a mom like her.

Life passed quickly. The wind moved the clouds and revealed the endless blue skies; plants grew, were uprooted, and grew back again. Life continued on, and Chad and Evelyn had their challenges, but they kept reminding themselves of how far they had traveled in life together. Life kept moving, but what remained was a scar on their hearts that reminded them of the little boy who they'd only known for a few months but who had changed their lives forever. He'd taught them to challenge their fears of love and of failure, and that it was okay to not to be in control of every emotion and situation. He taught them to appreciate life and enjoy today. Together, they rediscovered each other and love; they appreciated just breathing.

CB

The girls were jumping on the trampoline in the backyard when Evelyn opened the back door, allowing a cross breeze to come through the screen door on a warm August day. The girls' screeching with joy was heard throughout the house.

"You girls want a break and to have smoothies?" Evelyn called out to the bouncing girls.

"Yes, Mom!" They jumped off the trampoline and ran in the house to grab their homemade mango-and-tangerine treats.

Noelle stood tall and lanky with her mom's straight, limp, banana-cream-pie-colored hair. She was a serious girl and would do whatever it took to beat the boys in a race, which was quite familiar to Evelyn. She played tennis and took junior lifeguarding. She was fourteen years old, and Evelyn and Chad tried not to put any pressure on her for top grades or performance, as she was already self-motivated.

Her younger sister, Elise, was eleven years old and giggled incessantly. Everything was funny to her, and it annoyed her older sister to no end. Elise had solid legs, and her mother knew that, one day, she would outrun her sister. Evelyn cringed whenever she heard one of the girls call out, "race you," in fear the younger would outrun the older and she knew there would be life-long emotional healing just from a fair race. Elise's hair was dark brown, like her dad's. She could sleep on it, wear it in a ponytail the next day, then sleep on it again, and they could finger comb out the knots the next morning, and it would look like it had a few days ago. She brought so much life to the house.

When Noelle was young, and was regularly attending day care, Evelyn had started to realize that she herself was challenged by juggling a demanding job that involved spontaneous travel, while her husband could not be reached sometimes for hours while he was in surgery. She knew that one of the parents needed to be more available, and Evelyn wanted to be that parent. Plus, she had dreams of maybe setting up a gym and offering an overall wellness program to people. She decided it was time to quit her job and pursue her fitness-training dreams. On Noelle's first birthday, Evelyn went into Irene's office and gave her two-week notice.

For the first year Evelyn stayed at home, she took care of Noelle, wrote articles for the local paper, and was a faithful blogger, making money off her "Just Live It Out" blog. She took the project seriously and even set up interviews and asked for guest writers. She wrote about exercise routines, meal tips, and also the challenges and joys of being a parent. Her site grew, her daily hits increased, and she started making some extra money.

When she thought about how little money she was making, she felt a slight pang of inferiority, and her confidence wavered. She didn't like that she wasn't contributing more financially to the family, but Chad's job was more than enough for them to live comfortably, and they tried to live a simple life in their small Coronado home. Chad's job had changed. He had switched hospitals, which gave him a salary increase, although they still had to change their lifestyle with just one income. They traveled less, they sold their sail boat, and they ate almost all their meals in.

Evelyn also loved spending time with her husband, and they still got on their bikes together and took long rides along the streets and byways—as their girls trailed behind. They even traded in their mountain bikes for beach cruisers.

Both Chad and Evelyn were committed to showing their children how to give their time and energy to others, and as a family, they would drive down to Mexico to help build a house for a family in need or volunteer at an orphanage. The kids started learning Spanish and would play soccer with the other children. They also started going to church and financially supported a missionary family.

Evelyn put the last dish in the dishwasher, squirted the detergent in the container, twisted the dial to a normal setting, and set it to start washing in the early evening.. She went to the girls' room to collect their dirty clothes, then dragged the hamper to the garage to start a load of laundry. As she passed her front window, a flash of light caught her eye, and she saw a familiar car—a car she remembered being green. This one was black. She was surprised such an old car could still drive on a public road. It reminded her of her brother-in-law's old family Suburban, the very one that had been banished, once again, to the side of the shed—Brian just couldn't get rid of the vehicle that so many fond family memories, of trips and adventures, had been made in. When Evelyn had driven it, so many years ago, she hadn't seen the sentimental value of it, just the convenience of its size.

Today, on her way from one room to another, she stopped and looked out the window at the old familiar Chevy. It reminded her of that endless day years ago, but she decided that it was a different car altogether—it only reminded her of what had been, right?

As she headed back to the kitchen, she heard a faint knock on the door. It was gentle, and she could barely hear it from the back room. Then it came again, a little harder. She squirted ginger hand cream onto her hands and rubbed it in as she walked to the door. She twisted the doorknob, but her hand slipped, so she used the edge of her T-shirt to turn the knob. The sun glared into her eyes as she opened the door. "May I help you?"

"Hello, yes, um, are you Evelyn?"

"Yes, yes, I am. Can I…"—her hand dropped from the doorknob—"help you?" she finished lamely as her hand went to her mouth. She stood there, transfixed.

"Yes, ma'am, I'm, um, well, I'm Marcos."

Marcos, the boy with the red hair, who threw his arms out wide when someone called his name. Marcos, who shoved a spoonful of oatmeal into her mouth and made her laugh so hard she fell off her chair. Marcos, the boy who tucked a *Garfield* Pooky Bear in the crook of his arm, the very boy that sang "The Itsy Bitsy Spider" with her the first time they had met. Marcos, the sweet boy whom she had missed all these years.

She stared at him and didn't know how much time passed; she forgot where she stood, the time of day, and even what month it was. She stood there—and he stood there with a faint smile on his face and curiosity in his eyes.

She didn't know if she should hug him and kiss his cheek or take his hand and lead him in —like she had when he was little—or just invite him in. She couldn't hide her emotions and had to keep her hand to her mouth to try to keep from crying. She stared, blinking back the tears. She looked at his dark auburn hair that was a bit curlier than she remembered; she saw the freckles that danced across his nose and spilled over onto his cheeks. She noticed he was about four inches taller than she was, making him not quite six feet tall. His shoulders were wide and his hands square. He wore a plaid button-up shirt with faded, straight-leg jeans, and big sneakers with their wide shoelaces loosely tied.

She invited him in without a touch and without a word. He sat in their family room and met her girls and talked about how he had just graduated from high school and was planning on getting his associate's degree at Grossmont College and then hoped to get his nursing degree at UCSD. Evelyn smiled, remembering the convict who had been a nurse, the man who had sat next to her on her bus ride. Marcos told them that he lived with his godfather and that his grandmamma raised him— the very lady who had cleaned Evelyn's house every Friday.

Suddenly, the connections all made sense to Evelyn. She had never known that Rosita was actually caring for Marcos. She was confused and wanted to know why Rosita had never told her that she had Marcos all along. Rosita had seen Evelyn cry when there was no news on the boy who was taken from her. Rosita had been there when Evelyn had learned the police had scoured the neighborhood looking for a little redheaded Mexican boy but had never found him. She was there when they had packed up all of Marcos's toys and given them to Goodwill. She wanted to ask Rosita so many questions—but she had quit about a month ago and wasn't coming back.

Evelyn loved Rosita—they had become friends over the past fourteen years, and she enjoyed talking to Rosita when she came over. At first, when Evelyn was still working, Rosita would come over every Friday and then, when Evelyn decided to stay home with the kids, once a month. Evelyn knew that Rosita had a grandson who she was raising but would never have guessed it was Marcos. Evelyn smiled, knowing that a good person had been watching over their dear Marcos, and she was thankful that Rosita had kept their connection, knowing that one day she would be able to send Marcos back to her. But who had taken Marcos from Evelyn's house? Did Rosita know who that person was? She thought about all the things Rosita had told her about her sweet grandson, and now Evelyn knew that all those stories Rosita had told of the boy who played soccer in the streets and who had started playing on a competitive team; the boy who liked taking care of people, especially when they were hurt or needed help; the boy who the teacher would always sit next to the special ed children or the children who had crutches, who needed someone patient to help them; the boy who was always inviting kids in the neighborhood over to her house—this boy was actually the sweet little boy Evelyn once knew when he was only three years old.

Marcos calmly sat in the chair across from Evelyn and her daughters, a smile lingering on his face; he seemed pleased to see her. He said he remembered her singing to him and the warm sun shining down on him as he played with colored blocks. She listened to him ask her girls questions and watched as they invited him out to the backyard to jump on the trampoline. He stayed for dinner.

That day in August when Marcos came back, Evelyn walked him out to his black Impala that had been well taken care of by his godfather. She stood there as the sun set and watched him drive away, unsure if he would come back—she wondered if he'd meant it when he said that he would. She stood and watched him drive down their street, and suddenly the trees were not rustling, the birds were silent, and the world stood still.

The End

© Antoinette McIntyre-Anderson

ACKNOWLEDGMENTS

A big thank you to Lindy Brazil who encouraged me to write this book based just on the few sentences I shared about a dream I had the night before, and who helped me through the early process of creating a story; to Grace Volta and Phyllis Hartigan who were my big cheerleaders and encouraged me in many ways throughout the years; to Gris Alves who helped me with the details of Santiago's life and met with me through the course of writing those chapters; to Laura Johnson who met with me several times and helped me define the character of Evelyn; to my book group who openly shared their opinions, which changed the course of the story; to Terry Bono, Lilianna Hagewood, and Randi Clark who shared their stories with me and allowed me to insert them in my book; to my sisters: Melinda McIntyre Gunning who wrote the book-group questions, Marilu McIntyre Beattie who was very motivational and coordinated the publishing celebration, and Antoinette McIntyre-Andersson who encouraged me along the way and shared her cobweb photo; to my mom who read a very early version of the manuscript and inserted the proper Spanish words; to Chris Yanov who read an early unedited version and wrote the Foreword; to Olivia Taylor who created and re-created the cover; to my Kickstarter supporters who financed the three phases of editing; to my Facebook friends who named characters and gave me most of the food descriptions; to Ana Paola Rubio who helped with the Mexican pop culture and slang; to Julianna Volta who did the final read through of the book while juggling homework and celebrating her birthday; to my husband, Clif, whom I'm eternally thankful for his support as I took classes in the evenings for several years, and then stole away every Thursday night to write; to my boys, Asher and Samuel, who have been my biggest fans and have NEVER complained about my absence on many evenings, weekends, and vacation time as I wrote this book..

I couldn't have written this book without you in my life. Thank you.

BOOK GROUP DISCUSSION QUESTIONS

By Melinda Gunning

1. How is Santiago's choice of Evelyn as Marcos' new mama based on misinformation? What does the reader know about Evelyn's character that Santiago doesn't? What parts of Evelyn's personality does Santiago see accurately, if any? Do you agree with Santiago's opinion of himself as a good judge of character?

2. Given Santiago's family background, do you feel like he had any legitimate choices to live his life differently than involvement in a gang dependent on illegal activities? Do you see Santiago as a criminal for his gang involvement? Why do you feel that way?

3. Do you understand Evelyn and Chad's desire not to have children complicating their lives? How do you argue for or against their original choice to remain childless?

4. Why do you think Santiago wanted to choose a new mama for Marcos instead of Ruben, his long-time Mexican friend and godfather to his beloved child? Is there anything else Santiago could have done to make sure Marcos had a safe family/home environment, free of gang involvement and illegal activity?

5. Do you agree with Lorena's assessment that Evelyn is not ready for a child in her life because she doesn't understand what bringing a child into her life really means and because she and her husband do not have a relationship based on communication? Are there any earlier hints that Evelyn and Chad do not have a perfect relationship? What is your assessment of their relationship and Evelyn's motivation for wanting Marcos in her life? Is it really possible for someone to change priorities that drastically? Explain.

6. Santiago and Katiana also have a lack of communication in their relationship that causes the destruction of everything Santiago has wanted in life for his family. How are the problems of both couples similar and how are they different? Do you see any similarities in Santiago's job for the gang and Evelyn and Chad's commitment to their careers and physical fitness? Explain your answer.

7. Who do you sympathize with more: Evelyn for falling in love with Marcos or Chad for not being included in the decision to change the nature of their lives? What could Evelyn have done better to handle the situation of wanting to make a radical change in their marital life? What could Chad have done better to adapt to his spouse wanting to make such a change?

8. Which do you think is ultimately more important in a child's life: a connection with genealogical and cultural heritage or the stability of a parent earning a regular, crime-free salary? If you could have chosen the perfect family for Marcos, describe that family.

9. What were the fundamental changes evidenced in Evelyn and Chad after Marcos' disappearance? Evelyn says that "it's hard to grow in the midst of hurt. But we can do it." Which characters in the novel grow through hard times? Which ones are forever damaged by it?

10. Admittedly Rubén does his best for Marcos by separating himself from the gang and staying faithful to his new family. But do you agree that being reunited with his extended family was the best thing for Marcos? Do you agree with Grandmamma Rosita's decision to work for Evelyn but conceal the truth from her about Marcos' whereabouts? Explain your reasons.

11. How would you continue the story after the point when Marcos reunites with Evelyn?